D0927855

D.W. GILLESPIE

ONE BY ONE

This is a FLAME TREE PRESS book

FLAME TREE PRESS
6 Melbray Mews, London, SW6 3NS, UK
flametreepress.com

Distribution and warehouse:
Baker & Taylor Publisher Services (BTPS)
30 Amberwood Parkway, Ashland, OH 44805
btpubservices.com

Thanks to the Flame Tree Press team, including:
Taylor Bentley, Frances Bodiam, Federica Ciaravella, Don D'Auria,
Chris Herbert, Josie Karani, Molly Rosevear, Mike Spender,
Cat Taylor, Maria Tissot, Nick Wells, Gillian Whitaker.

The cover is created by Flame Tree Studio with
thanks to Nik Keevil and Shutterstock.com.
The font families used are Avenir and Bembo.

Flame Tree Press is an imprint of Flame Tree Publishing Ltd
flametreepublishing.com

A copy of the CIP data for this book is available from the British Library and the Library of Congress.

HB ISBN: 978-1-78758-166-1
PB ISBN: 978-1-78758-164-7
ebook ISBN: 978-1-78758-167-8
Also available in FLAME TREE AUDIO

Printed in the US at Bookmasters, Ashland, Ohio

D.W. GILLESPIE

ONE BY ONE

FLAME TREE PRESS
London & New York

This book is dedicated to my wife, Alicia.

As of this publication, we've been together for twenty years. In that time, she's been the first reader for more than a dozen books, many of which will rightfully never be published. There's little doubt in my mind that she suffered through some bad books, all the while encouraging, supporting, and helping me to get better. Without her, I wouldn't have made it this far.

PROLOGUE

I never wanted to come here.

Dad said it would be good for me. To get away from town, the concrete, to replace it with country and trees, tall grass and woods, to hear the owls always hoot, hooting out in the dark, telling each other secrets. But what secrets could owls have to tell?

I tried to like it.

No, really, I did. Mom is the same way, trying so hard to smile. I think a lot about what a smile is, especially when you don't mean it. It's a mask. Something that hides the truth. I know why she smiles all the time because that's the best way to pretend that she doesn't see. That she doesn't see what Dad is.

What he's done.

Peter loves it. He's a boy, so of course he does. He never wants to come inside, and when he does, the mud is so thick on his boots that he has to leave them by the door. Dad thinks it's funny, but Mom is tired of it. She says, "He's too old for this kind of shit." I think she's right.

I feel like I'm too old for this place, but it makes me feel like a baby too. At night, the way it breathes, the way everything creaks and pops, like the house is alive. The house in town never did that. All you had was the sound of traffic and horns, sirens somewhere far off. I miss that. Here it's all crickets and owls, like the woods are so full of bad things that all the animals can do is just scream at each other, like maybe if they're all miserable together, it might help somehow.

I hate the woods the most. Full of dark. Limbs that reach for you. And, of course, secrets.

I shouldn't have painted that picture.

I did it in the long hallway in front of the stairs. That place is almost at the center of the entire house, the place where every other hallway has to come together. I wanted it to be clear, easy to see, something we'd always notice when we walked to and from our rooms. A reminder of who we are, of what we could be.

It was a simple thing. I stuck with stick figures, just to make sure I could make it work. I was pretty good at drawing by then, but something about it, the act of drawing on the walls, was so childish, something a four-year-old would do, not a third grader. It was, up to that point at least, the most impulsive thing I'd ever done. That makes me laugh now, looking back on it. Jesus, the stuff I've done since then.

I used the leftover paints that I'd gotten the year before. Simple stuff, big bold, primary colors. It looked almost symbolic when I was done, which, in a way, was exactly what I was going for. It was like a logo of our family, a representation – anyone could tell exactly what it was.

Like I said, I was only seven at the time, so I don't think I was trying to be ironic. As childish as the drawing looked, it was genuine as well. I wanted to remember everyone, to remember all of us just that way. It was stupid, I knew that even then, but I hoped that maybe, just maybe, Mom would think it was cute. Like she used to.

But she didn't think it was cute. Honestly, I've never seen her so mad. She said I didn't care about anything. Didn't care about our house, the one she worked so hard to fix up. Said she should just forget it, that she should stop trying and just let us be hooligans, running around in our bare feet, tracking mud all over. It wasn't funny. It's never funny when she gets mad like that, but I caught Dad out of the corner of my eye. Dad stood back, sort of smiling, trying not to laugh.

He always finds something to laugh about, even when he's at his worst. "It's fine," Dad said when she finally stopped yelling. "We're putting the paper up soon, so what's the harm?"

"Don't you do that," Mom yelled, suddenly mad at him instead of me. Was that why he did it?

I could hear them the rest of the afternoon, the fighting rising and falling in waves, crashing like waves on the beach. I miss the beach. I wonder if we'll ever go on vacations like that again. I can still remember the nights, the windows open, the endless sound of the ocean all through the night.

A week later, Dad did exactly what he said he would do, and he covered up the drawing with long, ugly sheets of wallpaper. Mom seemed to calm down after that, but nothing was the same. Nothing was right.

I should have seen it all coming. Everything changed. Forever. The family that was painted on the wall was covered up too.

Buried.

I think, in hindsight, that was the point when things started to change. I was growing up after all, and you wouldn't believe how much I blamed myself for what happened next. If I'd stayed that little girl, that sweet, safe little thing, would any of this ever have happened?

Either way, Dad wasn't right after that. Then again, I don't think any of us were.

—Mary

CHAPTER ONE

The house snuck up on her as things often did. They weren't very far out of town, not by adult standards anyway, but for Alice, it felt like they had driven cross-country. She didn't know what to expect. The truth was she never knew what to expect. Her teacher would undoubtedly say that, out of every child in her fifth-grade class, she was the most absentminded. For some, that was a negative thing, but for Alice, it meant she was usually surprised by whatever happened.

"Head-in-the-clouds sort of girl," Mrs. Carmichael told her parents at their twice-yearly conference. Alice had been sitting out in the hall, iPad in hand, earphones in her lap. The adults hadn't thought she was listening. They never thought she was listening.

"Friendly," the teacher continued, "and smart as a whip, but would walk onto a train track if she was daydreaming."

Her parents, Frank and Debra, said nothing. After all, what could they say? They knew the facts far more than her teacher ever could. From what Alice could tell, they'd gone through the usual rounds that most parents with such a child went through. She could still remember the questions, the ones they whispered to each other when they thought she was in bed.

Was she going through a phase? Was there some medical reason, something as mild as attention deficit disorder or as serious as mini-seizures perhaps? Or was she, quite simply, a bit different, a phrase that most parents refuse to even consider?

The neighborhood that held their original home, the only home as far as Alice knew, might as well have been an ocean away, and so she stared out the window, dreaming, thinking of nothing and everything all at once, same as always. A song played on the radio, something from the Nineties, her parents' time. She didn't pay attention to the lyrics, but the music made a scene in her head, a vision of the house, the family, a sunny day without end.

It won't be like that.

A voice in her head, one of many, some of them bright and lively, but not this one. This one sounded a bit like Eeyore. She ignored it. Despite this gray stretch of winter, she knew the sun would be out soon enough, and everything dead would be alive again.

There was some discussion from the front seat as to whether or not this house was *the* house, the *final* house. It was clear to Alice, watching from a distance, that Debra, her mother, was far more cautious about the move. After all, their current house was a good house, a *fine* house, and things that were fine didn't need to be replaced. There had been more talk in the months leading up to the ultimate decision, talk about budgets and long-term goals, but it was clear that her father's mind was made up. All that remained was the tedious task of convincing everyone else.

"You have to use your imagination," her father, Frank, said from behind the steering wheel.

Debra, her mother, nodded, familiar with the line of argument. "I used my imagination last year with the camping trip. I seem to remember a cabin that was supposed to be quaint, romantic, and adventurous. I learned the limits of my imagination that weekend."

Frank laughed, a goofy sound, boyish despite the fact that he was nearly forty. "I stand by that decision," he said, grinning.

"You would," Debra said. "You didn't find the spider in the shower."

"How big was it again?"

"Bigger than my fist."

"Strange such a monster got away and you were the *only* one who saw it...."

Alice, drawn away from daydreaming, watched them banter back and forth. It was different now that the choice had been made and the papers had been signed. Before, there was an edge to them both, a strained, painful sharpness to the conversations. It had seemed to Alice that both of them wielded their true feelings about moving as if they were knives without handles, something that wasn't safe to hand off to another person without that person getting cut. The simple fact that they cared about not hurting each other seemed to stand for something. Even so, there was no denying the past few months had been bad.

Frank had lost his job as a training manager at a local factory the previous year, and his new one, a commissioned sales job, wasn't nearly as well paying. Debra, already a higher earner than him, was now the official breadwinner. But through some strange magic, Frank had convinced her to go along with this new house.

"It's a steal."

Everyone in the family heard that phrase so many times over the past few months that it was practically tattooed on the insides of their eyelids. Alice and her older brother, Dean, watched the whole thing from afar, occasionally objecting, but never really feeling the need to push too hard. Dean was, after all, a sophomore in high school, and at the apex of teenage self-centeredness. He was fifteen, and mere months away from driving, so he had more pressing things on his mind than getting involved in family affairs. It seemed like just another one of their father's schemes, up there with becoming a real estate agent and starting his own restaurant. Most of these flights of fancy would pass on their own, but this one – this house – seemed to hang in there longer. It was his first real scheme after losing his job, after the family "took a hit" as he liked to say. But the rest of them had less patience for schemes now, less room for them too. They were toeing a thinner line than ever before, and you could see it, their mounting anxiety hiding in plain sight, peering through the cracks of the family armor.

Dean and Alice had, on rare occasions, confided in each other that they were certain divorce was the final spot on the treasure map that was their parents' marriage. But now, after their father somehow persuaded their mother to go along on the new house, everything had changed.

Don't you wonder what it is? a whisper inside her asked. There were lots of voices inside her, and for years, Alice was convinced that there were lots of voices inside of everyone. Loud and quiet voices. Mean and sweet voices. And most of all, scared voices, little voices that were so soft they were barely voices at all.

Yes. She did wonder what it was that had swayed her mother and ultimately made her parents' marriage suddenly pull itself out of the dive it had been in for the past year or so. Now, they would laugh together. Flirt. Dance to whatever happened to be playing. And so it was now, a feathery back-and-forth between them that was as saccharine as a romantic comedy. Alice realized, the week of Thanksgiving of all times, that her mother was now part of her father's game. Her no-nonsense, practical mother was complicit. And with that fact out of the way, Debra was wrapped up in the fun of it all. Their marriage, unquestionably old and tired at this point, had something new, a little spice thrown into the recipe. Eventually, the arguments drifted off. The fights diminished. And everyone had a single goal to focus on for the near future.

The house.

They had, by all accounts, no business moving, but Frank, in his never-ending search for a project, a deal…

…*a purpose?*

…had come across the place while searching around online. He couldn't get enough of the house-flipping shows, and Alice could see the twinkle in his eye when he first started talking about the place. There was little doubt in her mind that he could imagine himself as one of those young, strapping hosts, barreling in with a sledgehammer to carve out the diamond hiding in the mess of an old, forgotten house.

Her parents were still bantering in the front seat, but Alice had seen enough flirting; she glanced back out the window. The sky, gray blue, melted into the winter trees, whose bark was a deeper gray. They passed by them too quickly, and the trees blurred, becoming something liquid, a mealy, gravel-colored slime that dripped from the sky, taking hold in the brown-and-yellow earth.

There are monsters here.

Another voice, darker, not nearly as easy to ignore as the gloomy one. This was the nighttime voice, the one that rarely snuck out when the sun was still out. The neighborhood wouldn't allow for monsters. There were patches of darkness, places where foul things might hide, but not nearly enough to sustain a grim ecosystem. Monsters loved the woods, places the streetlights never touched, where the only light was that of a sagging moon on nights when even the clouds were afraid to show themselves. If any monsters made it into the neighborhood, they would find themselves stuck, abandoned, struck dead by the sunlight. All you had to do was stay on the lit path; any ten-year-old knew that.

But out there, in the gray, passing landscape, it was different. This wasn't her place. It wasn't just her home she was leaving behind, but it was also everything that her home meant. Safety. The expected. The known. Out there, in the leafless gray woods, anything could happen.

No, Alice didn't know what to expect at all. But when she saw the house, she knew it was theirs. As they pulled up the long, gravel driveway, under a roof of old oak trees, the house came into view in its entirety. She wasn't sure if she gasped, but it felt like she did. It didn't so much as sit on the wooded lot as loom, a lovely, strange thing. It looked to her like a giant doll's house, something that was once pristine but had been left out in the garden for years, forgotten, then discovered once again. But the strangest thing of all was that, despite the dirt and grime, it hadn't lost its odd beauty.

"Here we are," Frank said in a jovial tone.

Debra sighed, a motion that started from the roots of her hair all the way down to her toes, the car's light atmosphere dampening slightly. From where Alice sat, she could tell that her father was pretending not to notice. She'd seen her mother's own excitement, stirred up by her father over the past weeks, but there was something different now, some greater finality to the moment. The excitement still existed, surely, but it was hidden behind the long hours of work that it would surely take to bring the house to life.

"Where's the front door?" Alice asked.

Frank laughed. "It's an odd duck of a house," he replied. "It was built before the main road was. Back then, there was a little dirt road that went down the side here. So, from the road at least, the house is sideways. The front door is over there." He pointed toward the side of the house.

"Weird..." Alice said, following his finger.

"It's got personality," Frank said, stepping out. "You won't find anything like that in all these cookie-cutter neighborhoods where every third house looks the exact same and you can piss out your window and hit your neighbor—"

"Frank," Debra said quietly. "We get it, honey."

Debra stepped out of the car and stared up at the house, taking in the abandoned enormity of it.

"What the hell were we thinking?" she said to herself.

Alice stood half in, half out of the car and just kept staring. She had never seen anything like it in her life. Their current home was one in a line of very similar homes in a neighborhood just a few miles away from her school. It was, as her father described it, an assembly-line house. Nothing unique, nothing different, and thus, nothing special. It wasn't until he came around to the possibility of moving that he began to talk that way about their home, and the idea that anything could be wrong with the house she grew up in seemed somehow sacrilegious to Alice. The thought had simply never occurred to her that her room, her own little slice of the world, might not be perfect.

She missed most of her parents' conversation as she stepped out of the car, lost in her own thoughts. The house wasn't just big; it was also absolutely massive, swallowing their house at least twice, maybe more. That alone was enough to catch her eye, but it was just the beginning. The shape of it was so subtly wrong that she couldn't quite wrap her head around why it was. A wide, bloated bay window marked the side of the house in the center, and beside it, a tiny porch made up of nothing more than a few brick steps and a concrete landing. The mere size of the house seemed to hint at something more resplendent, like a Gothic, Southern mansion. But this porch…it was pure utilitarianism.

Gone was the familiar warmth of red brick, replaced by layers of wooden siding, the off-white paint peeling in sheets. The roof was a mess of odd angles, a peak in the center followed by a precipitous drop on one side and a gentle slope on the other. There were no answers to the design or look of it, at least not to a ten-year-old, but the overall *feel* of the place was unmistakable. A gigantic weeping willow, whose trunk was dangerously close to the edge of the house, leaned over the roof, threatening to eat the entire thing. The wisps of leafless branches reached down from the highest point brushing across the front of the bay window. Just looking at it, admiring it, Alice was filled with a sense of bubbling anticipation mingled with dark revulsion. It felt like stumbling across a dead body, something deeply wrong yet impossible to look away from. In a few short moments, Alice was smitten.

"It's something, isn't it?" Frank said, appearing beside her. He leaned in close, whispering into the cup of her ear so that Debra, who stood twenty feet away, inspecting the siding, couldn't hear.

"Almost couldn't get her out here," he said, a conspiratorial tone in his voice. "I knew it was a long shot. Mom and Dean, they were the hard sells, but you…" He clapped a hand on her shoulder. "I *knew* you'd like it."

Alice couldn't keep the smile off her face if she tried.

"Come on," he said. "Let's take the tour."

The three of them made their way around, finding a long, wooden porch that stretched the width of the house. Alice took a few steps back to take it all in from a distance, and sure enough, she was looking at what would normally be the front of a house. From here, it was more symmetrical but no less odd.

"Now," Frank said as he held open the front door for them, "there are so many interesting little things about this place."

Alice walked in, staring at the cavernous hallways, the ceilings that seemed too tall, the blank walls and peeling paint. For the first time in her life, she thought about what their house meant to her, searched for the words that most perfectly captured the place where she'd spent the entirety of her childhood.

Comfortable. Safe. Bland.

But this house was so different, the change so drastic, that she struggled to make sense of it. The words that came to mind as she stared at the foyer were a far cry from what she was used to.

Dark. Cold. And most of all, mysterious.

"It might not look like much, but all the foundation is solid. No bugs, mice, anything like that. And this is an old-school building, so everything is solid...."

"You already said that," Alice whispered.

"Well, I'll say it again!" he said with a grin. "Seriously, though, all we need is paint, a little bit of refinishing on some of the hardwood. I mean, look at these floors."

He stomped up and down, apparently meaning to signify... something.

"Yep," Debra said, giving her daughter a side-eye. "They're floors all right."

"Okay, you need a little more to impress you, I can see that. Just let me give you the tour, and trust me, you'll be in love."

Frank led them through like a genuine realtor, showing off the finer points wherever he could find them and seemingly making shit up whenever he couldn't.

"This here," he said, tapping the doorframe, "that's oak. Can't beat oak."

"How in the hell do you know that?" Debra asked.

"Honey, I have a life outside our family."

Alice laughed at the show of it all, but she had to admit, the place was something to see. Nothing quite seemed to fit where you thought it should, but that only added to Alice's desire to delve deeper into the dollhouse. She drifted off from her parents, away from the guided tour to explore on her own. In the center of the house was a tangle of hallways wrapped around a staircase. Alice took the hall opposite the stairs and ventured deeper into the far side of the house. She stopped at the first room she came to, a bedroom from the look of it, and peered inside. It was small and cozy, the only room she'd seen with carpet up to this point, but it was somehow darker than it should have been. It wasn't the paint or the cramped confines but something in the gray light that shined through the windows. She stepped across the room and looked through the smudged windows, squinting. A sudden face appeared, and she screamed.

"Calm down," her dad said from the other side of the window. "I told you this place was amazing." He slid open the window.

"Dad, you scared the crap out of me."

"Well…sorry," he said, leaning against the window frame. "Check it out though." He gestured behind him. "This used to be the back porch, and they turned it into a utility room. The washer and dryer are in here."

"How is that a good thing?"

He stared at her, incredulous. "You have windows that open into another room…." He said it as if there could be no question as to why that was a positive thing. "I'm thinking this could be your room. If Dean won't get his ass here, he doesn't get to pick."

Alice's older brother *hadn't* been up there yet, and she could only consider it a bit of a protest against the move.

"Maybe I don't want windows that go into another room."

"What?" he said, laughing. "It's like a clubhouse or something. You kidding me? I'd have killed for something like this when I was a kid."

"It's kind of just…I don't know. Creepy."

"Creepy is good," he said, leaning in.

From somewhere behind him, Debra asked, "Are you coming?"

"Go on up, I'll be there in a second."

Frank waited a moment for her to leave, and then he leaned farther in. "Look at this place," he said, a childish excitement in his voice. "It's a small room, but just picture what you can do with it.

Think about the wall colors, what kind of things we can hang on the walls, where your furniture can go. Come here."

Alice walked close enough for Frank to rest a hand on her shoulder.

"This is *yours*," he said earnestly. "Make it whatever you want it to be, baby."

With that, he was gone again.

Alice continued exploring as her parents' voices seemingly rang from all directions, echoing across the hardwood floors and high ceilings. The hallway through the downstairs was circuitous, doubling back on itself in a series of small bedrooms and bathrooms. Even without electricity, she could see the tall, three-sided mirror in one of the half bathrooms that turned her into endless reflections, stretching in either direction.

"That's the beauty of it," Frank's voice filtered in from the hallway. "The entire house doesn't face the road at all. There was an older dirt road from years ago that it used to face. That's why it looks so weird when you pull up."

"You just said that like five minutes ago," Debra said. "And what's the beauty in having a house turned the wrong way?"

"It's unique."

Alice met them back in the hall at the foot of a narrow set of wooden stairs. Above them, a single, small landing glared down from behind a thin handrail.

"You don't see stuff like this in our old neighborhood," Alice said.

Debra glanced at Alice and cocked an eyebrow. "It's not our *old* neighborhood yet."

"Alice, come check out the upstairs. You got to. I promise, you'll love it."

The three of them wound up the tiny staircase, taking a sharp turn. Frank led Debra deeper into the farthest recesses of the house as Alice lingered behind, staring over the edge of the tiny guardrail. It seemed so out of place there, as if the builders had forgotten to add a wall. She leaned forward, glancing down at the floor a dozen feet below her. The guardrail groaned under her touch.

The upstairs hallway seemed endless, a narrow corridor with a bathroom on one side and a squat, half-sized door opposite. She leaned down, inspecting it.

"Dad," she called. "What's this?"

He peered out of a room farther down the hall, squinting. "Oh, it's a crawl space. It leads to the attic, I think."

"Why is it so small?"

"They used to build them like that," he replied, the confidence in his voice waning.

"That's right, honey," Debra said, peering out the bedroom. "You see, in the 1800s, everyone was three feet tall."

Alice laughed, and Frank shook his head. "There's another entrance to the attic from the master bedroom," he said with authority. "This is just another, smaller storage space. See. I know what I'm talking about."

Alice stared at the door as she walked past. It was weird, but then again, this entire house was weird. Why would it start to make any sense now? Her parents were exploring the master bedroom when she found them. It was gigantic, easily the largest room in the house. The ceiling was angled, about seven feet on one side and nearly fifteen on the other. Sunlight beamed down on them from a long, narrow skylight set in the center of the ceiling, warming the room. Alice walked farther into the room, standing under the bloom of sunlight and looked up, smiling.

"What the hell is that?" Debra asked.

"What?"

"That!"

She pointed at the window to the right side of the room. Just on the outside, what looked like a ladder rested against the window frame. Frank stared at it for a moment, as if not quite sure how to spin it.

"Oh, that," he said. "It's a fire escape."

Alice walked over for a closer look. The ladder was bolted to the outer wall, and it stood, solid and unmoving, about six inches away from the siding.

"Why do we need that?" Debra asked.

"Well," he fumbled, "this is an old house. This is the *only* bedroom on the second floor, soooo, you know, if you needed to get out quick..."

"Or get in quick," Alice muttered.

"Somehow," Debra said, "I missed this little gem on our first walk-through."

She strode over and slid open the window before grabbing the ladder and giving it a good shake. It was, despite the peeling white paint, still solid. "Wonder if we can take that down."

"Why?" Frank asked, almost wounded.

"I don't like a direct line into my bedroom from outside. We've got smoke detectors. That should be good enough."

Frank stood for a moment, mouth open, appearing completely at a loss.

"Well, if the two of you are done crushing my dreams, I can show you the real crown jewel." He walked to the far side of the room and pointed out the window. "Now, if you two find a way to piss on this, well, I'm just going to have to move into a hotel or something."

It took Alice a moment to realize what she was seeing. The roof on the back side of the house was so gently sloping that it was nearly flat. Alice realized she could have stepped out of the window and walked around on the thirty-foot span of rooftop if she wanted to. But beyond that was the real attraction.

"What do you think about that?" Frank said.

It was, or once had been, an in-ground pool. A small, concrete deck was lined with a tall wooden fence, and in the center was a green, muck-filled hole half filled with murky water.

"Oh, good Lord," Debra said. "You honestly thought *that* would hook your daughter in? You poor, stupid man."

Alice stared, squinted, tried to imagine anything other than a sickly pond, but came up short. "I don't know, Dad...."

"It looks bad, I know, but come down and get a closer look."

They trailed along behind him, back down the stairs and outside as he chattered on about more of the fine features of their wonderful find. On closer inspection, the pool looked far worse, but Frank's animated excitement was almost contagious.

"See, the hole, the concrete, the fence, even the pump! It's all here. The expensive part is already good to go. All we gotta do is clean it up and replace the liner. I'm talking a fraction of what putting in a new pool would be."

The winter breeze blew through the yard, and Alice shuddered, huddling deeper into her jacket. An in-ground pool was about the last thing she could think about at the moment.

"You said this place would save us money," Debra said.

"Well, you have to spend money to save money. You know that. And over time, if we fix everything up, we could flip it for a huge profit...."

Alice and Debra looked at each other, then back at the pool. Frank trailed off, as if realizing he was losing them.

"Picture this," he said, taking a different angle. "What if we don't go on vacation this year? We save all that money because the vacation is right here. I told you it would take a little imagination, but by the time spring comes around, this will be a sparkling blue diamond. Dean and his buddies will have a place to hang out, so he'll be home more. Alice, your sleepovers will be all-night swim parties. And, Debra...honey...light of my life, every single day, you'll be able to come out here after work and just relax. Maybe we could even put a little bar out here? And I, your loving husband, will be back there, making margaritas. We'll be floating around all summer without a care in the world."

Alice was smiling, half because of how silly her father could be and half because she was already sold. She glanced over and saw her mother trying not to grin. It was a weird place, a slightly unsettling place, but there was a gravity to it as well. It had already pulled her dad in, and it was getting its hooks into her also. This, of all the places she had ever seen, was a prime spot to daydream. The woods, still strange, still terrifying, pressed in from all sides. There were secrets there, secrets everywhere, and to most people, that would be a bad thing.

"I can't even think of moving before Christmas," Debra said.

"We don't have to," he said, his tone telling Alice that he'd already rehearsed this point. "We've already paid for the old house up through January. There's no rush! So let's take a few weeks to enjoy the holidays, relax, do all the stuff we always do. I'll start working on packing things up, doing whatever it takes to make this work. Then, the week after Christmas, we move in. The kids will still be out of school then, so there's less pressure."

Debra was shaking her head but in a playful way.

"One more Christmas at the old place," she said with a grin. Alice looked up at the strange house, wondering how much it might change in the next month. It was their home now, and it was clear that she needed to get used to that fact.

Frank turned from Debra to Alice back to Debra again. His eyebrows shot up a bit, and his smile widened.

CHAPTER TWO

Alice's room – the one with the strange, interior windows – was slowly gaining the appearance of an actual living space. The frame of the bed was set in the general spot it would finally live, and boxes filled with clothes, decorations, toys, and all of the other random knickknacks that made up her young life were stacked in an irregular pile near the door. The mental gymnastics had begun, the bare patches of wall being laid out in her mind with posters, her dresser, mirrors, and everything else she might need. It was, of course, a downgrade in size. Her previous room had felt more open, but the change wasn't necessarily a bad one. The new room was cozier somehow, the ceiling lower, the walls tighter. It felt, in some odd way, like a hobbit hole, a tiny place in the ground that was hers through and through. Only one real problem remained as far as she could tell.

Those windows…

Her father had promised to get some blinds up before bedtime, but the day was already half gone. Always full of good intentions, he wasn't the most efficient or handiest handyman in the world. She lay back on the mattress that rested on the floor, staring up at the ceiling, trying to get a feel for the place. The excitement was still there, still real and electric, but the night was coming fast. She knew, more than most, about how things changed in the dark, the things that shadows hid. Anything awful or terrifying that could be out there in the dark halls or gray crag woods, she had already imagined much worse. Nights were like that for a girl with an overactive imagination. Beautiful and terrifying in equal measure.

She glanced over at the pair of windows that looked out into another room, a long, bare corridor of unfinished wood. A bit of sunlight peeked in, but she could practically see the moonlight already, could imagine what it might be like in the dead of night. The moonlight wouldn't be so bad, but the cloudy nights, the black nights, those would be something else. How easy would it be for someone to break in through the back door, the utility room, as her dad called it, and peer through those windows? Alice could already see the face, the eyes glowing.

"I thought you were unpacking."

She turned back to find her brother, Dean, standing in the doorway, one earbud in, the other dangling in front of his chest. Alice wasn't sure if he refused to look at her or if there really was something interesting on his phone.

"Glad you joined us," Alice said, propping herself up on her elbow.

Dean looked up at her. He was tall, already taller than their dad, but he hadn't quite grown into that frame yet. He'd asked their parents for a weight set for Christmas, but they bought him a month long gym membership instead. He'd gone twice, but she figured it wouldn't stick.

"I had stuff to do," he replied.

"Yeah, I'm sure. You'd do anything to get out of work."

"Whatever," Dean said.

"Seriously, where have you been?"

"Over at Max's," he said, his tone going from bored to annoyed. Dean was one of the last of his friends to turn sixteen, a sore spot that Alice usually knew to avoid.

"You've been over at his house a lot lately," she snipped at him. "Bet he's getting tired of driving you around."

He finished up with whatever bit of internet nonsense he needed to before glaring at his sister. "Your room's smaller."

"I know," Alice said. "I like it like this."

He took a few steps and peered into the utility room through the windows. "That's…creepy."

"It's unique," Alice answered, parroting her father.

"Did Dad pay you to say that?"

"If all you're going to do is complain, just leave."

Dean shook his head, curling his lip into a sneer as if he had a sour taste in his mouth. He kept staring out the windows a moment longer before turning away.

"That's why I've been staying over at Max's so much.... This house sucks."

He disappeared deeper into the labyrinthine hallways, probably looking for his own room, farther into the recesses of the house. Alice sat on the bed a bit longer, stewing, wondering why her brother was always such a jerk. When she finally got back up, she heard the unmistakable sound of her father cursing while her mother laughed uncontrollably. Apparently, the fridge wouldn't fit through the front door.

"Well, shit! I guess I got to take the doors off this fucker...."

Debra was still grinning when she rounded the corner, holding a water bottle. She stopped in Alice's doorway and stared into her room.

"Getting set up all right?"

Alice bent over one of the open boxes and began digging into it in a poor attempt at looking busy. Debra laughed.

"Were you just lounging around in here?"

Alice shrugged. It was clear that her mom didn't understand her, that she always mistook her daydreaming for laziness. Alice had tried to explain how busy her mind was, that what looked like laziness was anything but. It was tough though, especially when she was compared to Dean. Her brother had always been a hustler, even if his teen years had brought on a sense of surliness that none of them seemed to care for. He had a drive that made him pretty substantial on the basketball court or the baseball diamond. It was an unfair comparison, her and her brother, especially considering how alike Debra and Dean were.

"You *are* your father's daughter," Debra said, smiling. "It's fine, honey. If I thought I could get away with it, I'd take a nap right about now."

It was a lie. She never took naps. Alice didn't care though, and when Debra sat down on the floor, clearly ready for a break, Alice sat back down on the mattress.

"Sooo…" Alice said.

"So what?"

Alice wrinkled her nose. "I dunno. You came in here. Had to be for a reason."

Debra sighed. "You're too smart for your own good," she said. "All right then…what do you think?"

"About what?"

"All this. I mean, it's a mess. I wouldn't have picked it in ten years, but if I squint, I can see some of the charm."

"It's okay."

"Jeez…you lie like him too."

"What does that mean?" Alice asked.

"It means your brother's the good liar. Don't sweat it. It's not a compliment to him. At least I know what you're up to." Debra popped open the top of her bottle of water.

"I saw it happen when we were out here a few weeks ago," Debra added. "It got you. Somehow, this hunk got its hooks in you just like it did your dad."

Even from a distance, it was clear to Alice that her dad had a tendency to drive her mom nuts, but somehow, over the course of eighteen years, her mom had learned to just roll with it – for the most part. Alice could see her struggling with all the craziness of the day, and all the craziness to come, but the simple fact that she could laugh at her husband as he wrestled a refrigerator told the story well enough. She was in, for better or worse.

"So I'll ask it again…what do you think?"

The smile on Alice's face had a mind all its own, creeping up from some hidden place, refusing to obey her command.

"That's what I thought. Ahhh, this place."

"I think it's just…neat, I guess. Like a mystery or something. The old house was fine, but this one…"

Debra laughed. "Lord you sound just like him…."

"What? It *was* fine, but this feels like…I dunno. An adventure."

Debra smiled that same, weary, been-here-before smile. "I get it. I need to be more fun. But fun can cost you. Adventures take a lot of work."

Alice slid off the mattress and sat down on the floor, letting her head drift over to her mom's shoulder.

"We'll make it work," Debra added. "But it will take a lot of elbow grease…from all of us. You and your brother included."

"I know."

"I'm holding you to that. This is your room," she said, waving the bottle around. "Unless there's something you can't do on your own, I'm not touching it. Hanging pictures or blinds, anything like that, I'll help you out. But all this stuff is yours. It goes where you want it to. You got it?"

"Yeah," Alice said, leaning a bit closer.

"Who knows? Maybe it will be worth it. Hopefully, by the time summer comes this will be home."

Alice nodded. "Better than home."

⋆ ⋆ ⋆

Alice spent the next few hours with a drive that she rarely had. She had turned on the Michael Jackson Pandora station and just let it play while she worked. Her clothes were still in the drawers, but most of her old toys, school supplies, picture frames, and everything else that she considered hers had to be sorted through and emptied. There were five deep boxes with her name on the side of them, and she diligently set to work getting the room as close to ready as she could. By the time she was ready for a break, her father appeared in the doorway, red-faced and sweaty with a screwdriver in hand.

"You ready for me to put the bed together?"

She left him in relative peace, ignoring the occasional *shits* and *fucks* that emanated from the room, followed by the sounds of the clattering bed frame. No doubt he'd be in there for a while; it was time to continue exploring the stranger corners of the place.

On the back side of the staircase, just across from the front entrance, was a green-painted door that she'd somehow missed until then. She tried the creaking handle, marveling at how heavy the door was as she swung it open. This was the type of door she simply didn't see in their old house, a sturdy counterpoint to the light, hollow doors she was used to. Within, a single light hung above her, and with a click, a sickly yellow beam lit up an absolute nightmare of a descending staircase. Each unfinished wooden step was black with slick-looking mold; the walls were an ocherous yellow. It looked like it led to less of a basement and more of a cave, something carved out of the earth itself. Alice heard, or thought she heard, a stirring from deep within the hellish corners below. For a moment, she leaned forward, never daring to place a foot onto the top stair. Then, something brushed against her leg. She squeaked out a quiet little scream, then looked down.

There was Baxter, the pitch-black family cat curling around her leg. He wasn't a particularly sweet cat. He had an almost endless supply of energy, which seemed to translate into a wariness with people that bordered on outright dislike.

"You scared the crap out of me," she scolded. He looked up, mewed at her, then stared down the stairs.

"Don't even think about it." She reached down to move him out of the way. He hissed, which was perfectly normal for him, before darting away. Alice was still staring down the steps when her father's heavy footsteps came clomping up the hallway.

"Looks like he's having fun," he said, watching Baxter flee down the hall. "We won't find him for a week if I had to guess. Oh, and you found the basement." He took one look down, wrinkling his nose. "Yep, lots of work to do down there."

"Do you hear that?" Alice asked.

He tilted his head, listening.

"Furnace, I think. There was a sump pump down there too.

I haven't plugged it in yet. Looks like it gets a bit of flooding whenever it rains for more than a day or two. Definitely some work to be done there. Probably won't be turning it into a guest room anytime soon."

Alice glared down, feeling like she were standing on the edge of a cliff, that sensation that you might be suddenly, uncontrollably compelled to leap to your own death. She'd had that feeling before on one of their camping trips, standing at the precipice of a hundred-foot bluff, wondering what the air would feel like blurring through her hair, how the rocky ground would look racing up to meet her. But underneath all of it, a stronger, more persuasive sensation, a question, *the* question.

What would it feel like to no longer exist?

The black voice, whispering in her brain.

"Careful now," her father said, putting a hand on her shoulder. Alice started and realized with some embarrassment that she was leaning even farther in. "Steps are a little rickety. Probably best to steer clear until I have a chance to straighten things up."

He drew her back, closing the door, and Alice felt the odd shadow over her heart lift a bit.

"I don't think I'd want to go down there anyway," she said quietly.

Alice didn't dwell on the basement. There were simply too many corners to explore, more bits and pieces that seemed at odds with each other. She walked through a tiled sunroom out near the pool, which boasted one entire wall of solid glass, clearly another late addition to the structure. The whole pool area was vaguely modern, the orange tiles summoning something from the late Seventies, unlike the vastly more ancient hardwood found throughout the majority of the house. The sunroom was ice cold, the winter sun doing little to warm it.

Even without a jacket, she decided to take a quick stroll around the pool and was greeted by a stench that made her gasp. The wall of foul air hit her the moment she came within five feet of the pool's edge. Hand cupped over her mouth, she leaned over, peering into the black water. A thin layer of ice was forming, but it did little to stop the smell. The previous week had been unseasonably warm, but now the weather was beginning to turn. Soon, she realized, this dark little pit would be frozen solid, maybe enough to lock all that stench inside until spring. But as disgusting as it was, she could still picture it all fixed up, blue and deep and inviting.

Alice stepped up onto the diving board, which creaked and moaned under her weight. She stepped nimbly to the edge of the board, hovering above the grotesque pit.

It shouldn't stink this bad, the gloomy voice whispered.

Alice considered the idea. She'd been around ponds and lakes, some of which were pretty foul, but this was something different. It reminded her more of the sewage backup they experienced a few years ago, the black muck bubbling up into the bathtubs and the stink that refused to leave your nose. The idea of falling into it made her shudder, and she shuffled carefully onto the back end of the diving board.

From her slightly raised perch, she could see over the fence that ringed the pool area. It was her first, fleeting glance into the woods that surrounded the house. The trees, tall and gaunt, drooped over the pool like a poorly kept roof. Past that, she saw mostly the same. Trees. Tall, dead grass. Silence.

And something else....

Yes. There was something else. A small, foot-worn path.

I bet it's deer, a brighter voice whispered.

Yes, of course. There had to be deer everywhere around here. And rabbits, raccoons, possums, a bit of everything.

Deer didn't make that path.

Alice shivered and stepped down from the board. Back inside, Dean talked on his cell phone as he carried in a tiny box, wedged beneath one arm, from the moving truck. There were footsteps here and there, random bits of conversation, and beneath it all, the creaks and whistling breezes that seemed like the heartbeat of the old house. She was lost in thought as she made her way through the house, thinking about the woods, the basement, the trails through tall grass. Then, she glanced up and saw it.

It was in the hallway leading to her room. On an empty patch of wall across from the stairs, she found a curling piece of wallpaper that she'd barely noticed before. Alice stared at it, gripped by that too-young feeling of wanting to break something just to see what might happen. She'd been there before, just like all kids were there at some point or another. Her mother had screamed herself nearly hoarse when she'd found a five-year-old Alice drawing on the wall with her lipstick. She'd been too old to do something like that back then, and her mother had let her know it, but it didn't change the fact that she'd felt powerless to ignore the idea once it crept in. Afterward, she could remember the feeling as she sat in bed, crying, her mother still fuming, her father telling them both to calm down, that it was fine, that he would clean it up. Alice wasn't stupid, but she had done something remarkably stupid, and she couldn't begin to understand why.

It was the same feeling now, staring at the wallpaper, wanting nothing more than to peel it away. There wasn't anything hiding there, no secrets, just the ever-present urge to see what happened. It was a scab, a loose piece of skin after a sunburn, a sore on the inside of her cheek, or a hangnail that was still dangling, still *teasing* even after it started to bleed. No amount of parental glares, no logical explanation of why it was a bad idea, nothing on earth would prevent her from picking at it until the pain told her it was time to stop.

Alice glanced back, checking if anyone was in sight. The voices were still there, but she was alone.

Besides, no one would notice it.

Was that the dark voice? There was darkness in it, but something new had been stirred in. Something playful.

Just do it. You know you want to, girl.

She did want to. More than anything in her life at that moment. The satisfaction in it, the crunchy, tactile sound of it ripping off. Everything had to be fixed in the house anyway, and that included old, yellowed sheets of wallpaper. It was ugly as sin, and her mother would never let it stay for long.

Then stop thinking about it and do it.

This new voice was confident and convincing, and Alice didn't want to argue. With a grin, she grabbed the corner and began to tug. The sheet came away in a dry hunk, pulling further and further with a shredding sound that set her teeth on edge. It was dangerous, she knew it, but the more she pulled, the more she *wanted* to pull. Like a sheet of dead skin, the wallpaper just kept going, peeling away. Any attempt to pretend it was an accident or had just been that way all along would be impossible to argue at that point. Even so, she just couldn't stop.

The wall underneath was dry and flaking, and the bits of drywall and old glue began to shower the tops of her shoes. Finally, with a satisfying rip, the sheet fell away. In her hand, she held a strip of curled paper over four feet long, and the exhilaration was instantly replaced with fear.

You'll have to explain this.

This was the glum part of her, returned to let her know that her bad idea was, in fact, a bad idea. A sick feeling began to bubble up in her stomach, but only for a moment, as it was replaced by some other, more powerful feeling of strange curiosity.

"Daaadddd. Mommmmm."

CHAPTER THREE

The four of them gathered close in the hallway, huddling together to get a better view of what Alice had discovered. Alice was struck by how tightly packed they were, and she realized she could smell them. It was a strange thing, a reminder of the four of them giving group hugs after ball games or funerals, the good memories and the bad mixing in strange ways. From the soft scent of her mom's deodorant to the sting of her dad's sweat to the cheap cologne that Dean had started to wear, she could pick each member of the family out individually.

"What the hell…?" Frank asked.

"Did you just find it like this?" asked Debra.

"Yeah," Alice replied, "I was just walking by, and a box snagged the corner and started pulling back the wallpaper."

Dean cast a cockeyed glance at her, skeptical, but he didn't say anything. He, like everyone else, was taken aback by the scene before them.

It was a painting, a crude, simplistic depiction of a family. It was hard to tell exactly what had been used to create it, either colored markers or some sort of finger paint. Most of the colors had been removed, stuck forever to the back of the sheet of wallpaper. All that remained was the dull, lifeless imprint of the original shapes, like a film negative. It was, Alice realized, an anti-picture.

"It's really creepy," Dean said finally.

"No," Debra answered. "Just a kid's painting. Probably soaked into the drywall, so they just had to put the wallpaper up."

Frank was grimacing, turning his head this way and that like a cat studying a laser pointer.

"No," he muttered, "it is pretty strange."

"Good Lord," Debra replied. "Once again, I'm the sane one. Come on, we've got too much work to do."

She turned to walk away, and the others did the same. Only Alice remained, still staring, still puzzling over it. She glanced down at the sheet of wallpaper, at the phantom colors still stuck there.

"Wait!" she said suddenly. "Come back. Look at this."

The others returned, Debra and Dean in eye-rolling defiance, Frank with bright, inquisitive eyes.

"Look," she said, holding up the old paper. It was a mirror image of the painting on the wall.

"Cool," Dean said, "still creepy."

"The colors," she said.

They all took a good, long look, but only Frank could see where she was headed.

"Ohhh..." he said.

"What?" Debra asked.

"Look," Alice replied, "the mom has blond hair. Just like you. The dad is tall with black hair," she said, pointing at her father. "There's an older son, tall and skinny with freckles...."

"I don't have freckles," Dean said defiantly. The others paused for a moment, staring without a word.

"What? I don't. It's a tan...."

"And then the youngest," Alice continued, ignoring him. "Black hair and blue eyes."

She gave a short pause, letting the weight of it sink into them. Of the three, only Frank seemed to understand the strange enormity of it.

"It's...it's us..." he said.

For a moment, no one spoke as the similarities became too much to ignore. Debra was the one who finally broke the spell over them.

"Nope," she said with assurance. "Look...there."

She pointed at the shape just off to the side of the family. A dog with floppy ears.

"No dog for this family. Cats all the way."

Debra smiled as she said it, but Alice wasn't sure what her mother was thinking at that moment. The confident grin could have been pride, but it might have been relief as well.

"Sorry to deflate the fantasy...for both of you," she said, putting a hand on Frank's shoulder. "I know how much you two like to stir up adventures, but the truth is this is just a coincidence."

Debra and Dean ventured off in different directions, leaving Alice and Frank to stare at the wall. Alice could hear Dean's scoffing little laugh as he walked away.

"I guess," Frank said finally, "they're right. Just a weird little coincidence."

"Yeah," Alice said. "I guess so."

Frank stood for a moment, placing his long, wiry hand on her shoulder. "Probably for the best," he said. "I think we have all the excitement we can handle at the moment."

When he walked away, he did so slowly, his eyes still on the painting until he disappeared around the corner. Alice watched him leave. Then, for a long time, she studied the picture with awestruck eyes.

⋆ ⋆ ⋆

Dinner was a sublime mixture of Chinese takeout, store-bought break and bake cookies, and bottled water. Alice asked why they didn't use the tap, and Frank assured her the "old taste" would wash out of the pipes soon enough.

"Should just be a day or two," he added. "Perfectly safe to bathe in though."

The work was far from done, but enough of the essentials were in place for the family to begin to get at least a little bit comfortable. The couches and loveseat were arranged around the living room, and even without an entertainment center or cable, the TV, cable box, and DVD player were in place. The calming, soothing drone of a movie they'd all seen a dozen times filled the quiet halls, changing the strange house into something familiar, comforting even. Dean, who was old enough to remember the first few times the family had moved, seemed apathetic, tapping away on his phone. For Alice, it was a completely new sensation. The new territory filled her with a deep, bone-aching feeling of homesickness blended with a surging fear of the night to come.

Soon, the sun was down, but the work continued into the evening. Debra went from room to room, putting sheets on each bed after Frank finally got them up. Beds were made, pillows arranged and piled up, and one by one, the family began to wilt. Even Dean, who had spent his day pretending to work, looked ready to fall into a bed, no matter how strange the room might be. For Alice, there came a final, ultimate moment of truth as they reconvened in the living room, where her mother yawned, stretched, and finally made it clear to all of them.

"I think we need to call it a night soon," she said, pouring herself a glass of red wine and sinking into the loveseat.

Frank scratched his belly, slid off his glasses, and rubbed his temples. "I'm pooped," he said. "So much more to do tomorrow." He glanced at his phone for a second, then slipped his glasses back on. "Well, shit . . ."

"What?" Debra asked through a yawn.

"Cold front coming in a few days. Looking like snow…maybe a lot of snow."

Excitement, at least for this moment, pushed Alice's nervous fear aside. They never got much snow this far south, and anything more than an inch was reason to celebrate.

"How much?" she asked.

Frank squinted. "Well, hell…if you believe the weather app, over five inches."

Alice's heart skipped a beat, and even the notoriously hard-to-excite Dean glanced up from his phone. Frank saw her perk up, but he was quick to let her down easy.

"I wouldn't get too excited," he said. "Probably been fifteen years since we've had snow like that. And about half the time they predict it, we end up with less than an inch."

"Yeah," Dean added, "no *way* we're getting five inches."

Alice deflated, and Frank backpedaled at least a bit. "You never know though. Weather does whatever it wants, so...you just never know. But...what I *do* know is we need to get some sleep. If it gets rough, we need to make sure we're comfy, which means there's a lot more to do tomorrow to get ready."

He looked at both of the kids, one after the other. "You kids good for the night?" He would never have asked a question like that before, but Alice understood. This was new territory, and being a little apprehensive was expected, even welcome. And despite the way it might look from the outside, Alice wasn't yet old enough to be immune to parental concern.

"Dean-o? You good?"

He nodded. "Yup."

Alice envied the unearned confidence of teenagers.

"Alice? You good?"

Her face couldn't begin to hide it, but what else could she say? She was too old to climb into Mommy and Daddy's bed, even if that was exactly what she wanted to do. The thought of the virtual miles between her and her parents sickened her probably just as much as it thrilled Dean. He had his own little corner of the place, complete with a side door in and out, closer to his room than any other room in the house. She could only imagine how much Dean would be using that on the weekends, especially after he was driving.

And, in her own way, Alice had her little corner as well. Her parents' room was upstairs, past windows that led into other rooms, a heavy green door that led into a cellar pulled from a horror movie, a narrow, harrowing set of stairs, and a half door that led into a shadowy crawl space and the attic beyond. Laid out in her mind, it reminded her of a level in a video game, the obstacles growing in length and complexity before hitting the finish line.

"I'm good."

Frank was still yawning, still rubbing his eyes when she answered. If there was any nuanced fear in her body language, he didn't notice it.

"Sounds good. Don't stay up too late, kiddos."

Debra sat a moment longer, waiting for her two boys to exit before she finally spoke.

"It's a little…different," she said, finishing off her glass of red wine.

Alice nodded, not quite able to find her voice. She was on unsteady ground, and she knew that if she said anything, she'd break. She wanted this. It was clear from that first day, with her and her father both like giddy children, drunk on the power of this place. That truth was clear to everyone, especially her mother, and to go back on it now would be a mistake she might never live down. She half expected her mother to pounce, to dig in and force a confession from her daughter, to make her admit, even if Frank never did, that this was all a terrible idea.

"Did I ever tell you about how much I moved around as a kid?" Debra asked, suddenly filling the gulf of silence between them. Alice cocked her eyebrows and shook her head, her voice still not safe to use just yet. Debra leaned back, staring at the ceiling.

"Yeah, my parents got divorced when I was eight. I bet Mom moved us probably ten, twelve times before I was old enough to move out on my own. I never really understood what it did to me when I was a kid. All I knew was how much I hated it, especially that first time. Our house was tiny, but it was all I ever knew. It had this little pine tree in the front yard, probably fifteen feet tall, definitely nothing special. But I was small enough that I could sneak in there, past all the needles, and just hide. It was like a clubhouse that nature built for me, and I used to imagine that I could live in there, you know? That if I ever got tired of the arguing and fighting, I could just take my blanket, some pillows, some food, and that would just be my new home."

Debra was staring off into some unseen distance with the saddest smile Alice had ever seen on her face. "I hated her for making me leave."

"I don't hate you," Alice said.

Debra laughed and wiped her eye. "I know that. That's not what I'm saying. I just know what it's like. Mom was always running from…well, whatever was around at the moment. It took me years to realize she wasn't just shitty with money, even though she totally was. She was just trying to make it work. Stay somewhere six months, a year, maybe two if you're lucky; then it's wheels up again, a few months late on rent, a few extra months' worth of cash in your pocket, and boom, onto the next one."

"Granny was like that?"

Debra smiled. "You've met her. You really that surprised?"

"No, not really."

"When I married your dad, I saw that he had a little bit of that… how do I even say it? Butterfly chasing in him. He would have been the type to up and move us on a whim."

"Is that what this is?"

Debra grinned, a sneaky thing that was full of grown-up secrets. "Oh no. I'm the one who crunches the numbers, and believe me, I crunched the hell out of these. We're coming out good here. And despite what your dad thinks about my lack of imagination, I can see what this place could be. I can see the sculpture hiding under all this…clay. This wasn't a quick choice on my part, honey. And I promise you, we won't be doing this twice."

Debra stood up, stretched, and added, "If you want to sleep out here, it's fine." She thought for a moment and said, "I'll even join you if you want me to. Make it a little girls' night campout."

Alice smiled. The idea sounded wonderful to her, but she saw this first night as something bigger. A sort of test. She had to make it through alone.

"Thanks, Mom. But I'm good. Really, I am."

"Okay then. You know where to find us."

* * *

Alice had every intention of heading to bed soon after she had the living room to herself, but a chorus of voices came into her mind, each whispering softly, "Just a few minutes more." So, she finished one movie, thought a bit, then popped in another one. By the time she finally awoke after dozing, it was already after midnight, and the house was a silent tomb. For a few minutes, she sat there, working up the nerve to even stand up out of the comforting groove she had made in the couch. That was when she heard the first pop.

In a flash, she was on her feet, scanning the well-lit room and the darkened corners just beyond it. The kitchen was a dim mix of shadows and hidden alcoves, the hall behind as black as the void of deep space. She waited, holding her breath, anxious and terrified to see if the sound would repeat. It never did.

The wind blew outside, not a howl but a whisper. She flipped on the kitchen light as she passed by, knowing full well that there was no way in hell it would be turned off again before she was in bed. A few extra dollars on the electric bill was a small price to pay for her safety against the unnamable things that hid in the dark. Slowly, she made her way across the living room, toward the hall that led to her bedroom, past the front sitting room with the wide, black aperture of a window, past the narrow staircase, past the silent closed door that was her brother's room. The two of them shared that end of the house, each of the separate rooms divided by a hallway. Dean's room had doors on both ends, one that led back into the sitting room and one to the house's side exit.

For a moment, Alice hovered in the room between, listening for signs her brother was still awake. Once more, from some deeper corner of the house, she heard a pop, and the hair on her neck stood up like a cat's.

"Baxter," she said under her breath.

It had to be him. Old houses were well known for how talkative they could be, but that nosy cat was no doubt making the place his personal playground. She could only imagine the tight corners he could squeeze into, and she fully expected him to disappear for hours, if not days, at a time.

Are you going to just stand there, girl?

The new voice again, a subtle, mocking tone. It was a fair thing to ask. This was, after all, her house, her room, her still-packed boxes of junk, and she wasn't going to be scared away from it, especially by nosy cats and creaking floorboards. With her courage firmly in place, she stepped into her room with the same teenage confidence that Dean had shown. Then, her heart sank like a stone. Her father, despite his best intentions, had not gotten the blinds in place as he said he would.

It was ghoulish somehow, the view from her safe, quiet room into the unfinished wood and moonlit windows of the long utility room. It wasn't any more dangerous than anything else she had seen in the house up to that point, and yet, it felt like a strange breach of her privacy, as if she'd be sleeping inside an aquarium.

"It's fine," she said to herself with a deep breath.

No, no, no, it's not, another voice said, the part of her mind that dealt exclusively in irrational fear. *Can't sleep like this, never, never, never!*

Alice closed her eyes and tried to empty her mind. After a few deep breaths, she opened them again, seeing the room with fresh eyes.

What do you see?

Boxes, filled with memories, her memories. A comforter, warm and soft, the years of use only making it more comfy. A bed, a refuge, a place to rest after a long day.

It's warm in there. Warm and safe.

Like a spell, a feeling of calm sleepiness began to wash over her. Her bed was a slice of her old house, carved out and slipped right into this new place, and all the fearsome creaks and moans couldn't keep her out of it.

She slid under the covers, hunkered down between the pillows, and sighed deeply. It was like being inside her own personal cocoon, so comfy and safe that she suddenly realized she had left the bedside lamp on. She considered ignoring it, just sleeping with the light on for one short night. What could be the harm in that? Alice didn't have nearly as much of her mother in her as she did her dad, but there were moments here and there. The idea of sleeping with the light on felt like the way her father might handle the situation. It would be a small concession made in the moment for a single purpose: to make herself feel better. In a way, it would be a bit like giving up, like admitting that she was, still in fact, a child. Her mother would have seen the silliness in it, and for once, Alice did too. Without a hint of hesitation, she reached up and flipped off the lamp.

The dark swallowed her, and she burrowed deeper into the blankets and pillows like a turtle receding into its shell. For a long time, there was nothing but darkness and the nervous, anxious sounds of her own body. Her breath coming in short, sharp spurts. Her heart thumping. Her ears ringing, filled with nervously pumping blood.

Alice couldn't begin to guess how long she stayed just like that, eyes wide, though seeing nothing but the comforter in front of her face. It might have been minutes, hours, but it felt more like years, unbroken in the silent dark. She might have stayed like that all night, maybe even forever, if it wasn't so damn hot. The comforter, a thick, pink wall of goose down, was like a shirt that was too tight. The more time that passed, the more impossible breathing felt, until she knew she couldn't stand it a minute longer. Finally, Alice peeled back the cover and stared into the midnight world of her room.

Now that her eyes had adjusted, it wasn't nearly as dark as she'd thought it would be, especially with the blinds not up yet. With a proper set of curtains and blinds, it might have been a true, deep black, but the moon peeked through the layers of windows from the utility room, coating half the room in a soft blue glow. She gazed at the wall, her eyes open and unblinking, refusing to look away for a moment. The minutes ticked by, and all at once, the mysterious fear of the room vanished, leaving behind only the growing sense of ownership she felt for this new chapter of her life.

"My room," she whispered, snuggling down and letting her eyes drift closed in contented silence for the first time.

★ ★ ★

Alice dreamt.

It was as strange and unreal as every other dream she could remember. The room, her room, was almost the same, but not quite. Bits stood out in strange, otherworldly ways, like the unopened boxes piled around the corner of her vision. And the fact that her bed wasn't positioned quite right, the ceiling farther away than it should be. And the way her windows, devoid of blinds or curtains, stretched wide, like monstrous mouths. These were false things, *dream* things, and she had experienced enough dreams to know not to fret too much over the weirdness. It was still *her* house.

Alice wanted to get out of bed, to wander, to see why she felt so bizarre, so *visible*. The idea rose in her mind that somehow she was in an aquarium, a feeling of being inside a glass tank to be gawked at and studied. It was a truly eerie feeling, but that still didn't explain the dread she felt, the cold hand massaging her heart.

No.

There was something else.

Something…wrong.

There was a darkness in the corner of her vision, something she couldn't quite place, that maybe she didn't *want* to place it.

Don't look. You won't see it if you don't look.

The truth was she couldn't look, not without moving first. It was gentle, a careful movement so subtle that it might not have happened at all. It was less than breathing, less than blinking, just a slight… turn. That was all it took for Alice to realize that the dark spot at the corner of the window was actually a silhouette. After that, it was the only thing she could see.

A face…

The fuzzy outline was hair, a wild mane of it. It was close, so close that Alice would have seen the fog of breath on the window if it wasn't so dark. She refused to move, refused to turn her head an inch, but she couldn't look away, not even for a moment. She was, without question, being *watched*. The fact that she was watching back did little to calm the throb inside her chest.

The moment lingered, stretched, and she became part of the darkness, one with despair. Never before had such a fear shadowed her heart, and in the eye of that terrifying storm, she would have welcomed death as a release from that heart-chilling terror.

No.

Alice studied the dark, featureless shape, focusing on the edges, and its utter, complete stillness. The dream seemed to congeal around her, the intangible nature of time making the truth clear to her after such a seemingly endless span.

It's not real.

How could it be? She almost laughed out loud at that moment, and a smile crept onto her face, invisible even in the darkness. Just then, the shape moved again, tilting to one side as a single, stunted hand rose to the glass and began to slowly tap.

CHAPTER FOUR

Alice was still screaming when her parents flipped on the light. The dream never ended, not really, but it didn't matter any longer. Her body wasn't hers to command in that moment. Something had shattered inside her, and control wasn't in her hands, so like a baby in a crib, she did the only thing she could. Her throat was hurting by the time they burst in, her mother in front and her father close behind in his underwear.

"Honey, honey, calm down!" her mother insisted, gathering Alice up in her arms.

"What is it?" her father asked.

It was ugly, the sort of scene that only ever seemed to happen in the dead of night when everyone is too tired and confused to make sense of it. By the time any of them got a hold on the situation, Dean had finally been roused from his room as well.

"What's her deal?" he asked as Alice huddled against her mother's chest.

"Where the hell were you?" Frank demanded.

"What?" Dean answered. "I was sleeping."

"You slept through that?" Frank asked, pointing at his hysterical daughter.

"I had my headphones in."

"There…there was someone there," Alice finally got out.

"Where, honey?"

She pointed at the bare window. Frank shook his head and stomped away, and moments later, the light in the utility room sprang to life. The three of them peered in through the window, searching for something that no one but Alice believed was there.

Frank appeared at the window and spoke loud enough for all to hear through the glass.

"Honey, I think it was just a dream. There's nothing in here. I promise."

"No," she said. "It wasn't. I know something was there."

Dean rolled his eyes and made for the door. "Hey," Debra called to him.

"What?"

"Keep your headphones out when you sleep. The damn house could be burning down and you'd never know."

"Whatever," he said as he walked away.

Frank was back a few seconds later, his eyes heavy and exhausted.

"So," he said, staring over the room. "First-night jitters, huh?"

"Go ahead," Debra said to her husband, her voice hard-edged and without sympathy.

"What?" Alice asked.

"Honey, I'll sleep in here with you tonight," Debra said.

For a brief moment, that old, silly pride snuck up in Alice's mind, but she brushed it easily aside this time. She was long past being stubborn.

"You…don't have to…"

"I know, baby."

Frank lingered in the doorway, mostly naked and growing increasingly awkward about it. Alice saw Debra flash him a look, one that she didn't quite understand. Either way, it got him talking.

"You two need anything?" Frank asked.

"No," Debra answered curtly. "We all just need some rest. This place has taken a lot out of us today."

Alice understood. This little moment between her parents was small, but it spoke volumes. Debra, she now realized, had spent the whole day wearing her own happy mask about the new house, and for the first time, it was starting to slip. Frank opened his mouth to reply, then seemed to think better of it. He turned to leave, stopping short once more.

"I'll get the blinds up tomorrow."

Soon, the two of them were alone in the darkness, curled around each other. Debra ran her hands through Alice's hair in long strokes that grew slower on each pass. She would be asleep soon, and even though she wasn't alone, Alice would *feel* alone. Eventually, Debra's hand fell still, and Alice worked up the nerve to peek over her mother's shoulder at the soft blue window. Everything was the same, except the terrifying visage was gone for good this time.

"It's okay, baby," Debra said, her voice barely a whisper.

"I…I know it wasn't real."

"It's fine," she yawned. "New houses can be a lot to get used to."

"It was… It just felt real."

"Dreams always do. Get some sleep, baby." She patted Alice's arm. Despite her fear, Alice felt herself growing heavy with sleep. At long last, she was safe, and she drifted away soon after.

⋆ ⋆ ⋆

The work on the house began the next day, long before Alice awoke. She never knew what time her mother had left her side, but the pillows and sheets were tucked in around her, the way that only a parent would do. She stumbled out into the hall, not at all surprised to see Dean's door still shut.

The kitchen had barely enough essentials to make it past the weekend, but she was able to scrounge up some dry cereal and a glass of orange juice. Her dad struggled through the front door, shimmying in with the small, metallic kitchen table.

"Need a place to eat?" he asked.

"No, I'm good."

He muscled it into place and leaned back with his eyes closed, stretching his lower back. "Second half of the night better than the first?"

"I guess so." She reached into the cereal box for a dry handful.

"So…you okay?"

"Yeah. I mean, just a nightmare."

Frank shook his head. "I know that. I mean, you okay with... all this?"

Alice smiled, not quite sure if he would buy it. The truth of the matter was that after last night, she wasn't sure what to think of the new house. It was, without a doubt, the most realistic dream she'd ever had, so much so that she was struggling to call it a dream at all.

"It's fine," she said after a moment.

Frank cocked his eyebrows. "Fine?"

"Good," she said, her tone suddenly sarcastic. "Great even. Perfect."

"Easy, killer," he said, throwing his hands up. "I was just asking."

She expected him to dig deeper, to crack a joke, to go out of his way to make her feel okay with everything. That was what he always did. Instead, he turned to leave, in search of more unfinished work, or perhaps just a more agreeable corner of the house.

He stopped, half in and half out of the room, and added, "Sit down and eat. That's what the table's there for."

* * *

The rest of that day was a blur of unpacking and settling as everyone wanted to get the work done as quickly as possible. There were months of actual repair work ahead, but for now, all the family could see was the task in front of them. There was a week left before Alice and Dean had to return to school, and neither of them wanted to spend it puttering around the house. Dean had a stack of new PlayStation 4 games that were still unwrapped, while Alice had twice as many books waiting for her to crack open.

While her mother and father flitted around, worrying themselves over where things went, Dean stuck mostly to his room. Once, around two o'clock, Alice crept to his door, wincing each time the floor creaked underfoot. She was greeted by the familiar sounds of virtual guns firing, along with the death moans of every enemy on the face of the earth.

Slacking off, she thought to herself.

Alice had spent the first half of the day steadily at work, and by noon, her room was enough "hers" to make her feel comfortable again. She didn't want to put her dad out, but when she glanced up at the still-bare windows, she knew there was no way in hell she would sleep in there again without the blinds. Newly resolved, she ventured out, following his voice, prepared to pour on the guilt if she had to. Her dad was remarkably easy to break, and if he said he was too busy, it wouldn't take much more than a tilt of the head and a "*Please, Daddy*." She was lost in her head, practicing what she might say to him when she saw it.

"Moooommmm!"

Both of her parents came bounding down the stairs, and Alice suddenly realized that she hadn't yelled for her dad like she normally did. He was almost always her go-to parent, even if no one would ever admit it. She wondered if anyone else noticed.

"What is it?" Debra asked, out of breath.

Alice winced and pointed at the crude family drawing on the wall behind her. It looked almost the same as it had the day before, but someone had added something new on top of the family dog. It was an irregular, crudely painted black X.

"What?" her mother asked. "Why did you do that?"

"Me?" Alice yelled incredulously. "I didn't."

Frank stepped forward, eyeing it carefully. "The paint," he said to himself, "where'd it come from?"

"Why are you asking me?" Alice asked.

The three of them glanced from one to the other, each person's face so earnest with confusion that the answer seemed clear.

"Dean!" Debra called down the hallway.

"What?"

"Dean, get your ass out here," Frank demanded.

Debra and Alice turned to each other, confused at his sudden burst of angry energy. It wasn't that he never cursed; it was just rarely pointed at anyone other than whatever sort of project or repair he was working on.

"It's okay, Dad," Alice said, but her father didn't seem to hear her.

"Hang on," Dean said from behind the closed door of his room. It seemed to Alice that he walked as slowly as possible out into the hallway. "What is it…?"

Dean joined them in the hallway – and at the looks on their faces, he stiffened defensively. "What?"

Debra took her hand off her hip long enough to point at the painting. Dean stared at it, then raised his eyebrows.

"Who the hell did that?" he asked.

"That's what we're trying to find out," Debra said.

"Cut the shit," Frank ordered.

"Honey, calm down," Debra said.

"No. If he's trying to scare his sister, he needs to own up to it."

"What, you seriously think I did this?" Dean asked.

"Are you saying you didn't?" Frank asked.

Dean looked from his mom to his dad and back again. Alice could see him biting the inside of his lip the same way he used to do when they played cards together and he had a good hand. He glanced over at Alice, but just for a second before looking away.

"Yeah, sure…it was me."

Debra sighed, but before she could say anything, Frank led off.

"Go to your damn room," he said.

"Whatever," he said, adding as he walked away, "This fucking house sucks."

He punctuated his exit by slamming the heavy wooden door, the sound echoing throughout the house. It was a blatant attempt to get a reaction, and Alice half expected her father, in his abnormally angry state, to take the bait. Instead, he walked away without a word.

"What…was all that about?" Alice whispered when she was alone with her mother.

Debra shook her head, dumbstruck. "I really don't know. Usually, I'm the one yelling and Dad's the one calming me down."

Alice laughed, a bit too hard.

"What are you laughing at?" Debra asked with a smirk.

"Nothing. Nothing at all. What's his deal, though? He snapped at me earlier too. Yelling isn't really his style. Sounds kind of weird coming from him, to be honest."

Debra nodded. "It *does*, doesn't it? I don't know. He didn't seem to sleep very much before…all the excitement." She glanced down at Alice but didn't say anything about last night's episode, a fact that Alice appreciated. "You been working on your room?" Debra asked.

"Yeah. Pretty much got it, I think. Except for…well…the blinds."

"Let's check it out."

Alice led her in, and Debra nodded in approval. Alice's trophies, pictures, and favorite toys were all laid out in place. On her shelf, next to a picture of her school camping trip with her friends flanking her on both sides, was her small collection of Funko Pop figures, which included Hermione, Frankenstein's Monster, and Max from *Where the Wild Things Are.*

"Nothing left but empty boxes," Debra said. "Very nice. It's pretty cozy in here with all the stuff put up. What do you think?"

Despite all the unpleasantness of the last twenty-four hours, Alice had to agree.

"I think it will work," she said, trying not to look at the window.

"Look, about your dad and Dean," Debra said, closing the door softly behind her. "I don't know how much you've picked up on, but it's pretty tense between them. Your dad is putting everything into this house. So much so that if it doesn't work, it won't just be a little thing. He'll feel like a failure. And on the flip side, your brother *really* didn't want to move."

"He said that?"

"No," Debra answered. "He never says anything. But I know. I can tell, even if your dad can't. I still don't know why the hell Dean did…that, with the paint. But I'll find out. Either way, I'm pretty sure it doesn't have anything to do with you, if that makes sense."

"Soooo, don't take it personal if Dean acts like a dick?"

Debra closed her eyes, no doubt remembering the dozens of times she had cursed in front of her daughter over the past few days.

If there was a lecture in there, it shriveled up and died before she got it out.

"Yeah. That's one way to say it."

Debra turned to leave, and Alice followed her out. She wanted to look at the painting one more time, in all of its creepy glory. She couldn't quite explain the urge, but she wanted to study it closer, to stand there in front of it, alone.

"Ugh," Debra said as they walked past it. "I need to get some paint before next weekend. I can't stand looking at that thing."

Alice waited for her mother to leave, and then she leaned closer. The brush stroke and black paint of the X *did* seem to match the original, which was an odd coincidence. She imagined the lengths her brother must have gone to for…what exactly? To get her back because she was more into the idea of this place than he was? To try to force the family to move? None of it made much sense.

There is no sense to it, a voice whispered. *Because he's lying.*

Alice gave it a few minutes before she approached Dean's bedroom. Everyone needed time to cool down, and any attempt to move in too soon would have ended with her on the receiving end of her brother's wrath. When she finally worked up the nerve, she tapped so softly that she was certain that he hadn't actually heard her.

"What?" he yelled, so loudly that she was sure her parents were about to come stomping down the hall.

"It's me," she said as she eased open the door a crack and peeped in. She waited a moment for him to invite her in, and when he didn't she rolled her eyes and added, "Please."

Dean stomped across the room and flung open the door; he silently stared at her, eyebrows up, as if to say, *Can I help you?*

"Why?" Alice asked.

"Why what?"

She pushed him into the room and pulled the door closed behind him. Already, it had the teenage boy smell to it, the smell of sweat and feet, and not a single box was completely unpacked.

"Why did you lie?"

"Just go," he said. "I don't want to get in trouble for being mean to the golden girl."

"Let's see the paint," Alice demanded.

"What the hell are you talking about?"

"If you did it, show me the paint. I want to see it."

"I threw it out. Jesus, what do you want from me?"

Alice sat down in his recliner, better known as his gaming chair, and crossed her legs.

"Are you telling me you studied that picture, went to the store, bought paint, snuck out of your bedroom…" She reached over into a box and fished out a pair of – hopefully clean – underwear. "…and you did all of this before you even unpacked your clothes?"

Dean rolled his eyes. "Fine. No. It wasn't me."

A wave of fear and excitement washed over Alice in a flash.

"Why did you say it was?" she said, her voice rising.

"Because Dad's been all over my ass about moving. I don't know what his deal is, but have you ever seen him act like that? Mr. Sweetness was going off on me like I fucking stole a pack of cigarettes at a gas station."

Alice barely heard him ranting. She could only sit there, shaking her head in disbelief at what her brother's admission actually meant.

"What, are you going to give me a guilt trip too?"

"What?" She looked up. "No. I don't care about you lying. I just want to know who did it.… I mean, if you didn't do it, who did?"

"You mean it wasn't you?" Dean asked.

"No!" Alice said, leaping from the chair. "I was terrified last night. You honestly think I'd do something like that?"

By then, Dean had his phone out, and he was flipping through pictures on Instagram. If he was even remotely interested in the conversation, he was doing a wonderful job of hiding it.

"I dunno," he said. "Figured you were trying to get me into trouble or something. Seems like something you'd do."

"What makes you say that?" she asked. "I never get you in trouble."

"Whatever."

Alice leaned over Dean's phone, pretending to look at it. Before he could pull it back, she snatched it out of his hands and hid it behind her back.

"Heeeyyyy," he said.

"You know, you really need to learn something new to say. 'Whatever' is getting pretty old."

"All right, give me my phone back now."

"Stop it," Alice said, holding a hand out in front of her and pushing her brother back a half step. "For one second, just stop."

Dean took a deep breath and glared down at her. He looked like a bull preparing to charge.

"Before you fly off the handle, just think for a second. Think about what it means. If you didn't paint it, and I didn't paint it, then who did?"

"I never said I believed you," Dean snapped.

"I never said I believed *you*," she replied. "But let's just pretend we both believe each other. Do you think Mom or Dad did it?"

Dean shrugged, "*I don't carrrreee...*"

Alice rolled her eyes. "It wasn't them. And it wasn't us. So..."

She paused, leaning forward, waiting for Dean to finish the thought for her. When it became clear that he wouldn't, Alice did it for him.

"Maybe I *did* see someone last night. Someone...*in our house*."

Dean's mouth fell open in apparent horror. It was enough for Alice to drop her guard, and she pulled the phone from behind her back as she nodded.

"Amazing," Dean whispered before snatching his phone back, shaking his head derisively. "You're too old for this shit. If you wanted to get me in trouble, there were easier ways to do it."

"But—"

"Get out of my room."

"*Dean*—"

"I said," Dean spat as he pushed her forward, "get out of my room."

He didn't quite slam the door, but he didn't need to. He had made his point loud and clear. Alice stood there out in the hall for a moment, her eyes beginning to water, not out of sadness but frustration. There was something strange going on, but, for the moment, it seemed she was going to be left alone with it, without her big brother's help. She turned and made her way back to her own room to hide her eyes and let the moment of pitiful anger pass.

CHAPTER FIVE

By the time Alice realized she hadn't seen Baxter all day, the sun was beginning to dip in the sky. More than ever, the house seemed to be more glass than wood; the deepening dark seeped in from the outside, making her stomach churn. The realization that the cat was missing led to a quiet but frantic hunt through the house. Alice went room to room, conducting her search quietly at first, mainly because she didn't want anyone to know how scared she was. There were too many coincidences in this house for her to ignore, and she hated the feeling that this place was somehow getting the better of her.

"Baxter," she whispered quietly into each room, fully aware that he ignored everyone in the family. So, she dropped down on hands and knees, checking under every bed, behind every curtain, inside every empty box. She had completely cleared the downstairs, making sure to close doors behind her, when her father bounded down the steps, coming to a halt in the hallway just outside her room. He had that exhausted, almost manic look in his eyes again, and she expected him to dart past her. At first, that looked like exactly what he planned to do, but something about the nervous glare in her eyes must have pulled him back.

"Ah, shit," he said suddenly.

"What is it?"

"Your blinds. They're on my list.... I'll do them right now!"

"Oh, yeah," she said.

Frank eyed her for a moment, then asked, "What's up?"

"I...uh..."

Alice didn't want to speak, didn't know if she even could speak. What if he was actually missing? Just behind her father, the creepy drawing peeked out over one shoulder, mocking her. Was the black X over the dog in the drawing bigger now?

No, a calm voice whispered. *Don't start that. It's all just a nasty trick. Don't turn it into something bigger than it is.*

Her attempt to calm herself failed miserably, and she felt herself begin to tremble. If she didn't do something, she would be crying again any second.

"Alice?" Frank asked.

"I can't find Baxter," she said in a syrupy voice.

"Umm…hmmm…I thought I saw him upstairs earlier," Frank said, putting two fingers to his chin as he always did whenever he was thinking. "Actually…maybe I just heard him pawing around. I figured it was him. If not, we've got some squirrels in the attic."

Alice stepped past him, still not wanting to talk, afraid that her fear would burst out of her.

"Give me a second, and I'll help you look," Frank called after her.

"It's fine," Alice replied, without looking back. She didn't care about the cat, not as much as she'd cared about Patty, the ancient, endlessly sweet cat they'd buried a few years back. That one had floored her, hit her harder with a dose of mortality than she was ready for, but Baxter…was just a cat. He was a pain in the ass, never very friendly, and prone to vanishing for hours at a time. No, it wasn't concern for him that made her feel so suddenly frantic; it was what the cat represented. If he was gone, if she couldn't find him, it meant something bigger was going on. Something that her darkest imagination had only begun to hint at.

She made her way upstairs and continued checking every room, meticulously closing doors behind her. She walked slowly, back down the hall, and found her eyes turning to the half-sized crawl-space door. It was small, only about three feet tall, and even she would have to duck to squeeze into it. It had a small latch, which, she noticed for the first time, hung curiously open.

"You almost ready for dinner?" Debra asked from behind her, close enough to make Alice yelp in surprise.

"You scared me to death!"

"Sorry," Debra said. "What are you up to anyway?"

"I was looking for Baxter. I can't find him anywhere."

"Why are you so concerned with him all of a sudden?"

Alice rolled her eyes, a skill that seemed to grow in her each day as she too approached her teens. "I don't know. I just haven't seen him."

"Well, unless he knows how to turn handles, I don't think he's in there."

"You didn't go in there, did you?" Debra asked.

"No," Alice said. "Have you?"

Debra reached for the handle and turned, and for a brief second, Alice winced. She didn't know what to expect in there, but the possibility of what could be inside was enough to put her on edge. The door swung wide, and the meager, yellow hallway light poked a few feet in. There wasn't much of anything beyond a plywood floor, some bits of loose insulation, and the occasional mouse dropping. Less than a foot in, a wall of junk rose up, creating a solid roadblock. Alice dipped down onto one knee, peering through the spaces between the boxes, deeper back into the dark. It seemed that the crawl space stretched the distance of the hallway, and on the far end was a tiny staircase leading up to the attic.

"I don't know who the hell designed this place," Debra said. "Supposedly, there's a ton of space up there for storage, but you have to fit it through this little damn tiny door. I bet it'll take a day's worth of digging this trash out of there before we can even get to the attic."

"Why would they do that?" Alice asked.

"Like everything else in this Frankenstein of a house, it was added later. The old owners wanted to finish out the attic overhead. Apparently, most houses this old don't have actual attics, just empty space. But this was the only way to get up there, besides the entrance in our closet."

"Wait, your closet has an entrance too?"

"Yeah, the walk-in. Just a tiny hole, boarded up at the moment. No stairs or ladder or anything. They must have given up before it all got finished up."

Debra closed the door and latched the lock. "If I had to guess, the cat is probably running around in the woods, eating birds. He's a city cat, so he's probably going wild out there."

Alice looked out the hallway window, into the gray woods beyond. "But it's so cold out there."

"He'll come home soon. Come on, let's get something to eat."

★ ★ ★

Debra had been baking a frozen brick of a lasagna, the kind that takes half a day to finish, and the smell of it was drifting so heavily through the house that even Dean had no choice but to heed the call. They sat around the couch once again, watching movies.

"Satellite should be in tomorrow," Frank said, answering a question no one asked. "It'll be a pain in the butt to relearn all those channels again."

"They have cable in town," Dean said as he finished off his food and left the room.

"That's your sole contribution to the conversation?" Frank asked bitterly. Dean was gone before anyone had a chance to follow up in any meaningful way.

"Why?" Debra glared at her husband.

"Don't you start too."

Alice took that as her cue to leave the living room. She could hear everything as she walked back toward her room. They fell in on each other, whispering at first, before their voices bloomed into hushed semi-screams that might have been funny if they weren't so sad. The two of them retreated into the kitchen as their voices grew louder and louder.

"It's because you didn't even hear him. He's old enough to have an opinion...."

"Oh, his attitude is my fault now? The last I checked, a fifteen-year-old isn't paying the fucking mortgage...."

The general dance wasn't new to Alice, but the tone was. She still couldn't quite wrap her head around how sharp and casually cruel her usually bubbly father had become in the past few days. She tried her best to remember what her mother had said, about how hard he was being on himself with the new house, but it wasn't enough for her to excuse him. From the sound of it, her mother was done looking the other way herself. Alice had seen them go a few rounds countless times in the past, and it didn't really matter who was right. Her mother had a resolve in arguing that her father simply didn't possess. Eventually, he would burn out and end up apologizing long before she would.

Alice had heard enough; she slipped into a pair of fuzzy slippers and grabbed her coat from the wall hooks just inside of the kitchen. She never made eye contact with her parents, but the argument died just long enough for her to enter and exit.

"Where you going?" Frank asked, clearly beginning to tire and looking for an out.

"Just some fresh air out back. Maybe listen to the frogs."

"Honey, there are no frogs this time of year," Debra said.

Alice didn't stop to listen, and the arguing started back up as soon as she was out of their sight. It was too cold to be out there in pajama pants, but the bracing wind was a nice change from the surprisingly sturdy central heating unit that blasted out of the old wall and floor grates. Before her, the concrete deck shined under a single, blue light that hovered from a pole a dozen feet away from the dark, gaping hole of the pool. The wind whipped through her hair, and Alice pulled her hood up, sinking further down into the jacket. It was, as she expected, a bit creepy out there. The blue light shined down, reflecting off the ripped sides of the pool liner, blending with the gray concrete, and casting the entire area in an otherworldly glow. It reminded her of a sci-fi movie, the way everything looks just before a flying saucer lands and the aliens start killing everyone.

Alice whistled as she walked, trying to match her tone to the wind. Together, she and the frozen breeze made a strange music that mixed with the endless moan of the woods. Once, the wind grew to a howl, and she stopped, listening. Never more had she been convinced that the woods themselves were alive, that this house, this pathetic stamp of humanity, was just a boil, a tumor, a cancer on something larger, older, wilder. They were trespassers here, fleas on the back of something they could barely even comprehend. The only question was, would they be strong enough to dig in and stake their claim, or be driven back, beaten, and maybe even broken in the process?

Alice made a round toward the back of the long, rectangular pool, checking out the deep end. How cold had the night grown when she wasn't looking, wasn't expecting it? There were a few days in the previous week when spring teased them, promising to come early, to bypass the coldest months of January and February altogether. But the night had gone from simply cold to bitter, and in a few moments, she was shivering. She passed by the diving board, taking a second to peer into the darkest depths of the black water. A gust of wind raced through the pool beneath her, whipping up a sudden, unexpectedly foul smell that nearly made her gag. Just like before, it reminded her of sewage, but there was something else. Something deeper.

Something dead.

The wind died, and she looked closer, leaning forward to catch a glimpse of something glimmering at the bottom of the pool. Something too bright to be part of that grimy water. A plastic bag caught in the wind maybe? Some random bit of trash that ended up in the pool?

No.

Something glistened in the darkness, a pair of dim beads that still managed to shine in the moonlight.

No.

* * *

Alice didn't politely wait for her parents to stop arguing as she normally would.

"Where's the flashlight?"

Frank and Debra both stared at her; the panic in her face must have been clear, unmistakable.

"Honey, what's wrong?" Debra asked.

"Jesus, you're shivering," Frank added.

"The flashlight," Alice demanded, her voice breaking a bit.

"I…I don't know," Frank answered. "Probably in a box somewhere."

"Mom, let me have your phone."

"Alice, what's going on?"

"Just let me have it," she said, nearly yelling now. "Please, come with me."

Debra handed it over, and Alice flipped on the flashlight app. Then, she dashed back toward the back door, her parents following closely at her heels. Her mother kept firing off questions from behind her, but Alice didn't even glance back. She needed to see what that oddly light shape was in the pool, even if, deep in her heart, she already knew the answer. Without a word, she walked to the diving board, leaned over, and held the light over the lip of the pool. There, at the bottom, was Baxter's glassy-eyed corpse.

CHAPTER SIX

Alice nearly hyperventilated when she saw it clear in the light. There was a moment, a short one, when she tried to talk herself out of it, when one of her inner voices, a soft motherly one, tried to convince her it was all okay.

It's not Baxter. No, not him at all.

Alice couldn't hear the voice clearly, not when her heart was pounding so dangerously loud. As awful as the moment was, Debra didn't waste any time. She grabbed the phone, slapped a hand onto her daughter's shoulder, and marched her back inside, back where it was warm, back where dead cats didn't stare up at you with green, dead eyes. Whatever awful work was left to be done, it would be up to Frank to handle it.

"Calm down," Debra said, pulling a chair out from the kitchen table. "Just breathe, just breathe."

Debra stood in front of Alice for a moment, rubbing her shoulders, letting her calm down bit by bit. She touched Alice's face once and winced.

"You're freezing," she said. "You want some tea? Something to warm you up?"

Alice hated tea, but not knowing what else to do, she nodded. Debra turned to the sink and began to fill up a coffee mug to heat in the microwave. Alice, still dazed by it all, glanced back toward the living room and the pool beyond. There was a clear line of sight from the kitchen, through the living room, and past the sliding glass doors that led out to the pool. Even from the kitchen, she could see her father balancing the net on the end of a rusty pole some twelve feet long. He was leaning back, struggling with the weight of it, moving slowly and steadily to keep the load on the end from falling. And there it was, rising out of the darkness, a mass of slick fur.

"Oh *god...*"

Debra hurried back to Alice's side.

"Jesus Christ," she replied. "Come on. You don't need to see this."

Dean, who had been roused by all the commotion, walked into the kitchen.

"What's her problem?"

"Go out by the pool," Debra said. "See if your father needs help."

Dean did as he was told, but he moved as slowly as humanly possible. Alice saw the pair of them huddled over the lump that had once been the cat.

Why did it smell so bad? He couldn't have been dead for long.

"Come on, honey," Debra said as she led Alice away from the kitchen. "You don't want to have nightmares."

Debra made a quick stop by the bathroom, just long enough to wet a washcloth in the sink. When the pair finally made it to Alice's room, she dabbed her daughter's forehead as they sat on the bed. Alice stared down at her comforter for a moment, and when she glanced back up, she saw something strange in her mother's eyes. What was it? Grief? Fear?

No. It was expectation. Debra was clearly bracing herself for something, some flood of emotion to pour out of Alice, and when it never came, the expectation had changed to confusion.

"You...okay, honey?" Debra asked.

Alice was still struggling a bit to breathe, but she was able to recall her old asthma days, the slow, steady in and out. It was muscle memory at that point, the kind of thing that would never leave her regardless of whether or not she carried around an inhaler. Alice took a deep breath, readied her response, then faltered.

"I know that Baxter meant a lot to you...."

Did he? a cynical voice whispered.

Alice didn't have an answer for that. Something deep in her chest seemed to hurt, but Alice wasn't the stoic type. Just like her father, she had been known to tear up over made-for-TV movies, pop ballads, even commercials from time to time. She would never admit it, but she was a crier. So why wasn't she crying now?

"I imagine he just slipped off the edge...probably trying to get at a bird or something," Debra said. "It's so cold out, and it's icy out there around the concrete...I bet he slipped in and just couldn't..."

Did any of that make sense?

No, it doesn't. But I'm sure you'll play along. It will be easier for everyone to play along.

Alice tried to quiet the voices long enough to think through it herself. Her mother's version of the story wasn't a real answer, wasn't anything based on evidence or truth. It was just an explanation, the kind of thing you turned to when there wasn't a satisfying answer. That was what people did to stay sane because if you started looking for what-ifs, you'd go crazy. You'd get buried in new questions.

"Honey, are you sure you're okay?" Debra was staring into her eyes now, her growing concern written across her face. "Alice? What is it? Please say something."

What to say? How to say it? The problem was her mother still thought it was about the cat.

Why can't she see something so fucking obvious?

It was a fair question. Why were adults so in tune with the complex things in life that they missed, or worse, ignored, the simple things? Why was it so difficult for her to see such an obvious truth? Alice didn't want to remind her, didn't feel like she needed to. Once the words were said, once the truth was uttered, it would be out there, and then no one could pretend not to know.

"M-mom..." she said, her lip quivering.

"What is it, baby? Please just tell me."

"Th-the painting..."

Debra's brow furrowed in confusion, her head gently shaking as she struggled to find the archive in her brain that would let the word make sense.

"Painting?" she muttered just as her eyes grew wide with the memory.

* * *

Alice stared at the ceiling, realizing for the first time that she actually hated the way it looked. At their old house, the ceiling showcased a swirl of ridges and rises, like the surface of an alien planet. She used to stare at it, glowing soft blue from her nightlight, and she would imagine it actually *was* an alien planet. She would picture spiders, the ones so tiny that you could barely see them, trekking across that endless, barren terrain in search of…what exactly? Another wall?

They say those spiders are so small that you eat them in your sleep, that they just crawl into your mouth and disappear forever, and you never even know the difference.

Who says? she thought.

They do.

Debra was somewhere out in the hall. Alice could hear her still milling around out there. She could tell from the footsteps that her mother had looked at the painting, walked back to Alice's bedroom door, then repeated the process several times. Her mother hadn't known how to respond when she'd brought it up, but Alice couldn't blame her. She wasn't jaded or bitter about any of it, not the move or even the cat. The simple fact was Alice was just old enough to know that her mother wasn't magic, that she couldn't pull answers out of thin air. None of this made sense, and she pitied the idea that her mother might soon walk into her room and try to convince her that it did. Moments later, Debra tried to do just that.

"Honey," she said quietly, "I think…"

Alice tried to imagine herself coming up with an excuse, and it occurred to her that maybe this was what being an adult was all about. Lying to yourself and those you love even when the truth was the only thing that seemed possible.

"This whole situation with Baxter. It was just an accident."

Alice looked at her, wondering. Did she actually believe it? If she had heard, from Dean's own mouth, that he hadn't painted on the wall, would she still say it? Alice considered that, trying to decide the exact moment when a kindness became a lie, or when an accidental lie became a knowing one.

"Have you talked to Dean?" Alice asked.

"About what?"

"The painting."

Debra shook her head. "What does it matter?"

"Because he didn't do it," Alice said as Debra began to shake her head, refusing to hear it. "He told me he didn't."

"Alice…"

"Go ask him—"

"I don't have to ask him!" Debra snapped, stomping her foot. "Even if he didn't do it, then you did."

Alice leaned away from her without realizing it. She was surprised by the sudden outburst, but more than that, she was disappointed; this was exactly what she thought might happen. It was another one of those moments, one of too many, where her mother didn't believe her even when she was telling the truth.

"How can you say that?" Alice cried. "I didn't do anything."

"One of you did. If it wasn't you, then Dean was lying to you."

"Lying about what?"

Debra turned around; Dean was in the hallway behind her. His face was red and chapped from the wind, and his nose was still running.

"Tell her," Alice said.

"Tell her what?"

"About the painting. Tell her what you told me."

Debra stared at him, a hand on one hip. "Tell me."

Dean shrugged and rolled his eyes. "Fine. It wasn't me."

"Why did you lie?" Debra asked.

"Because Dad was up my ass about it. It's easier just to say I did it than to stand there arguing."

Footsteps began moving toward them, and Frank appeared, still out of breath from what she could only assume was shoveling.

"It's done," he said. He looked past his wife into Alice's room. "You okay, honey?"

Debra answered for her. "We're having a little bit of a mystery here," she said. "And we're not leaving until we get to the bottom of this."

Alice sat up from her bed and walked to the doorway. She didn't always see eye to eye with her mother, but Debra knew how to fix things, and this was a moment she wanted to see fixed immediately.

"No," Frank said sharply. "Not at all."

"What?" Alice asked.

"I'm *exhausted*," he answered. "I just buried the damn cat. All I want, more than anything else, is to just go to bed."

"But Dean didn't paint that X on the picture."

Frank had already turned to walk away, and he turned back, throwing his hands into the air. "So?"

"What do you mean?" Alice asked.

Dean was shaking his head. "Someone painted an X over the dog in the picture," he said sternly, his assertiveness surprising Alice. "The next day, our cat is dead. Do you need me to draw a diagram?"

"Watch your damn mouth."

The tone of her father's voice was deeper, harder, more uncaring than Alice had ever heard, and from the looks on everyone else's face, they felt the same.

"No one in this *fucking* house is going to talk to me like that," he continued. "Do you understand?"

At Dean's stubborn silence, Frank reached out and grabbed him, bunching up the shoulder of his sweatshirt and giving him a sturdy shake.

"Dad, what the hell—"

"Do. You. Understand?"

The knuckles of Frank's hand were white as he gripped Dean's arm, but the truly disturbing sight was his other hand. It was balled up and raised, the unquestionable symbol of a man about to swing.

"Yes," Dean answered, a deep fear in his voice.

Frank loosened his grip, and Dean slipped a few feet away. For a moment, Frank just stared at his hands, as if wondering how they had gotten away from him.

"That's it for tonight," he said, his voice flat. The fire was gone now, but no one else seemed to know if it was gone for good. "Tomorrow, we can sort this out. But it's been a long day. A very long day."

Alice didn't know what to do, what to say. Her father was a gentle man; he always had been. Frank was a dreamer, just like she was, and she'd seen him shoo spiders out of their living room at the old house. "Ohh, a nice big boy like this," he'd say. "It'll keep the roaches away."

Never in her life had her father laid a hand on her, and as far as she knew, it was the same for Dean. And now, at this new crossroads, none of them, Debra included, knew quite how to respond.

Frank backed away and receded into the dark hallway. Alice stared, trying to understand what she was seeing. Was it sudden guilt in his eyes, the realization that his obsession with this house had soured into something ugly and dark? Moments later, he was gone. Dean waited a few seconds longer before retreating back to his room, avoiding Alice's eyes. His usual door-slamming was replaced by a nudging of the door, so gentle that it barely made a noise at all. Alice, still standing in her own doorway, looked up at her mother's face. Debra was shaking, but Alice couldn't quite tell if it was with anger or fear or some delicate mixture of the two.

"Mom?"

"Go to bed," she said, her voice quivering. "We'll talk about it tomorrow. I've got to go…talk to your father."

Alice stood half in and half out of her room, staring down the hallway. The picture was just out there, just out of sight. All she had to do was walk around the corner and see it, but she didn't dare. The house seemed to breathe as it always did whenever she was alone, and suddenly, for the first time, Alice felt certain that she *wasn't* alone. The moment came and went quickly, something too easily dismissed in her well-lit bedroom, but there was no question in the matter. Even behind the closed door and newly hung blinds, she didn't think she was being watched. She *knew* it.

CHAPTER SEVEN

That night, Alice slept with the light on. When she awoke, she sat up suddenly, the overhead light blocking out any sight of the sun or moon, leaving her confused as to what time it actually was. The clock, green and beaming, told her it was 6:15 a.m., less than an hour before her normal wake-up time for school. Once the break was over, that time would probably be pushed back half an hour or so, thanks to the new, longer commute.

Alice climbed out of bed, turned off the overhead light, slipped back under the covers, and stared up at the ceiling Everything that had happened since they moved in, each and every event, stretched out like a line of marching ants. She moved them around in her mind, rearranging them, trying to make sense of everything. After what she assumed was, at minimum, a solid hour of daydreaming, Alice looked at the clock again. It read 6:29 a.m. She could track the sound of footsteps somewhere in the house around her.

Overhead. Heavy. Boots…no, dress shoes.

Dad.

Alice didn't realize he had to work that day, but it didn't surprise her. Another set.

Down the steps, creaking one by one. Lighter. Barefoot.

Mom.

She rolled over, deciding to give sleep one more try, when she heard another set.

Closer. Solid. Tired feet dragging.

Dean's awake too.

Alice crept into the hall, staring across at Dean's still-closed door. He was still asleep then, but there were footsteps in the kitchen and the familiar scent of coffee; the solid thuds down the stairs signaled that Frank was making his way down. His new sales job was for an insurance company, and about half of his days were spent on the road. The downside was that the job paid on commission, and if he wasn't selling, he wasn't making money. He was always the first out the door, but this was early, even for him. Alice waited, considering whether or not she even wanted to see him.

As she thought, she heard the old, heavy side door creak open and closed roughly and the grumble of her dad's truck starting up. He was gone then, and for the first time she could remember, he left without saying goodbye to any of them.

He didn't want to say goodbye, a soft voice whispered. *Must still be mad at you.*

"Is he gone?" Dean was peering out through his doorway like a kid spying on Santa Claus, nervous that an adult might catch him.

"I...I think so."

She walked over to his door, and Dean let it drift open the rest of the way. He looked a bit like a ghost, something vaporous and not totally there.

"You...okay?" she asked.

Dean scowled, a familiar face that spoke of his desire to call her an idiot, a child, a brat. Then, the frown softened and she saw her brother again, the one who used to play monster with her when she was only six years old, the boy who seemed to revel in the fact that he had a younger sister, someone to look out for.

What happened to that boy?

"No," he said in a moment of surprising honesty. He rubbed his shoulder where Frank had grabbed him. "My arm still hurts. I've never seen him like that before, at least not with me."

"What does that mean?"

"I've seen him screaming at Mom before. A long time ago. He looked mad enough then to...I don't know. Do something." Dean shook his head and looked at the shining floorboards under his bare feet. "What the hell is going on here?"

Alice shook her head. "I don't know."

For a moment, neither spoke. A question was burning a hole in her, but though she didn't want to ask, she had to get it out.

"Are you sure it wasn't you?"

Dean's face momentarily blurred with frustration again, but he kept it under control. "No, it wasn't." He thought for a moment, then added, "Was it you? Tell me the truth. If it was, I won't even be mad...."

"It wasn't," Alice squeaked. It was clear that both of them wanted the other to be responsible, not so they could score a petty win. No, they just wanted answers. They wanted this situation to make sense, and now that they finally, truly believed each other, silence hung between them. They both drifted off to their separate corners to think.

A bit later, after Alice had brushed her teeth and made her way into the living room, her mother appeared. Her eyes were a bit puffy, but otherwise, she seemed no worse for wear.

"Do you want some breakfast?" she asked from the kitchen.

"I'm fine," Alice answered from the couch, her tone shaky, unsure.

Debra, despite her occasionally tough demeanor, picked up on the thread. "Alice, come in here."

Alice did as she was told, and when Debra pulled a chair out from the kitchen table, they both took seats.

"You're not fine," Debra said. She took a deep breath and glanced over her shoulder, back down the narrow hallway toward Dean's room. "You talk to your brother this morning?"

Tears threatened to spill out of Alice's eyes; she didn't dare speak. Instead, she nodded. Debra seemed to recognize her daughter's usual, sensitive fragility, and she stuck to yes or no questions.

"Is he okay?"

A tough one, not easy to answer truthfully without words. Rather than lie or explain, Alice just shook her head no.

"Yeah," Debra replied. "I wouldn't guess so. I'm going to go talk to him in a bit, but I wanted to catch you first. Let you know what was up. You ready to hear that?"

Alice swallowed, loudly. Then she nodded.

"The man I married," Debra began, "your father…I've never seen anything like that from him in my entire life. He was…"

She paused, seeming to remember that she was talking to the daughter of the man in question, a girl who still loved her daddy, despite what he had done.

"He made a mistake. He's acknowledged that. He had some obligations at work that he couldn't break, but he promised me that we would have a long talk about it tonight. That he would sit down with you, and with Dean, and try his best to make this right."

Debra's voice faltered a bit on that last word, and she took in a sharp breath, holding it together, staying strong when it mattered, like she always did.

"But," she continued, "I told him that he wouldn't put a hand on either of you *ever* again. And I told him that, if he did, it would be the last time we slept under the same roof as him."

Alice shivered at what this could mean. She loved her dad, and deep down, she always saw more of herself in him than she ever had in her mother. It was a deep, unspoken connection that everyone was fully aware of, just like the relationship between Dean and Mom. The idea of not having him around was so foreign, so bone-chilling, that Alice couldn't quite comprehend it.

"Do you understand what I'm telling you?" her mother asked. Another softball yes or no question, right over the plate. Alice nodded yes.

Debra took another deep breath, staring up at the ceiling, hoping, perhaps, for some deeper, supernatural assistance to help her make it through the next few minutes. Alice knew that the conversation with Dean was coming soon, and there was little question that she dreaded the prospect.

"We're a family," she said, still gazing upward. "We'll get through this."

She finally looked back down at Alice, and her smile was forced. Alice smiled tightly back.

"I love you," Debra said. Alice followed Debra out of the living room and lingered in the hall as her mother spoke to Dean in his room. She couldn't pick up any of the details, but it sounded the way she would have expected it to. Dean saying little, her mother trying her best to be as soft as possible. It was strange, the way that the roles had been suddenly reversed because there simply was no other option. Her father was always the peacekeeper, always the one to swoop in whenever tempers reached the boiling point. He was good at it, and Alice realized she was pretty good at it too. The two of them might struggle to stand up for themselves or they may just decide to eat a wrong meal at a restaurant rather than send it back. But the fact was you needed people like that, people who were less likely to rock the boat. That was what made a family work, a mixture of fighters and peacekeepers. So what do you do when suddenly, without explanation, the man with the olive branch becomes a man with a gun?

Dean snorted loudly from inside his room, but Alice didn't think it had anything to do with a cold. The door handle began to turn, and she darted into her room, sliding the door closed as her mother stepped into the hallway.

"You didn't do anything wrong," was the last thing Alice heard as the door closed.

She waited, tracking her mother's footsteps back upstairs and into the bathroom. Moments later, she heard the faint hum of the shower. When the coast was clear, she emerged once more and approached Dean's door with a slight tap. He grunted from behind the door; she opened it slightly, peering inside.

"What is it?" he asked as he rummaged through one of his boxes of clothes.

"Nothing," Alice said, stepping into the room.

"Then go. I'm busy."

Alice nodded but refused to move. When Dean looked up again, he threw his hands out to his sides.

"What?"

"I don't know," Alice said truthfully. "I don't know what's going on with any of us. I just…wanted to talk about it, I guess."

"Then talk."

Alice realized, to her surprise, that she didn't know what to say. "It's just…I…I…"

They stood two feet apart, her brother hulking over her, a surly, teenage giant. His face was blank, a mask of utter malaise that met every moment in life, the good and bad, with nonchalant complacency.

"I…I…"

The longer she looked at him, stumbling over her words, her thoughts bubbling into a mess that even she couldn't decipher, the more alone she felt, stranded on an island in the middle of the sea while her brother stood in a boat just offshore, too stubborn to come save her.

"Spit it out."

"I mean…" She paused. "I don't know what to say. Her lip quivered. "Maybe Dad was right. Maybe we all deserve to be roughed up. If all that we can do for each other is just stand there and stare, then maybe our dumb family doesn't deserve to be happy at all."

Alice intended to turn and stomp away, to escape the room with the final word before the tears actually started to stream down her face, but Dean never gave her the chance. He swept over her like a tidal wave, wrapping her up in a big brother hug that she couldn't hope to escape. Alice melted.

"It's okay," he said as she cried tears onto his chest. "It's going to be okay."

They stayed like that for a while, neither of them quite able to break away. More than once, she could hear him sniffing as well, and Alice knew the boy who played with his little sister was back, at least for a moment. When she finally did push back, her eyes were red.

"Thanks for being my brother again," she said.

Dean rolled his eyes. "Shit," he muttered, "I always was."

Alice scurried off to the kitchen, feeling surprisingly better. The entire situation was still a mess, but the sun was out. Things would get better for all of them; she had to believe it.

Unless, the dark voice whispered, *they get worse.*

CHAPTER EIGHT

"Shit."

Alice stepped into the kitchen, the smell of apple cinnamon oatmeal with granola filling the air. It was her favorite breakfast on workdays when her mom was in a hurry. Weekends were for homemade waffles.

"No, no, no...*shit.*"

Debra was standing at the stovetop, slowly stirring the oats that had been warming on the stove. She was already dressed for the office, and her job as the director of finance at a corporate shipping company was never one to let her have too much time off. She and Frank both tried to take off as much time as possible during the winter break between Christmas and New Year's, but occasionally, she had to make an appearance. She held her phone in one hand and glared at it as she stirred with a wooden spoon.

"Shit, shit, shit!"

"What?" Alice asked finally.

Debra turned and gave a frustrated half smile. "Sorry...didn't realize you were in here yet."

"What's the emergency?"

"It's the damn weather," she said with a sigh.

Alice perked up. "Snow?"

"Yes," Debra replied. "The forecast is still calling for a lot. Ugh. I have so much crap to do at work, and there's not nearly enough food here...."

She launched into a list of what she needed to get done before making it home that day, but Alice didn't hear most of it. She was too occupied with the very exciting development that there might be snow. Their part of Tennessee didn't get much snow. For them, half an inch was enough to close schools, so the potential of a real blizzard was beyond exciting.

"How much?" she asked.

"How much what, honey?"

"Snow?"

"I shouldn't even tell you."

"Why not?"

"Because you'll probably be disappointed. Whenever they predict this much snow, it hardly ever turns out."

Alice's eyebrows shot up. "How…much…?"

"Six to eight inches."

The most snow Alice had ever seen was probably a solid three inches. That was enough to get them out of school for four straight days, and every one of them was spent sledding. But *six to eight*? She imagined building entire igloos with that.

"Go tell your brother to come eat if he wants something hot."

Alice did so with a bounce in her step that she wouldn't have thought possible mere minutes earlier.

"Dean!" she said, poking her head through his door.

"What?" He was still working on the box of clothes, and Alice couldn't help but think how odd it was to see her brother proactive for once.

"It's going to snow."

He tilted his head. Any remnants of their earlier moment seemed to have melted away, but Alice didn't mind. Now, she knew that the big brother was still hiding inside the teenager if she ever needed him again.

"Cool…"

"Six to eight inches!" she squealed.

He tried not to smile, and she wasn't sure if it was from her news or from her bubbly reaction. "I'll believe it when I see it."

She told him about breakfast before she raced back into the kitchen for a bowl. She filled it up with brown sugar and granola and sat at the table, bouncing in her seat and crunching away. Halfway through her bowl, Dean strolled in as well.

"You're in charge today," Debra told him.

"I know," he replied.

"I've got to run. I'll probably be home early, but I have to run by the store.... Who knows what kind of a mess *that* will be. Keep an eye on each other. Don't go outside."

"Why?" Alice asked with a full mouth. "What if it starts snowing?"

"Fine," Debra said. "Just don't go out alone." She had her purse over one shoulder and was nearly out of the kitchen when she stopped, seeming to consider something.

"Don't go out by the pool."

Neither of the kids argued with that.

"Love you two...have a good day."

And then, she was gone, and the two of them were alone with the giant, silent house.

"No way in hell it's snowing," Dean said as he filled up his bowl.

"It might," she replied.

The wind was picking up outside, so strong that she could almost feel the house shuddering around her. Dean took his breakfast into the living room, and Alice followed along behind him. They ate in silence, surrounded by the wide windows. She didn't pay any attention to the movie he turned on. She only stared out into the gray day, up at the heavy sky.

It's going to happen.

"All right," Dean said suddenly. "Going to get my game on."

"Why?" Alice asked. "What if it starts snowing?"

"Don't care. Come get me when it hits eight inches."

She tried to convince him, but he wasn't hearing it. She let him go and stared at the screen for a minute. It was a movie she'd seen a dozen times already, but she didn't feel like changing it to something else. It was cold in there, colder than most of the house, so she wrapped herself up in a throw and sank down into the couch. After the last two restless nights, it felt good to finally relax, and if she closed her eyes, she could easily imagine she was back in the old house.

Back home…

No. Home was gone.

The snow's coming. And then, after that…

★ ★ ★

"Alice!"

Confusion. The day outside too bright.

I'm in bed….

No, not in bed, on the couch, the same place where she drifted off. Dean stood at the edge of the couch, but he wasn't looking at her. He was looking out the window.

"Alice, wake up!"

Excitement in his voice. A strange sound. A forgotten sound. She sat up and blinked once, twice. Then she saw it.

"Holy crap!"

The ground was already mostly white, and the air was so thick with fat snowflakes that she could hardly see the woods.

"I'll be damned," Dean said as he sprang past her toward the sliding glass door. He wrenched it open, and the wind raced inside so quickly that it reminded Alice of sci-fi movies where someone opens a door into space. The cold wind hit her with a whoosh that blew back the throw blanket. It was terribly cold, and both of them were barefoot, but they didn't care. Even a fifteen-year-old could still be excited by snow, and so they ran outside, leaving bare footprints on the white concrete.

"I can't believe how fast it's coming down," Dean said as the snow coated his shirt.

Alice was beaming. "Holy shit!" she yelled out into the blizzard. Dean turned to her, his eyebrows cocked, a sneaky grin on his face.

"Holy *fuck*!" he yelled back. They stood out there, taking it all in as long as they could before they felt like their toes had turned to ice.

Dean cocked his head and held a finger to his mouth.

"Shh...you hear that?" he asked.

"Hear w-what?" she asked through her chattering teeth.

Dean stared out into the woods beyond the fence, and Alice did the same. There it was that familiar, creaking sound of bare tree trunks rubbing against each other. It was a grotesque sound, like a room full of empty rocking chairs moving by themselves.

"Th-the t-t-trees..." she added.

Dean stared for a moment longer. "Maybe," he said finally.

The two of them ran back inside, chased by a plume of fresh snow that blew through the open door. They were both giggling once they slammed the door behind them, their frozen toes wet on the doormat.

"Holy shit," Dean repeated.

"I know," Alice replied, feeling giddy with the snow and the parent-free house. "It's...fucking crazy."

Dean doubled over in laughter as he locked the door behind them. "Damn, we need to get Mom and Dad to leave us home alone more often."

They walked into the kitchen, and Dean, as always, raided the fridge. "Hope Mom's going to the store. There's *nothing* to eat."

"When are they going to be home?" she asked, suddenly aware of how freakishly quiet the house was. Usually, there were voices, footsteps, and the ever-present sound of electronics squawking in every room.

"I dunno," he said, pulling out a plastic tub of sliced turkey and eating it straight from the pack. "With all this, they better get home soon, or they might be spending the night at work."

Alice saw from the clock over the stove that it was already after ten.

How did I sleep that long?

"You should call her," Alice said.

"Why?" Dean asked with food in his mouth.

The correct answer – the *proper* answer – was, because Alice wanted to make sure her parents were okay. The honest answer was, because Alice could already imagine being snowed in without any parents around. All that darkness, combined with the knowledge that there might not be a way out, was more than she wanted to consider.

"To make sure she goes to the store," Alice said in a moment of inspiration.

"All right." Dean drew out his cell phone.

As Dean dialed their mother, Alice walked into the living room. Snow was drifting around the pool, and already there were several inches pressed up against the glass doors.

"Yeah," Dean said in the kitchen, talking through a mouth full of food. "Are you kidding me? *Yes*, I'm keeping an eye on her."

Even with the talking, Alice could hear the house breathing deeper now. It was wind. It was always wind, but it felt too strong. Too purposeful. A strong gust blew across the roof, and it brought with it a rattling sound overhead.

Sounds like footsteps.

Nonsense.

Dean was just stirring up her imagination, the way he kept staring into the woods, as if he were suspicious of the trees. Something vibrated and clanked, and Alice looked up to see a picture frame dancing and jittering on the wall above the entertainment center.

Not your imagination.

Maybe not. But it was still just wind, just the house responding to the weather. Suddenly, the sound stopped, and Alice was aware of the fact that she was holding her breath.

"Hang on," Dean said, sounding annoyed from the other room. He stomped in and handed Alice his phone.

"Here," he said, "calm your momma down."

"Hello?" Alice said.

"Hey, baby," Debra replied. "Everything okay?"

"Yeah," she said. "It got crazy out there."

"You're telling me," Debra said. "I'm really hoping I don't get stuck in this mess. Traffic is already a nightmare. I'm leaving work now, but I still need to run by the store."

"Milk and bread?" Alice asked, grinning.

"Something like that. You two stay put, and I'll be there soon."

"Mom?"

"What is it, sweetie?"

"Is...Dad coming home?"

Debra sighed. "He's good. He's heading home too." She paused, seemingly considering how far to go. "He might be there before me...so we'll see."

"All right. I'll see you soon," Alice said. "Love you."

"Love you too. Put your brother back on."

Alice sighed. "Fine."

She handed the phone back to Dean and listened as he got the same message. He drifted out of the room, giving his mom the usual series of *Yes...No...Yes*

Once she was alone again, Alice dropped onto the couch and picked up the remote. She didn't want to watch anything, but she needed noise, needed distraction. Just something to cut the unbroken tension of being in this house without parents. She hit the power button. Hit it again. Then she slapped it against her hand and hit it a third time.

Nothing.

Alice walked into the kitchen and tried flipping on the light.

Nothing.

The fridge had been on earlier. She'd seen the light, so she knew it was working, but when she opened up the door, it contained nothing but more darkness. Alice gasped, and the house creaked in response, the sound like a cold, guttural laugh.

No power, she thought as she dashed from the room, chasing Dean down.

"The power is out!"

"Are you shitting me?" Dean said, cupping his hand over the phone. "Mom, the power is out."

He squinted, listening as she spoke. Then he sighed the way that only teenagers could, summoning all of the annoyance in his body.

"Fine," he said. "Love you too."

"Are you sure it's out?" he asked after ending the call.

Alice followed him through the house, trying lights, remotes, and finally, the fridge.

"Dammit!" he said. "I almost just went over to Max's house. Now I'm stuck here all day with jack shit to do."

The house creaked and moaned, and Alice stared up toward the ceiling.

"What *is* that?" she asked.

Dean stared up as well, but when he spoke, the confidence had drained from his voice. "Wind."

"What should we do?"

"I don't know," he said, retreating back to his room. "I'm taking a nap."

"What?" Alice asked. It was almost as if the last twenty-four hours hadn't happened at all. Her old brother, the lazy, sullen teenager had returned, replacing the sweet guy who let her cry on his shoulder.

"What do you want me to do?" he asked. "I'm bored. There's nothing going on. We might as well just chill and wait for the power to come back on."

"What if it doesn't come back on?" she asked, following him. "Shouldn't we get some candles or flashlights?"

They passed a pile of boxes in the hallway, still unpacked. He pointed at the stack. "Go nuts. Good luck actually finding anything."

"What about…the painting?"

He rolled his eyes and continued back to his room without a word.

"How can you be so…so…?"

"So, what?" he asked as he walked away.

"So like this?"

"I don't know!" he said, turning on her suddenly. "You expect me to have answers, and I'm really sorry to disappoint you. But I don't. I *don't.*"

There was a familiar glare in his eyes, but it wasn't until that moment that Alice realized what exactly she was seeing.

He's afraid.

There was no denying it. He'd been avoiding the situation, but not because he didn't care. Dean was, quite simply, terrified, and this was his attempt to hide it. While her instincts told her to track down the truth, Dean stayed true to form, taking the path of least resistance.

"I just want to chill out," he added. "I don't want to think about all this shit, okay? Mom will be home soon, and everything will be fine."

The two of them turned the corner, Alice nipping at his heels like a tiny dog, both pretending not to see the crude family portrait when they walked past it. It was the same as before, the thick, black lines, the unfortunate X over the family pet. Alice wanted to stop, to study it, to puzzle out what exactly was going on, but she didn't dare, not by herself. She wanted Dean to jump in with her, to create a plan, to help her find a way to make it all make sense. There was an answer, there had to be, but she didn't think she could find it alone. Dean's pace quickened, and he refused to so much as glance at it.

"What should *I* do?" she asked as he approached his room.

Finally, he stopped and turned, an exasperated look on his face. "Just relax," he said. "Go to your room, lie down, read a book. Everything will be fine. I promise. You just have to calm down because honestly, you're making it worse for both of us."

Alice sighed and let her head drop. There was no fighting him, not at the moment at least. Without another word, she turned and walked back to the dim, half-light of her room.

"Mom'll be home in a minute," Dean called after her, a hint of guilt rising in his voice. She shut the door, refusing to respond.

Alice dropped back onto her bed, wondering if she would ever actually begin to feel at home there. It was so different, even from the night before, when her mother piled in next to her, the two of them sleeping off the bad dream.

Bad dream.

The house creaked, seemingly summoned by the thoughts running through her head. She considered a nap, but it was a foolish idea. She was exhausted from the night before, but sleep wouldn't come, not until some of the unanswered questions in her mind were finally settled. The painting, the cat, and, though she hated to admit it, the face at her window. Any of them alone might be enough to overlook, but together, they combined into something darker and impossible to ignore.

Alice turned to one side, her eyes closed as she considered it all. The house moaned, and the familiar sound of crackling wind and snow sounded more and more like footsteps on the roof, in the upstairs bedrooms, maybe even in the crawl space. She closed her eyes tighter, trying to will herself to sleep, to skip through time like a scratched DVD to the moment when her mom arrived home. After a few agonizingly slow minutes, she rolled over to her other side.

And that was when she first saw it.

There was a tiny, green book sitting on the bedside table. It was so small, so inconspicuous in the darkened room, that it was a miracle that she saw it at all. She tried to remember putting it there, wondering where she might have gotten it. But a few moments later, she realized what she already knew. It wasn't hers. She had never seen it before in her life. She crossed the room and glanced back out in the hall, checking for Dean, wondering if this might be some kind of trick, before she hurried back in and pulled the door closed.

Alice picked the book up and turned it over, studying the worn-out cover. At first, she thought it might be an old library book, until she saw the clasp. Before she could second-guess herself, she popped the clasp, and the cover fell open. It was a diary. She flipped through the pages, noticing the interesting progression from a child's awkward scribbling to a slightly more refined hand.

"Weird," she said as she tried to make out some of the pages. She spied a name that ended all of the entries, written with a neat, light script.

Mary.

The name echoed through her mind, and the wind gusted, angry, until the word forced its way out of her lips.

"Mary."

She said it aloud, the sound of her own voice frightening her in the dark of the room as the wind threatened to tear the roof off the house.

"Mary."

She said it once more, unable to stop herself for reasons she couldn't understand, and somewhere above, separated by layers of ancient wood and nails, she heard a moan.

In the silent moments that followed, she tried – *dear god* how she tried – to convince herself that it was just the wind. It still whipped furiously, still tore at the shingles, threatening to pry them free, to fling them away like old scabs. The moment stretched, and Alice realized she wasn't breathing; she'd been holding her breath so long that it actually hurt. She finally exhaled, and the sound of herself, something other than the wind, only further convinced her that the moan hadn't been the wind at all.

So she sat with the book in her lap, unmoving, poised like a small animal, a rabbit or a squirrel whose only defense is to *not move*. Her heart pounded, and when Dean swung open her door, she screamed.

"What was that?" he asked.

"You heard it?"

He nodded, his eyes drifting upward. The two of them stood silently, waiting for it to return. Finally, when the silence washed over them, Dean spoke.

"Should we…go check it out?"

"No," Alice cried.

"What if a branch fell on the roof or something?"

"What are we going to do about that? You gonna climb out there and fix it?"

But Dean ignored her, staring at the spot above his head as if he expected the ceiling to come to life.

"I'm going up there," he said as he strode out of her room and back into his.

"Wait," Alice said, her voice more of a whine than she meant it to be. She met him back in the hall, just as he emerged from his room with an aluminum baseball bat. "What's that for?" she asked.

"I don't know," he replied.

"I thought it was a damn tree."

"Just…be quiet."

They walked up the narrow staircase, Dean in front, bat at the ready, and Alice behind. She walked too close to him, one hand on the back of his shirt as if the two of them were walking through a haunted house, each afraid to lose the other. He glanced back once, casting his eyes at her hand, her tiny fist gripping the fabric.

"What?" she asked.

"Nothing."

They crested the top stair and peered down the long hall to their parents' room. Dean started taking a few steps when Alice pulled him back by his shirt.

"What is it?"

She pointed to the crawl-space door. The latch was still in place. Dean shook his head. "I'm not touching that."

"Should we check it?" she asked tentatively.

"Hell no."

Alice, despite her curiosity, couldn't help but respect his honesty. They passed the bathroom, taking time to glance in and check the dark corners before moving on. Their parents' room was one of the brightest in the house, and the white light shined down through the skylight overhead. Snow, loose and windblown, was beginning to pile up around the window. By the time the storm ended, Alice wondered if there would be any light shining through at all. They checked behind the doors, in the closets, even under the bed, but found nothing of note.

"Happy?" Dean asked.

"You were the one who wanted to come up here."

Regaining a bit of his usual swagger, Dean turned and walked back the way they came. Alice lingered for a minute, staring up at the ceiling and the snow dancing on the skylight. It seemed alive somehow, and she had the sudden urge to go out there, to climb out onto the flat span of roof and stare at the wisps of flakes.

CHAPTER NINE

Alice stared at the small book on her end table for a long time before she worked up the nerve to open it again. She had the strange, impossible feeling that the book was somehow alive, that it *wanted* her to pick it up, that it wanted someone to see whatever secrets might be inside. It was silly, even she knew it, but the idea took hold in her brain with barbed little claws, refusing to let up. She'd already flipped through it once, and nothing bad had happened, but that fact did little to calm the ominous feeling that stirred inside her.

Mary.

Was she someone who lived here before? Though worn, the book was still in good condition, the spine still sturdy and sound. A leaf was embossed on the cover, though Alice didn't know what kind. It reminded her of similar diaries her mother had bought her in the past for Christmases or birthdays. The faux leather was scratched in spots, but overall, it was in mostly stable condition.

She wanted to read it.

A million questions were spinning through her head, the most pressing being, how exactly had it gotten here? She didn't know, and in some deep-seated part of herself, she didn't care.

Does it really matter?

That wasn't the usual Alice whispering to her. That Alice, the sweet one, followed orders and stuck to the plan. That Alice was a perfect combination of her father's optimism and her mother's pragmatism. Doing the right thing simply got you further in life, and even at her age, she knew it. Maybe it was because she wasn't quite as cute as some of the other girls her age. They were learning as well, figuring out the best way to get ahead in this little puzzle called life. She'd seen it firsthand. They got what they wanted by acting cute, by batting their eyes, by playing some ageless, unspoken game. But not Alice; she played a different game, the good-girl game. And that game did not include this book. There was something about it, the idea that it might contain someone else's thoughts, dreams, or secrets. It didn't sit well with her. Finding strange books was a creepier version of finding a filthy dollar bill on the floor of a fast-food restaurant. Sure, it might be something you wanted, but it just wasn't the type of thing that she, or her mother, would approve of.

Who knew where the book had been and, even worse, what secrets might be lurking beneath its cover? In a sickening rush, her mind flashed back to the time when she was walking around the state fair by herself. It was one of the few times she'd ever been allowed out of her parents' sight in a public place, and she reveled in it, feeling big, grown.

It was hot that day, over ninety degrees, but she didn't mind. She never noticed the boy coming toward her, not in the crowded throng of people that flowed from place to place like water, gathering and pooling like puddles in front of rides and food trucks. He was probably fifteen, and he was flanked by a few other boys his age. Alice remembered thinking he was tall, taller than her father at that point. Something about that detail still stuck with her.

He'd slipped his phone out of his pocket, and as she walked past, he held it in front of her face. She didn't have to look. After all, he was at least fifteen, and he and the rest of his friends scared her. They weren't the types that good girls talk to.

But she *did* look. And what she saw was a naked woman splayed out with men surrounding her. They were all naked as well, and something in the way they looked, closing in on her, made Alice think it was some sort of ritual, that the woman in the picture might be dead by now. She knew what they were doing. She was plenty old enough to at least grasp the basics. But that picture looked less like what she imagined sex to be. This wasn't a shared moment of love. It was an offering.

It was just a peek, but it was enough for her to fill in the details. Her face was, apparently, enough as well, and the boys fell onto each other, laughing deliriously as they ran away.

Was it a game then? Walking around the fair, showing porn to kids? Alice thought about it the rest of the day, asking herself why they did it, what it meant. She couldn't get the picture out of her mind. It was a glimpse into a dark, adult world that she wasn't ready to think about yet. She spent the afternoon talking to herself in a voice that was remarkably like her mother's.

What is wrong with people?

This is why you don't go walking around without your parents.

And yet, that night, she thought of the picture again, the image filling her mind, her room, taking her somewhere she'd never been, never asked to go. She was afraid, but there in the dark, Alice didn't fight it, and when she slipped her hands between her legs, it wasn't fear she felt but something stronger, something brighter. Alice slept hard that night, and when she woke up the next day, she went straight into the shower and stood there, letting the scalding water peel the wrongness off her.

She had done a good job of burying that memory, stomping the dirt down on top of it, doing her best to keep it from rising up once more. But in that moment, looking at the book, she could think of nothing else. Her skin was alive in a wave of prickling goose bumps when she finally touched the cover. Once she lifted it from the end table, a bead of sweat dripped down her head, and she sighed.

Still holding the journal, she pushed her heavy door closed, leaning her shoulder into it, listening to it hiss across the thick, old carpet. When it finally clicked into place, she turned the lock gently. Dean didn't seem to be around, and even if he was, he wouldn't care what she was up to. Still, if he heard the door lock, it might be enough to pique his interest. She'd held the doorknob for a moment, ears perked, listening to the sounds of the house, trying to figure out where he was. The knob, cold and brass, wiggled a bit in her hand as she turned it, easing the latch closed as quietly as possible. All the inside doors seemed to do this, as if they might just pop off in her hand without warning. It was, she assumed, on her dad's ever-growing list of things to fix.

Once she was certain she had complete privacy, she crept back to the bed and opened the clasp on the front of the book. The book fell open in her hands, and at once, she could see how worn it was. The earliest pages near the front had begun to yellow and wrinkle with age, some of them so much so that it was hard for her to read them. The others near the back were still crisp, the scrawling print still legible.

Alice flipped to one of the earlier entries, studying it. The pages weren't dated, which appalled Alice on some deep, unspoken level. The entire purpose of a diary, as far as she was concerned, was the steady documentation of days. It had to be specific, tangible, a perfect little snapshot of that mood, that moment in time. This diary was, well, just messy. A list of things that happened. The idea that Mary was so unkempt almost killed a bit of the magic and mystique that the diary allowed to swell up in her mind.

Even so, she picked a random page and began to read.

I'll never know what it's like to be a parent. I know that now. I can only watch from the outside, wondering what it's like, daydreaming about the details, the changes, the sleepless nights, the unconditional love that makes it all worth it. That's the idealized version, of course. That's how it begins.

I know how it ends.

I think a lot about what a parent's ultimate goal would be. I once heard that the idea is not to raise children but to raise adults. To create something that can sustain itself. I wonder how many parents think like that, who have the foresight to always think of those kids as future adults. I don't see it, at least not in my life, not moment to moment. It becomes something different, something more like survival when kids begin to think for themselves. When "they come online," as my dad used to say.

They're little people, even when they don't seem like they are. I always thought kids were stupid, just because they didn't make good decisions. For adults, making good choices is everything. But even the smartest kids are capable of stunning lapses in judgment. The next thing you know, they've got kids of their own, and we all like to act surprised when they keep on acting like fools.

No, I'll never understand parenthood, at least not from the other side, but I think I understand what the job is all about. You can blow it up, tear it down, stack it in whatever shape you like, but there's really only one true goal for a parent.

Make sure the kids make it out alive.

It's a simple measuring stick, but a powerful one all the same. I won't know for sure until it's too late, but if I had to guess, my parents will end up being failures by that measurement. I just can't imagine still being alive at eighteen.

Alice let the final sentence sit in her mind. Who the hell *was* this girl? Everything about the diary had made her think the writer would be someone near her age, but her words? They went deeper than anything Alice had ever seen.

You don't have friends like that, a voice whispered, only to be immediately answered by another, darker voice.

You don't have friends at all.

An idea swirled in her mind. Alice at school. Awkward. Mostly alone. There were people there. Acquaintances. People who seemed to like her fine, but nothing like what other girls seemed to have. There was always Alice, struggling to make friends. Jealous of the breezy way other girls seemed to fall in with each other.

Then, there she was. Mary. Swooping in, taking her by the crook of the arm and whisking her away.

"Come on," she might say, "let's get away from these little girls."

But you're a little girl.

It didn't matter. She let the fantasy run its course. Mary was older, deeper, more interesting than any of the other girls at school, and she was probably tougher than any of the ones who picked on her.

They would *be jealous.*

Of course they would.

It reminded her of movies and TV shows where the good girl suddenly falls in with the new girl in town, the one who listens to weird music and pisses off parents just because she can. It was all beyond silly, but it was wonderful too, more real than most of the actual friendships she had.

She kept reading.

Dad never got around to fixing things like he said he would. The house was older than all of us combined. It was falling apart all around us, but he wouldn't hear it.

"A man takes care of things," he'd say, smiling.

He wasn't smiling for long.

I wonder if I should have seen it coming, the way he changed. The way Mom changed. The way we all changed.

I was too young to see anything. How could I have known what he would do? What we would all do?

It was a short entry, but the brevity seemed to make it even more special and mysterious. Was this the family that had lived here before them, a family full of secrets? The dad sounded a lot like her own dad in some ways. Eager. Self-assured. Ultimately in over his head.

But that last bit. *How could I have known what he would do?* That line chilled her. She let herself imagine what that might be about, but only for a moment. Then she turned to another page.

One time I bit into an apple and tasted something…wrong. I spit it out and stared at the spot I bit. It was brown inside, nearly black in places. Something moved inside there. A worm maybe, but I never knew for sure. I screamed and threw it across the yard, into the dead leaves.

Every once in a while, I remember that apple. How red it was. How perfect it looked. The rot inside perfectly camouflaged.

Had it always been there?

I remember the house when the paint was still new, still red and bright.

I can't remember how old I was when I saw it start to peel. Maybe twelve? It doesn't matter.

Once I noticed it, that was all I could see. The gray underneath the red. The real color trying to get out. It almost felt like the house was waiting for me to grow up. Like I had something to do with peeling paint. Like I made it happen.

They painted it white. Maybe that white would change things.

I keep thinking about that apple.

Dad should have never had a daughter.

Each page led her deeper into the weeds, and the questions swirled around her, like flies circling a rotting piece of fruit.

Who was this family?

A thought occurred to her, something so obvious that she felt foolish when she remembered it. The picture in the hallway, drawn by a child's hands. A little girl's hands. Was it her? Was little Mary the one who'd painted it, who ruined an entire section of wall so dramatically that her angry father had to cover it up with wallpaper?

She read on.

Dad has his own little place. It's out in the woods, a ways past the tree line. I think it was a smokehouse from back in the days when you couldn't just buy meat at the store like you can now. There wasn't much to it. Four sturdy wood walls. A leaky roof. Some wooden tables and things like that.

Dad always complained about how there wasn't enough room. So, he started putting things out there. Shovels and tools, stuff like that. He even put new shingles on the roof and put a fresh lock on the door to keep people from stealing out of it.

I would say, "Daddy, who would want some old tools?"

He never had much of an answer for that.

I went back there one time with some of my paint and wrote on the door in big black letters.

DADDYS ROOM.

I did it for him. I thought he'd like it, but he got all nervous, told me to leave that place alone, to make sure, extra sure, *that I didn't tell anyone about it. I don't know why he liked it so much. It always smelled funny to me anyway.*

Even so, I liked the idea of everyone having their own little places. I think I wanted to find a little place for myself. Somewhere quiet and lonely. I could make a sign for Peter and put it on his door. Then, I'd make one for Mom. Maybe put it in the kitchen, since that is more her room than anyone else's. And then, I'd write one on my door, with big, blocky letters.

MARY'S ROOM.

Mom would have a fit over that. I could see her stomping up and down the halls, just like she did when I painted the picture. I was younger then. I wouldn't do anything that stupid now.

Alice closed the book. She sat in the room, her eyes narrowed. Something about this felt wrong. Felt like an invasion, like sifting through someone's underwear drawer after they died. But even beyond that, it felt strange…maybe even dangerous.

All of this family drama and dirty laundry. These were the things that you weren't supposed to see, the things that lived and died behind closed doors. She thought of a friend she had in third grade, Carole. Alice could remember going to her house, how excited she had been to have a real sleepover. And what a house it was, bigger than hers, nicer. It was perched up on a hill with a long driveway, looking like a little cottage from a movie. Only, it wasn't little at all, and she found herself getting lost in the rooms, and before night fell, Alice was suddenly and terribly jealous of her new friend. She wondered why her own life wasn't so lavish, why her parents hadn't been more successful in their lives. She especially thought of her father, of the way that Frank seemed almost childlike and foolish all the time, less a parent than a kid himself.

That faded away in an instant when Carole's own father came home. The girls had been in the playroom all day. The very existence of a separate room dedicated to children's toys and dresses, dolls and babies, it thrilled her, and before she knew it, the tidy room was a complete disaster. Alice didn't really notice it, partially because of how much fun she was having, but mostly because this was how her own room looked most of the time. The idea of getting bent out of shape about it was as foreign to her as having a playroom in the first place.

Suddenly, Carole's father was there. Alice couldn't remember his name, but it didn't matter. He clearly didn't remember hers either. He came through the door, looking worn and stressed. He was wearing a neatly pressed white shirt, still crisp at the end of the day. Alice noticed that he wore cufflinks, both of them tipped with black circles like little shark eyes. She'd never seen a man in cufflinks before. The extra decoration made him look very fancy and important, like a manager at a bank.

"What is this?" he asked, his hands perched on his hips. Something in his posture, the way he jutted out his sharp, smooth chin, the angle of his arms, and the tilt of his head, made Alice think of some kind of giant, ill-tempered bird. He scowled down at the two of them.

"*I said*, what is this?"

"We're just playing, Daddy," Carole said in a voice that Alice had never heard from her before. It was softer than normal, but there was more to it than that. It was pathetic somehow, at once babyish and submissive. It sounded like a two-year-old asking for another cookie while she still had crumbs in the corner of her mouth.

"This damn mess better be cleaned before bed, do you understand?" Before she could answer, he repeated, "Do you understand?"

"Yes, Daddy."

He stomped off into some other corner of the house, and all at once, Alice saw the room for what it was. Nothing magical. Nothing even special. Just a room that happened to have more space and more toys. They spent the rest of the time before dinner quietly putting things back, and when it was all said and done, Alice never stayed the night with Carole again.

Something about that night swirled up in her mind, like a breeze catching last year's dead leaves in a gust. This book, this window into the past, reminded her of that little moment with Carole's father. No one got hurt. Nothing much was lost. But somehow, she had seen into a dark corner that wasn't meant for her eyes. Carole's dad burst in and brought all of that grown-up baggage with him.

But the book. The book was different. This was something she could put down, something she could turn away from, something she could toss into the trash. And yet, even the idea of such a thing terrified her. This was someone else's property, someone else's deepest thoughts thrown together with paper and ink. Keeping it was wrong, but throwing it away, not reading it word for word, well that was unthinkable.

Her hands felt suddenly dirty, covered with germs. Like whatever secrets the book held might infect her somehow. Like they might escape if she didn't keep the cover latched and locked.

With a blooming hum, the power returned to the house, and moments later, she heard her brother milling around in the hall. Without thinking, she slid the diary under her pillow. Seconds later, she emerged, out into the hallway.

Dean passed by her, a bag of tortilla chips in hand. Alice did her best to look casual, which instantly had the opposite effect.

"The hell are you up to?" Dean asked, though he never even slowed down, not waiting for an answer. He retreated into his room, and seconds later, the sounds of violent, virtual death began to blare out from within.

Alice spent the next ten minutes walking around the house, once again trying to look casual even though there was no one around to witness it. She sat in the living room for a moment, looking at the TV but not turning it on. Had Mary's family kept the television on the same side of the room? Was it as big as the one her dad had insisted on getting? She tried to imagine what the family might look like sitting around the room.

"Were they happy?" she asked the empty room, wincing at the sound of her voice in the silence. It seemed to echo within her, a slightly deeper voice asking, *Are you happy?*

She went to the kitchen and stared into the fridge, then the pantry, then the fridge again, all the while knowing that she wasn't actually hungry, just anxious. The wind kept whistling outside, the sound of it growing as the day dragged on, and she pictured this house like a cabin built of twigs and sticks, all full of holes, easy for things that crawl and skitter to come in and out whenever they pleased.

But the secrets are here to stay.

Alice had already made up her mind to keep the book, but she wouldn't read it anymore, not just yet. She knew, in her rational, logical, motherly mind, that it was a book and nothing more, that having it, reading it, keeping it were all perfectly acceptable things. There was a reason that it ended up in her room. Her mom or dad must have found it tucked into a drawer somewhere, and if they had, it would have made perfect sense to give it to Alice. Of course she'd find it interesting. She loved old things, loved to write, loved to wander and daydream.

That was the solution. She'd tuck it into a drawer, maybe hidden under some pictures or old papers, and she'd wait. Tonight, when everyone was home, they'd mention it. Ask about it. And she'd play coy, saying she glanced at it but didn't give it much mind, and that would be that. When the house quieted down, she'd dive back in, alone.

CHAPTER TEN

Everyone knew that Alice had a problem with focusing, but no one really understood why. Unlike most kids her age, who tended to drift around from subject to subject, staring out the window during math class, she had the opposite problem. She would focus so intently on a single thing that she would get lost in it and the rest of the world would disappear around her. When a teacher started lecturing on the Fertile Crescent, that mere phrase would stir images in her head so intense that she'd lose the next ten minutes dwelling on what it might mean. It drove her dad crazy, especially when the family gathered around the TV to watch a movie on Netflix or to catch up on the latest episode of whatever show they were watching. It was, inevitably, Alice who would tilt her head, squint, and ask, "Now what's going on?"

This earned her the reputation as a daydreamer, the girl with her head in the clouds. And, she supposed, it was a fair way to see her, at least from the outside. But on the inside, it was a completely different story. An actor's face, for example, might stir a bit of recognition. Had that person been in something else she'd seen? That face would linger, like the negative of a photograph, blurring out the background, distracting her from watching the rest of the scene as she mentally went back through every scene she could, cross-checking for the image of that face.

So it was in the hours that passed after finding the diary. The TV was on, Dean was busy in his bedroom, and the wind continued to blow bits of loose snow onto the bare tree limbs. A show she liked was flashing across the screen, a cartoon about a talking dog and a boy named Finn, but she didn't see any of it. Her mind was a pinhole camera, blotting out the rest of the world except for one thing.

Daddy's place.

The woods back behind the house waited, silent, watching. The gray, craggy trees loomed over the top of the fence around the pool, leering over like headless skeletons. If Alice walked around from the gravel driveway, she could get back there. There was a little path between an old storage shed and the fence, but she never considered actually venturing out into those darkened woods. Frank and Dean had been back there the day before to bury Baxter. She could have gone back there to see the grave, but she simply didn't want to. She could tell that her mom thought it was because she was too sad. The truth was she just didn't like the look of those woods.

Daddy's place.

If the diary was telling the truth, there was something back there, something hiding, waiting in the woods. Alice knew it was foolish, but she wanted to see it. Wanted to know if there was some piece of Mary back there, some deeper clue into the strange family that had lived there before them. She glanced at the clock on the wall. Her mom could be home at any time, but that didn't matter. She had a fine alibi for being back there. Alice was already dressed in her coat and boots before she even thought the whole thing through. Just as she walked back out of her room, Dean stepped out of his own room, empty chip bag in hand.

"Where you going?" he asked.

"Nowhere."

He rolled his eyes. "Come on," he said. "I'm not your babysitter, but if you get into some trouble, I'm the one who'd get all the shit for it. What are you up to?"

She considered the book, wondering why she felt so compelled to keep it a secret. Maybe it was just the simple fact that it was *her* secret, something she didn't have to share with anyone else. Whatever the reason, she wasn't ready to let it go yet.

"I want to go check out Baxter's...place."

The word "grave" stuck in her throat, not from grief but from all the images it conjured. She was already afraid of the woods. Her imagination didn't need any extra encouragement.

Dean sighed. "You know, we didn't even have him for that long."

He'd misread her. They *all* seemed to misread her. She pushed down the urge to get upset about it. In this case, it helped her.

"I know. I'm fine. I just want to see."

She saw something on Dean's face then, his mask slipping a bit. It was the look of a brother dropping his bike and running over after she had taken a spill. The look of a brother who began to truly panic when she choked on a hot dog one Fourth of July. It was concern, true and unspoiled by teenage surliness.

"Give me a second," he said. "I'll go with you."

When he spoke, the teenager had returned, but it wasn't the same now. It was all just smoke, his attempt to hide the fact that he did actually love his sister.

"Don't worry about it," she replied, trying to tamp down the swell of emotion in her chest.

"No," he said, retreating to his room to suit up for the cold. "If you go out there and break an ankle, tripping over a tree stump, I'll be the one to hear about it."

She waited in the living room, staring out the wide, sliding glass door to the swimming pool and the woods beyond. Alice could hear the cold, even inside, the way that the wind blew, the soft dust of snow that was just then beginning to stick to the tree limbs. It would take a long time for such a light snow to coat the ground, but the news promised more of it, maybe a lot more. Normally, it was exciting to think about, but something about this place, the strange, dreamlike feel of it, made her dread the snow. The prospect of being stuck here made her stomach curl, like being marooned on an alien planet.

"You daydreaming again?" Dean asked.

He was standing right next to her. Somehow, she hadn't even heard him walk up.

"No. Just thinking."

"That's what daydreaming is, genius."

"You don't have to be an ass."

Dean laughed, enjoying this new side to his sister. Alice didn't curse very often. Usually, it was the opposite. She was the one getting on him, telling her brother that he needed to watch his mouth, that one of these days he would slip up and say *ass* or *shit* or something even worse in front of a teacher. Even so, Alice knew that a well-timed bad word would work wonders with Dean.

"Calm down," he said in that easy way he had whenever someone else was getting upset. It made Alice even madder, the fact that he could bring himself back from the brink when he was angry. For her, losing her temper was like sliding off the edge of a cliff. Once she was over, it might take hours to scale her way back up. For Dean, it was more like jumping off the cliff with a balloon on his back. He might end up even more relaxed once he leapt.

Alice sighed, pushing herself back from the edge. She wasn't mad, but she knew herself well enough. If she kept going in circles with him, she might end up mad before it was over with. What she didn't have was a plan for getting Dean to walk even farther back into the woods, but she didn't worry too much about that, now pretty confident that he would follow her wherever.

"Let's go," he said, sliding the door open. "We don't need to stay out here any longer than we need to."

The wind blew the cold day in, greeting them before they ever actually took a step out. Alice had known it would be cold, but she swore it had already dropped a few degrees in the past few hours. Dean led the expedition past the frozen pool.

"Ugh," he said as they passed by it. "Smells like shit."

"Why do you think it stinks so bad?"

"Who knows? Dad thinks the septic tank might have leaked into it. Maybe something else fell in and died before it started to freeze. Either way, that shit is gross."

To the right of the pool was a gate that led to the driveway. Dean had to muscle it into moving, but it swung forward, shrieking on its rusting hinges. The drive stretched from the main road all the way up to a small path between the fence and a storage shed. Dean led them on, Alice's heartbeat quickening as they walked. This was it: the path into the woods that had loomed over everything. Past the shed, a yellow clearing greeted them, and there, tucked back close to the fence itself, was a small patch of dirt.

"Here it is," Dean said as they walked up to the unmarked grave.

Here lies Baxter, the cynical part of Alice whispered. *The asshole cat.*

The reality of the grave, the pomp and circumstance of it all, that it concealed something that was once alive; before coming back there, she'd wondered how it would affect her, if she would get sad, start crying, start reminiscing about the good times she had with the surly cat.

She didn't.

But, even so, her nose was running from the cold, and when she sniffed, Dean shuffled his feet uncertainly.

"He was…a good…cat?" he said.

The sentence that escaped from his mouth was perched on the narrow divide between statement and question. Alice didn't even know if he knew for sure which it was. Of course, Baxter was an asshole. He'd bitten every member of the house more than once. He was, in many ways, the most *catlike* cat any of them had ever seen. He'd liked being stroked behind the ears from time to time, but only when he wanted it, and only for as long as he wanted it. Anything outside of those parameters was asking to get nipped. The rest of the time, he spent his days in a perpetual panic, running from room to room, always careful to never get trapped between any human being and an exit. Alice's friends had dogs, big, dumb, simple things that poured love out on anyone who happened to be in the vicinity. But Baxter. Baxter was as close as you could get to having a completely wild animal living in your house for years on end. If anything good came out of a situation like that, it was by pure chance alone, and it was hard to mourn something that felt so random.

"I'm fine," she said after a few moments.

"It's okay," he replied. "I mean, if you're not fine."

"I'm serious. He was a pain."

She'd been through worse a few years earlier. Patty, Baxter's predecessor, was a loving, gray momma cat who gave birth to kittens every chance she got. That was fun, sweet, and the kind of thing kids thinks of when they think of pets. And, when she died, it *had* been rough. That was a true loss, the kind of thing that kept her in her room, thinking about life and death for a solid week. Baxter, in many ways, was just an attempt at replacing Patty. She'd never really seen it in those terms before now, but with his sudden death, she was almost thankful that things had gone that way. At least this didn't hurt.

"You sure?"

Alice shrugged. "I think so. I just wanted to see it."

"It was a bitch to dig the hole," he said. "Me and dad took turns. The ground is almost solid now from the cold."

Alice looked up away from the dark patch of earth and stared into the yellow field and the deeper woods beyond. She still didn't have a plan, but she hoped she might be able to come up with something, to see some small detail that might drag them farther into the gray crag trees, to *Daddy's place.*

"It's kind of spooky back here," she said, fumbling for something else to say.

Dean looked around as well. "I guess so. It was dark when we were back here before. Never really got a good look at it." He took a few steps forward, closer to the looming branches that hung low overhead. Then, without warning, he began to walk toward them.

"Where you going?" she asked, following at his heels.

He tilted his head as he walked. "I thought I saw something."

About fifty feet away past the fence, they stepped into the line of trees. There was a neat little path, the sort of thing that would disappear in the middle of the summer when the grass was at its highest. Now, with most of the brush killed off from the cold, they could walk between the trees without even touching the branches.

She followed along, excited and nervous that her plan was working so well without even being a plan at all.

They walked in silence for a moment, and when they finally stopped, Alice glanced back. Even without a single leaf on the branches, the house was barely visible through the trees. Had they come so far? Surely it had only been a few steps, but the feeling that they had somehow stepped off the edge of the earth overwhelmed her.

"Did you hear that?" Dean asked.

She turned back around, ear cocked, eyes wide. The wind blew. A few close trees leaned against each other, that familiar sound returning, like an old rocking chair. Dead leaves stirred around her ankles. The woods were simultaneously alive and dead, and Alice wanted nothing more than to be back inside, back in the warmth and the quiet, back where the wind was just an abstract, something you heard but never felt.

"Let's go," she whispered, but Dean shushed her with a wave of his hand. All thoughts of the diary, of undiscovered family secrets, fell away. She was only cold and afraid and ready to go home, to drink some cocoa, to forget that she ever wanted to come out here at all. The trees whined again, and it sounded like the woods were full of rocking chairs, each of them slowly rocked by invisible hands.

"I swear to god, I saw something."

Alice was standing behind him then, almost hiding in his shadow, and she peered around his shoulder and looked deeper into the woods.

"What?" she asked softly, afraid that someone or something other than her brother might hear. "What did you see?"

For a long time, Dean said nothing. Then he spoke in a whisper. "It was…pink."

Alice furrowed her brow, and some of the dread of the place seemed to lighten. "Pink?" She tried not to laugh.

"Shut up."

"What, like the Easter Bunny or something?"

"I know what I saw," he said. "It was like something blowing in the wind. Like…a dress or something."

Alice shook her head, but she didn't move. The world held around them, quiet and still. Finally, Dean began to walk again, not back to the house like she hoped but onward, deeper.

"Where are you going?"

Dean waved a hand again, refusing to look at her. "Go back," he said.

"I'm not going alone. We need to stick together." She stood, feet planted, eyes narrowed against the wind, watching him walk away. "You're responsible for me!"

It was a bit of a low blow, but she was desperate, and she knew where to hit him. It worked. Dean stopped, turned. "Come on then. I want to look around a little bit more."

Alice bit her lip. She was caught then, balanced between two worlds, between the fear of how the woods made her feel, and of the strange draw of the diary, of the secrets that had yet to be revealed.

Do it now, or you'll never do it.

Without another word, she ran to her brother's side, and they carried on in silence, each footfall echoing around them in the empty woods. Alice kept scanning the horizon, looking for…what exactly? A pink dress? The idea of it was so silly that she wanted to laugh out loud.

Mary.

Her inner voice whispered the name, soft as the wind on her cheek.

Girls love pink.

She owned one herself, a cute little springtime dress that made her feel grown up even if she did only wear it to church. Her mom made her take it off the moment she walked in the house, but Alice always managed to make a detour to the bathroom to stare at herself in the mirror, to pose and make duck faces like some kind of pop star.

And as absurd as it was, an idea had planted itself, was already sprouting deep roots. The face pressed to her window, the outline of a person peering in, looked to be a figure with long, wild hair.

Mary.

Alice let the name echo in her mind, curl in her brain like the wind that curled around her legs. What if, in some distant way, Mary was all around her, in the house, at her window, in the woods itself?

"I didn't see anything," she answered, pushing away the frightening images swirling in her brain. Mary was gone, just a memory at this point, but Alice could feel something lingering, like eyes watching her sleep.

Dead eyes, a voice whispered. *Her eyes.*

"Come on," Dean said as he kept plowing in. There was a trail, a faint one that became clear once they passed into the veil of trees. She kept expecting to see a deer or a raccoon pop up and sprint away from them, but beyond the wind, the woods were silent.

"How much longer?" she asked, feeling the cold in her toes for the first time. She had dressed warmly enough for a short stroll, but the farther they trekked, the deeper the cold bit into her, so deep that she was ready to abandon *Daddy's place.*

"A little farther, I think," he said. "You can do it."

He seemed to realize how sweet he was being, and he immediately backtracked. "Don't blame me if you're cold. I told you to go back."

Being alone in the house at this point was like flipping a coin. It was warm and relatively safe to be sure, but the otherworldly strangeness of the place had only grown in her mind. The last thing she wanted to do was walk back alone, regardless of what horrors might be waiting ahead of her. She trudged on, head down, so focused on putting one foot in front of the other that she didn't notice the shed until they were nearly upon it.

"What's that?" Dean asked, stopping them both on the trail. Alice looked up and gasped at the sight of it, a dingy gray skull of a building hidden among the trees.

Daddy's place.

"What the hell?" Dean said as they walked into the small clearing that held the shack. It was tiny, maybe twenty feet wide and half that deep. It was constructed of old, unfinished wood planks that had gone gray from the weather. The roof was a mismatched array of shingles that looked like they had been scavenged from various jobsites over the years. Her original impression of the building as a half-buried skull wasn't far off base. A pair of small windows marked the eyes, and the dark wooden door could have been a mouth.

"What *is* this place?" Dean asked, but Alice didn't have an answer. She barely heard the question at all as she kept staring at the wooden door. The paint might have been dark green at one point, but it had turned a sickly gray. In the center, right at eye level for a young girl, was a patch of white. It was just enough to cover up the words that Mary had painted there years before.

She looked back up the path. The house was out of sight, but she didn't think it was as far as it seemed. During the summer, when the woods were warm, the walk down here wouldn't be so bad at all. Mary's father could come and go as he pleased. Dean walked up to the doorway and tried the handle. A metal clasp held it in place, and hanging from it was a chain with a sturdy steel lock.

"That's a heavy-duty lock," he said, jangling the door.

"Yeah," Alice said, finally finding her voice. "I wonder what's in there."

The windows were blacked out from the inside.

"It's newspaper," Alice said, leaning close. "Look…you can see the print."

"That's some weird shit," Dean said, leaning close.

They walked the perimeter of the shed, checking it for other ways in and out. There was a tree growing close on its back end, and a tree stand for deer hunting leaned against it. It still looked sturdy enough to use.

"I bet this was like a little hunting shack or something," Dean said.

"Why?" Alice asked. "I mean, the house is just up there."

"Maybe they just liked the quiet. A chance to get away. I mean, I get that."

Alice considered whether or not the statement was directed at her, but she didn't linger on it. There were piles of sheet metal stacked against the back of the shed; Dean tilted his head and stared.

"What a junk pile." He gave the stack of metal a solid kick. As he did, a rabbit shot out from underneath; Alice screamed.

"Jesus," Dean said. "You're so jumpy."

"Let's go back," Alice said. "I'm freezing to death."

They walked back around, and Dean reached for the lock once more. "This is still in good shape," he said. "I bet we can break it open. I think I saw a sledgehammer in the shed by the house."

"Later," Alice said. "Let's go back, please."

Dean seemed to be ignoring her. He was scanning the tree line around them, listening for something. There was a stirring in the distance, closer to the house. For a long moment, neither of them moved.

"Rabbits," he said to himself. "Feel sorry for them in this weather."

"They can d-d-dig…we can't. Let's get b-b-back."

Alice was seriously considering leaving him if he didn't agree, but to her relief, he turned and began to lead them back the way they'd come. They walked in silence, or at least as much silence as the woods would allow. There was a feeling now that Alice couldn't shake, that the woods had tried to hide that shed and that by finding it, she and Dean had done something they weren't supposed to. Now, the woods were watching them, following them, trying to spit them out like gristle stuck between two teeth. Dean kept scanning, kept looking left to right like a bird, or a groundhog on its haunches.

Like prey.

Alice thought of the rabbit, alone out here in all this cold, surrounded by things that wanted to kill it, chief among them, the woods itself. Something rose up in her mind, a memory of a book she once read, a book about talking rabbits running away from all the things in the world that wanted them dead. The memory filled her with a sick feeling, a tension that felt like a rubber band inside her that was being stretched tighter and tighter. Alice kept waiting for something to happen, for all that tension to suddenly break. But it never did. Dean never stopped her again, never pointed into the woods, never claimed to see any little girls in pink dresses.

Little girls.

He had said that, hadn't he? Or did Alice just think that?

The house came into view, huge and fading, like a sad little sunset, and the sight of it calmed the tight, crouching feeling in her stomach. They were almost totally past the fence when Dean noticed the hole.

"Aw, shit." He stopped in his tracks, and Alice nearly bumped into him. His voice wasn't filled with fear or dread. Rather, it was the voice of an exhausted homeowner who comes home to find that raccoons have torn through his trash.

"What is it?"

Dean sighed, a heavy, tired sound, as he stepped aside and pointed. "That."

The spot where they buried Baxter had been, a few minutes earlier, a smooth circle of dirt. You could even still see the boot prints on it where Frank and Dean had patted it down. But now, it was an open hole. Dirt had been tossed aside, and as far as she could tell, the grave was completely empty.

"What in the world?"

Dean shook his head. "Coyotes. Or maybe dogs. Jesus Christ, I can't believe they'd do this in broad daylight. Dad said we should have looked for some rocks to put on top of it. I thought we got it deep enough though."

For the first time since finding the cat, Alice began to tear up, not from sadness but from the simple grotesqueness of it all.

"Come on," Dean said, putting a hand on her shoulder. "There's nothing left to see out here. Let's get inside before whatever did this comes back."

★ ★ ★

Frank was the first to arrive home. Alice had just begun to get all the feeling back in her toes when she heard him coming in, the thump of his heavy footsteps distinct from her mom's. She considered getting up from the couch to see him, to tell him everything that had happened that day, but she wasn't ready to just yet.

From the living room, she could see he was carrying half a dozen plastic bags looped across his arm. It was a mishmash of supplies picked up from the hardware store. Paintbrushes, painter's tape, drop cloths. Dean and Alice were sitting in the living room together, a Harry Potter movie playing in the background. Dean was on his phone, not really watching the film, but both of them in the same room was no doubt a strange sight.

"What are you two up to?" Frank asked awkwardly as he set down the painting supplies. The cans of primer landed on the hardwood with a thud, and Alice looked up from her daze. She watched him with a wary eye, still a bit on edge from the blowup earlier.

"You painting?" she asked.

Frank half shrugged, half nodded. "Well, it wasn't part of the plan…at least not at first. But, if we're going to be snowed in, I figured I'd make the most of it."

Dean looked up from his phone. "Starting on the hallway?" he asked without blinking.

Alice was stunned by how much gall her brother showed to their father. Frank looked from one to the other, measuring the moment. He somehow managed a smile.

"Good a place as any," he said.

"I suppose so." Dean looked back at his phone.

Frank stood for a moment, half in and half out of the living room. Then he seemed to find his voice.

"Look, I've been pretty uptight about this place. No sense in acting like that's not true. Things got heated last night, and I just want to say that I'm sorry."

Dean didn't look up. Alice glanced between the two of them, waiting to see who would be the first to say something, anything.

"Sorry about what?" Dean asked finally.

Frank actually laughed at that, a genuine, sweet laugh that made Alice feel better than she would have thought possible in that moment.

"How about, I'm sorry for being a dick? Will that work?"

Dean never looked up, but he did grin. "It's a start."

Frank had that way about him. Even at his angriest, he'd go out of his way to prevent a war in the family. In some ways, Alice didn't understand that at all. It made him look weak and afraid to deal with things. But on the other hand, the older she got, the more she appreciated her dad's easy way. They were, whether any of them liked it or not, all in this together. So, why not be cordial?

"The snow looks like it's picking up," he said as he began to organize his supplies. "Weatherman says we might even get half a foot. Pretty exciting, huh?"

Despite herself, Alice felt her heart flutter. "Really?"

"I guess we'll have to see," Frank replied. "So…what have you been up to today?"

Dean and Alice looked at each other, both of them seeming to dare the other to tell their father what happened.

"What?" he asked when no one spoke.

"We went down to the woods," Dean said finally.

"What did you do that for?"

Alice answered, cutting her brother off. "I wanted to see Baxter."

Frank nodded. If there was anything else to be said, he didn't seem to know what it might be.

"We found this weird little shack way back in the woods. Like *way* back."

"Well, the property goes back for ten acres or so. Hell of a deal. You hit a fence back there?"

"No."

"There's supposed to be one at the edge of the property. Maybe it wasn't as far back as you thought. It's easy to get lost once you lose sight of the house."

"There wasn't any fence," Dean said.

"Okay," Frank replied. "I might take a stroll down there myself in a bit and see what it's all about."

Alice was staring at her father, at the unsure look in his eyes.

Up to something, a voice inside cried like an alarm.

"You see anything else?" Frank asked.

"Yeah," Dean said. He glanced over in Alice's direction, but he didn't make eye contact with her. He paused for a long time, but she finally spoke for him.

"Something dug up Baxter."

She said it plainly, without a hint of emotion in her voice. To hear her tell it, the event was just a thing that happened, not something worth getting worked up over.

"What?" Frank said, incredulous.

"She's right," Dean said.

"Must have been a coyote. Dammit, I meant to get back out there today and put some rocks on it. Son of a bitch."

Frank left the supplies where they were for the moment. Normally, this was the type of big, family excitement that everyone would want to be a part of, but Alice and Dean just sat there and watched as he strode back outside.

"You didn't tell him about the dress."

Dean's face scrunched up into a sneer. "I never said it was a dress. I just thought I saw something."

He stood up, retreating finally to his room. Now that he wasn't the oldest one in the house, the one in charge, Alice knew he was ready to be alone once again.

"Besides, there's nothing to tell."

Alice waited for a moment before turning of the TV and venturing back to her room as well, pausing just long enough to stare at the painting in the hallway. She wanted to look at it longer, to study it, to imagine the hand tracing it on the wall. But just then, the front door banged open again, and she walked into her room without a word. She pressed her ear to the door, listening as her dad shook off the cold and snow. Night would fall soon, and that reality swirled inside her, darkening her insides like old coffee poured into a cup of milk. Unless something strange happened, they were all here to stay, snowed in for at least a few days. That was more than enough time to paint over the picture in the hallway, to cover it up for a second time, to erase it from memory for good.

Except. It felt wrong, the idea of the history of this place painted over. It felt like kicking over someone's tombstone.

Why?

It was a fair question. One she hadn't considered before then. The diary wasn't necessarily a memorial. It could have just been a keepsake left behind, something that her parents stumbled across. Maybe the diary had been long forgotten and Alice was just dwelling on someone's abandoned history, puzzling over details that Mary herself had already put in the rearview mirror of her life.

It's not that simple.

But it could be. Whatever was happening in this old, strange house didn't have to be some grand adventure, even if part of Alice's heart longed for it to be. Mary could be a teenager now, living somewhere else, somewhere warm, the beach maybe. She could be even older than that, a college graduate, maybe a wife or a mother. Maybe she even had a daughter of her own.

She's dead.

No, she's not.

She might even be buried out there, buried and forgotten, like a cat that no one loved enough to cry for.

Stop it.

Or maybe, whatever is left of her is locked away in that shack, moldering, covered with maggots, her eyes rotted away.

She tried to banish the thought, tried to chase it away like a rabbit, but she couldn't. The idea was too powerful, the clues too enticing.

Mary was dead.

Someone had given Alice her diary.

Someone had been peering in through the window.

Someone had followed them through the woods in a pink dress.

And someone had dug up Baxter.

No. None of it made sense.

Of course it makes sense. The dead get hungry, you know. And they aren't picky. She probably went for the cat because it was still fresh.

Alice heard the outside door open and close once again, followed by the soft sound of conversation between her parents. Normally, her parents had an almost cute way of arguing in the most polite way possible, but lately, that had begun to change, get meaner and more heated. Alice told herself it was just the stress of the move, though if she was being honest, it had been getting worse for months – long before they finally decided to move. She never understood grown-up problems about money or work or anything like that, but she had hoped in some deeper part of herself that the house would actually be a good thing for them. And for a while, at least, it had seemed to be the Band Aid her parents' relationship needed. Now, that idea felt amazingly naïve.

Debra almost always made the rounds through the house after the small talk was over, so Alice decided to preemptively head out and greet her. She caught the tail end of the conversation, a whispered retelling of the scene with Baxter. Both of them stopped talking when they heard her footsteps. Debra turned and managed a tired smile, the stress of the move, the cat, the snow all visible in her mother's eyes.

"Hey, honey," she said, smiling. "You okay?" She stopped short of actually talking about what happened, but the implication was clear enough.

"I'm fine," Alice said, letting her mother wrap her in a hug.

Debra leaned back, studying Alice's face for some hidden details that might have slipped out. Finally, she shook her head. "This place," she muttered darkly.

"What does that mean?" Alice asked. Frank leaned closer as well, ready to pounce at anything negative that his wife might have to say.

Debra ran her fingers through her hair, her eyes closed, the stress just leaking out of her. Somehow, she found the will to push it back down and manage a smile.

"Just crazy times," she answered. "We're good though. We're all good."

Her repeated phrase made Alice think that she was trying to convince herself, but she didn't linger on it for long.

"And," Debra continued, "on top of everything else, this damn snow."

Frank's face loosened up a bit. Alice knew the look in his eyes, the way that his lips thinned out whenever he was preparing himself for a fight. He didn't like to argue. He much preferred the path of least resistance, but he had a bit of badger in him, the kind of thing that could bite when cornered. His face told Alice that he was happy this wasn't going to be the moment.

"Oh yeah," he said cheerfully, "it's piling up out there."

The conversation continued, but Alice didn't pay it much mind. It was clear that everyone, Dean included, had forgiven Frank's lapse the night before. For a brief moment, the thought offended Alice. Surely her father deserved more punishment; he hadn't really done anything more than say he was sorry.

You're a family, a soft voice whispered. *It's better if everyone is just happy.*

She recognized that part of herself as something very similar to Frank's own personality, and for just a second she hated herself. But she saw the dark truth at the heart of it. They *were* a family, and it was just simpler if they all got along.

After all, he'll probably never act like that again.

A lie perhaps, but a comforting one. Her parents tag teamed a quick dinner of chicken Alfredo pasta, salad, and garlic bread. All except the chicken was either frozen or from a bag, but if Alice squinted, it looked like the real deal. They sat around the living room couches, eating with plates in their laps as they flipped around for something to watch. Christmas had come and gone, but Frank, the eternal child he was, didn't like to let it go. Before anyone had a chance to object, he'd snuck in the stop-motion Rudolph special they'd been playing since he was a kid.

"Dad, come on," Dean complained.

"Hey, this is a classic."

That was all it took to break up the evening's festivities. Dean slunk away to his room. Debra started cleaning up the dishes in the kitchen, cursing at how small and ineffective the new kitchen was, banging pots and pans like she had to hammer them in place.

Frank and Alice, the two stragglers, stayed and watched till the end, till the toothy monster was tamed and Rudolph learned his place in the world. The wildness of the past few days had taken a toll on Alice, and though she longed to fall into a quick sleep, she knew it wouldn't happen, at least not for a while. There was work to do, and as the credits rolled, she felt something dark stirring up within her, like a coyote digging at the fresh dirt.

"I'm sleepy," she said, feigning a yawn that soon turned into a real one. If her dad noticed, he didn't say anything.

"Tomorrow, we'll get some real work going. Make this place feel like a home."

Alice perked up a bit. "Who lived here before us?"

"Hmm?" Frank said, as if he didn't understand the question. "Oh, just a family. Probably like us, I'd guess."

"You bought it from them?"

"Well, no. I bought it from the bank. They foreclosed on it, after the family stopped paying. Pretty normal stuff really, and a hell of a deal."

Alice measured every word, testing every syllable, trying to find why he seemed so nervous. So unsure. Finally, she asked, "Do you know anything about the family?"

He coughed. Whatever else came out of his mouth from that point, Alice knew he was holding something back. He did the same thing whenever they were playing cards. Didn't matter if it was poker, Uno, or old maid. When he had something he didn't want you to know about, Frank would clear his throat, just a tiny bit.

It was the kind of thing you would miss unless you were waiting for it.

"No, not really. I think there was some falling out. Divorce. You know. Grown-up stuff. Bad for them, I guess, but good for us. This place will be our home, a real home. Something with personality, not just a cookie-cutter subdivision where every house looks the same. It'll be great."

Unlike with her mother, Alice didn't have to wonder if her dad was trying to convince himself. He had already done that months ago. He was all in on this place, for better or worse.

Alice didn't say anything else. This was the perfect opportunity for Frank to mention the diary if he had been the one to put it in her room. But the moment passed. Alice told him good night, and she went into the kitchen where her mother sat, bathed in the blue glow of her laptop, her reading glasses firmly in place.

"You going to bed, sweetie?"

"I think so." Alice stood there for a moment, picking at the edge of the tablecloth. It wasn't subtle.

"Something on your mind?" Debra asked.

Alice peered back over her shoulder. Her dad was already wrapped up in whatever else was coming on, and the TV was too loud for them to be overheard. She had done a decent job of keeping her secret all day, but she couldn't hold it any longer. She had to find out who put the diary in her room.

"Mom," she said, sliding into a chair next to her. "What do you think about this place?"

Debra laughed, but there was no humor in it, just a sharp hiss through her teeth. She shook her head, almost as if she were shaking off the sarcasm before she talked.

"It's fine, baby. It will be great once we get settled. It's just…a lot to deal with."

"Yeah," Alice said, trying to figure out how to guide the conversation to where she wanted it to go. "It's just… It almost feels like there's more going on here, you know?"

Debra leaned around the side of the laptop and peered down over her reading glasses. "What do you mean?"

'I don't know. I mean, the stuff with Baxter is bad, but you know...things like that happen. But there's something else. Like, there's something here."

"Honey, the other night was just your imagination."

"I know. I just feel like part of the family that lived here before is still here somehow."

That was it. That was as good as she could do without coming right out and mentioning the diary. If her mom had found it, this was the perfect opportunity to talk about it.

"It's just the new house," she said with finality. Something in her voice had changed, gotten sharper somehow. She didn't intend to continue this conversation, even if Alice couldn't quite figure out why.

"Now," she said, turning back to her laptop, "head to bed. Get some sleep. You'll feel better in the morning."

Alice didn't know what to make of any of it, of her parents' knowing glances and deflections, of the strangeness of the house, of the painting and the cat, of the shed and loose dirt. If any excitement about the house remained, it had faded, changed, been replaced by something much closer to pure fear. She had spent the entire day, ever since she had found the diary, expecting her mom or dad to pull back the curtain, to reveal the truth hiding in plain sight. But now, it seemed they were just a part of the sleight of hand, and the realization that she was in this more or less alone twisted knots inside of her.

Without another word, Alice crept to her room. For the first time, she didn't glance up at the picture as she passed it. She didn't want to see it, not then, not at this sudden low point. She closed the door behind her, blocking out the sounds of Dean's room across the hall. Her first instinct was to grab the diary, to spend the entire night poring over it, studying every detail for the answers she so desperately needed.

Instead, she sat down on the bed and waited patiently. Her room was near the center of the house, a small little nexus that had other rooms on each side. Close to her door, all she could hear was Dean's TV, blaring. But, if she crossed the room and slipped into her small closet, she could hear the TV from the living room. There were no details to pick out, nothing specific, but she didn't care about that anyway. She was waiting until the TV in the living room was turned off to make her move.

She didn't have to wait long. Frank had probably kept the show going as he waited for her to leave the room. Now that Alice was officially in bed, she listened as the TV clicked off and her father's footsteps lumbered into the kitchen.

Alice slid her door open, but instead of going left, which was the direct path to the kitchen, she went right. There was a small hallway that opened up into a bathroom, and behind that, that strange, unfinished hallway, the "utility room," whose windows peered into her room. It was like a gray tunnel, unfurnished, unpainted, home to nothing more than some bare storage shelves and the washer and dryer. On the far end was a folding, slat door, the kind usually attached to closets. It was closed at the moment, just like she remembered it.

This door led right back into the living room, completing the odd architectural loop. She crept forward, breath held, and tilted her head to the slats. Her parents, still in the kitchen, were easily within earshot.

"…she must have heard you talking about it," Debra said, the irritation clear in her voice. It was a familiar voice, one that made Alice wonder if her mother had ever respected her father at all.

"I haven't said shit in front of them," he replied, voice raising.

"Keep your fucking voice down."

"I'm not even talking louder."

"Jesus…just be quiet," Debra said, her voice dropping. "All I'm saying is that they heard about it somehow. And it sure as hell wasn't from me."

"I think you're overexaggerating," Frank answered.

"Am I? She's specifically asking about the family that lived here before us. How else would she know about it?"

"She's a kid. Kids ask questions."

"Oh, sure, they randomly ask questions about the girl who died in this house."

Alice gasped and clapped a hand over her mouth.

"You know it was her, right?" Debra asked.

"Her, what?"

"She was the one who drew that picture. It had to be her. It's like she left her stamp here before she…Before it happened."

"Look, you're letting this place spook you."

"I'm not doing shit," Debra snapped. "The cat, the picture, now Alice asking questions. Something is *off* here. I don't know what it is, but it's the truth."

"Oh, come on," Frank said. "Of course you'd go that way with it."

"What the hell is that supposed to mean?"

"It means you thought this was a bad idea from day one. I found a deal here, something we can fix up, something we can make amazing for our family, and all you see are the negatives."

"How the hell do you think you got that deal?"

"Don't be so dramatic," Frank said. "There was a tragedy here, yes. An accident. They happen every day. And when the family packed up and left, the bank took over."

"And it sat empty for two years because no one wanted to buy a house where a teenage girl died."

Alice felt her throat tighten. They had danced around it, neither of them wanting to voice the truth of this place. But there it was, out in the open, impossible to ignore any longer.

The fire in Frank's voice faded, replaced by sarcastic defeat.

"I should have known," he said. "I should have known that this was a mistake. That you'd throw it back in my damn face the first opportunity you got."

Footsteps left the kitchen, and for a brief moment, Alice thought her parents might be coming to get her, to put her in the hot seat and demand answers for her sudden curiosity. Instead, a second set of footsteps followed.

"Oh, you'd like to put the blame on me, I'm sure, but you know full well…"

The voices faded, the argument carried upstairs like a leaf on the wind. The heavy footsteps carried on overhead, but the squabble faded to nothingness, mixing with the groan of wind and softly drifting snow.

Alice went back the way she'd come, and jumped – Dean was standing in the hall between their rooms.

"Jeez, I didn't see you standing there…."

"They'll get a divorce," he replied, seeming not to hear.

"You don't know that."

"I didn't know before. I mean, I thought they might. When you were little, Mom was working two jobs, and Dad got laid off for the first time…. I thought it would have happened back then."

He walked to the hallway door and peered up the crooked staircase. "They got better though. I don't really know how, but they did."

"It's just stress," Alice answered.

"They don't do good with stress."

"Does anyone?"

Dean shook his head and waved a dismissive hand. "You were too young to remember. They came close to splitting up once, really close. This shit show of a house might be enough to finish the job."

"They're fine. Once we get settled…"

"You feel settled?" he asked, looking back at her. "I wish we hadn't come here."

He left her standing there to ponder what the future might hold for them. Dean stopped at his door and turned around. The light from his room lit half his face but hid his expression from her.

"Don't listen to me," he said. "Who knows what could happen? Things'll be fine."

Alice wanted to smile at that, but the sentiment was too weak, too half felt for her to buy into it.

"Either way," he added, "we got each other."

He closed the door behind him, too quickly to see that she was smiling.

CHAPTER ELEVEN

The footsteps grew quiet, and the new house creaked and moaned all around her as Alice slipped into bed, table-side lamp on, diary in hand. It felt even stranger to hold it, and she couldn't help but wonder if it was tied to Mary somehow, as if her soul was trapped inside it like Tom Riddle's soul in the Harry Potter movie they'd watched that afternoon.

If she felt absurd about the way her imagination was getting away from her, it was hidden under thick layers of apprehension and fear. She snuggled down under the comforter, feeling warmer and safer than she had all day, as if cotton and polyester could somehow protect her from the madness of this place. She opened the diary. This time, instead of flipping around from page to page, she started from the beginning. The page was ragged and worn, but still readable.

I can't believe my birthday is over. I didn't even have fun at my party. I told Mom I was too old for an actual party. It was all little kid stuff. Balloon animals. A big, huge cake that looked like a dress. It was nice, but silly. I just wanted friends over. Just wanted to do something that wasn't so kiddy. I'm ten, not six.

That confirmed one detail Alice didn't know. She wasn't sure how many years Mary had written in the diary, but now at least, she knew when she started. Ten years old. Same age as Alice herself.

She remembered her own tenth birthday party. It probably wasn't very different. No balloon animals, but still very childish. It was at a local place that rented out huge rooms full of inflatables.

She'd had a few birthdays there, and it was always a good time, one of the few times that everyone in the family seemed to get on the same wavelength. Even Dean would put up his phone and jump down one of the huge, bouncy slides.

But there was something else there, something she hadn't considered much before reading that page. She had, in her own way, felt the same as Mary. She wouldn't have dared tell her mom the truth though, especially once she'd seen the excitement in her mom's eyes.

"Want me to book the bounce house?" she'd asked.

She imagined what it would have taken to stick a pin in her mother's excitement, to watch it deflate in front of her. Alice had gotten her ears pierced for her tenth birthday, years later than most of her friends. She'd wanted a makeover party that year, something where she could pick out new earrings, get her nails done, get pedicures. Most of her friends were doing birthdays like that. None of them made any pretense to actually be grown-ups, but it was time to start pretending, to start acting like you understood what was coming.

Women made themselves up. It was a skill, an important one even. Alice didn't have it in her, not yet at least, but the makeover party wouldn't have been for her anyway. It would have been for her friends, pretty girls, prettier than her, each of them somehow already understanding this strange, frightening new aspect of life. She was only now starting to realize, several months later, that her friends hadn't been frightened at all. They were, somehow, brought into young adulthood knowing exactly what the strange world of boys, sex, and looks was all about.

Mary seemed to be that type, the type that took to junior high like a fish to water. A sneaky idea crept into her mind. She imagined what it would have been like if the two of them had been friends. She could actually see it, Alice as a lost little puppy, Mary as her chatty guide into adulthood. As she read on, the notion remained, firmly planted in her mind.

She did get me this though. I rolled my eyes when I opened it. A diary. Such a little girl thing. I promised I'd sit down and write in it, just to make her happy. So, here I am, writing, killing time, waiting for her to stop walking by my room so I can toss it into a drawer.

Oh, Mom. So predictable.

That was it. The first entry from start to finish. No revelations. No grand truths. Just a little girl writing to appease her mother. She flipped to the next page. This one was written with a different pen, now in purple ink.

Wow. This will be interesting to look back on one day. I threw this thing in a drawer and lost track of it. Mom must have given up on me quicker than I thought she would have. No surprise there.

All right, just for the record, here I am, three years later. A thirteen-year-old! Hold your applause for the teenager. This thing looks different to me now. Still a little silly, but...different.

For starters, I actually like English class now. We have to write essays in Mrs. Carmichael's class. I expected to hate it, but the fact is I'm good at it. It's all basic stuff, things like picking out the meaning in Beowulf *or* Othello *or* The Red Badge of Courage. *And Mrs. C thinks I have real talent. I mean, I'm eating shit in geometry, but that's life for you.*

Alice laughed out loud to herself, her voice harsh in the quiet room. Mrs. Carmicheal. Could it have been the same one? Were she and Mary even more alike that she even imagined? Alice did the math in her head, trying to figure out how old Mrs. Carmichael was, if it was possible that she could have been teaching that long. She hated geometry too. She read on, the strange connection between them deepening.

I'm surprised by how well this little book has held up. I couldn't appreciate it back then, but this was a good gift. Did Mom see something in me? Something I didn't see?

Either way, I think I might start keeping up with this. Not an everyday thing. Just when I need it. Who knows, after everything that's been going on with Mom and Dad lately, I might have plenty to write about.

They'll get a divorce. I know it.

All Mom does is talk about him when he's not around. How lazy he is. How worthless.

And Dad...all he does is go off into the woods on his own. Wander around. Says he's hunting, but you never see any animals anymore. Never hear any shots.

I don't know what's going on between them, but I can tell where it's going. Doesn't take a teenager to know that.

Something shuffled out in the hallway, and Alice closed the book for a moment, listening to the house, listening to it breathe. She froze, expecting to hear something that never came. The clomp of Dean's big feet as he went to the kitchen for a snack. Her parents' whispered voices as their argument continued.

Baxter.

Yes. With a grim sense of humor, she realized she was waiting to hear him as well.

He's back. Just like Pet Sematary...

Alice shushed that part of her mind. She didn't need to hear that, not now. But instead, something worse entered her mind, a tiny seed of an idea that she couldn't dig out once it started to grow.

The painting...

Yes. That was what she heard in the hallway. Someone, maybe Dean, maybe Frank, maybe even Debra, was crouched in front of the wall, paintbrush in hand. Someone was responsible for the entire thing, and at this point, even if it felt impossible, she clung to the image, clung to the hope that everything that had happened was just some kind of trick, a cruel practical joke that everyone else was in on.

You won't like what you see, the dark part of her mind whispered. She fanned the thought away like smoke. She didn't just want to see the picture again; she *had* to.

Alice climbed out of bed and opened the door slowly. The only sound past the pounding of her heart was the brush of carpet as the door slid open. She stood like that for a while, letting her eyes adjust to the darkness and, above all else, listening for movement.

She heard nothing, so she slowly crept out into the hallway. The house was silent then, and even the familiar light peeking out from under Dean's door was dark now. The house, in all its strange glory, was hers. And yet, more than ever before, she felt eyes on her, felt a presence, something so close she could touch it.

Alice rounded the corner, still fully expecting to see her parents, her brother, *someone* crouched there in the dark.

Someone in pink…

But the hallway was empty.

The painting glowed blue in the moonlight spilling in from the bay window. She looked down at her feet, positioning herself just right, just where Mary must have been those years before, kneeling down to the height she imagined she must have been. She reached up, imagining the brush in her hand. How long had it taken her? Did she have a plan, or did she just start painting the way that little kids do? It felt like Mary had left her brand on this place, something indelible, something that would be there when she was gone.

When she was dead.

"Mary…"

Alice said the name aloud, and the house seemed to groan in response. She turned and took a few steps forward, peering into the blackness of the front sitting room. There was nothing in there, no furniture yet, nothing at all besides boxes. It was one of the several rooms that expanded her family's footprint, one that would stay empty until the springtime sales started hitting the furniture stores. She stood in the doorway, certain that there was something inside the room, that there was *someone*. The room was sliced into a grid of blue light and black lines from the window panes, and beyond that, the edges of the room were black as pitch.

With a deep breath, she took a single step in. Something shuddered within. A shape stirred in the darkness. A shadow passed in front of the moonlight. Alice didn't move. Didn't breathe. For a long time, the house was frozen, a broken watch, a moment pulled out of time.

Was it minutes of her standing there, not moving a single muscle? Was it hours?

Finally, when she couldn't stand it any longer, Alice stepped back out of the room, into the hall, and the world un-paused. She noticed the snow falling out the wide window. It was white everywhere – the ground, the trees, everything covered in a fresh blanket, glittering like handfuls of quartz.

She never heard anything else move, never saw another shadow, and when she made it back to her room, the clock told her that nearly two hours had passed since she had left. It seemed impossible, but then again, this was no normal house. Something was here, she knew that, and the longer she stayed, the more convinced she had become that it was guiding her. That *she* was guiding her.

Sleep overtook Alice the instant she was under the covers, and she dozed fitfully, dreamed of faces leering in through the window, of a girl with wild, unkempt hair in a pink jacket, beckoning her to some unknown place, some unknown time.

CHAPTER TWELVE

Alice could hear her parents in the kitchen when she opened her eyes. It didn't sound like they were arguing, not completely. It was more of what her father called an "enhanced conversation." Heated, but not angry. They were like that a lot in the morning when both of them had to be somewhere. Alice sat up, her body aching, not quite feeling rested yet. The first thing she did was look over to the bedside table, at the diary that still lay there. A small bit of her feared it had all been a dream, feared and hoped at the same time. Mary was real to her now, as close as the bed, the floor, the walls themselves. There was more work to be done today, and she was actually excited to get to it.

Alice walked into the hallway, glancing over at Dean's room. The door was ajar, just slightly, but none of the usual sounds bellowed out from within. She shrugged and walked toward the kitchen, toward the sound of her parents.

"It will be fine," Debra insisted. "It's front-wheel drive."

"I know, but the truck would be better. I don't mind letting you take it. I promise."

Both of them had to work that day, but Alice was confused for a moment about what they could be arguing about. Then she caught a glimpse outside. The snow. The night before returned to her, the sight of it, blue and glowing. It was still falling, and already, there was enough of it to cover every surface in sight, turning the lawn a flat span of white.

Unstoppable, childlike glee stirred up in her. They rarely got much more than a dusting of snow, but this was the real deal. This was sled snow, snowman snow, snowball war snow. For a brief moment, all the fear and uncertainty of the new house disappeared, and she was just a ten-year-old girl, excited to see the world transformed.

"Wow," she said as she entered the kitchen. Her parents kept talking, neither of them completely acknowledging her. "I mean, how much is it? Is it supposed to keep going?"

Debra turned to her, eyebrows raised, lips narrowed. It was a familiar look, one that Alice had seen her entire life. It seemed to say to her, *Yes, dear? You've interrupted me, so what's so important?*

That look usually came without any actual words attached, and it was no different this time. Alice repeated herself.

"Yes, honey. It's a lot of snow. Your dad and I have to get some work done today, at least for a few hours."

She trailed off a bit, mumbling to herself, picking the thread back up in Frank's direction instead of Alice's. They were close to an argument from the looks of it, both of them stressing about work and oblivious about the once in a decade snow they were getting.

"Is there anywhere good to go sledding?" Alice interrupted.

Debra shook her head. "I don't know.... For god's sake, can you go get your brother up?"

"Why?"

"Because he doesn't need to sleep all day for one thing, but I need him to get those tubs in off the porch – they'll get soaked through if the snow starts melting. It's all his crap in them anyway."

"It's not melting anytime soon," Frank said, looking at his phone.

"Jesus." Debra stared at the ceiling. "Please just go get your brother up."

Alice sighed, frustrated that the fun of the day was already draining out, spoiled by her family's familiar, boring nonsense. She took one last, distant look at the snow and walked back down the hall, past the stairs.

Then she screamed.

The conversation in the kitchen died, replaced by footsteps, hurried, panicked. And there they were, one at each side, Frank turning her face toward his, Debra checking her as if she were a piece of fruit that might be bruised. Neither of them saw. How could they not see?

"What the hell is it?" Frank asked.

Alice raised a finger and pointed at the wall in front of them. Debra saw it first. She didn't scream. She didn't seem to be able to. Finally, Frank saw it too. While Alice and Debra stood, aghast, he was the one to make a run for Dean's room.

"Dean!"

Something in the sound of his voice must have brought Debra back as well, and she followed along, leaving Alice alone to stare at the painting on the wall, at the fresh, black X drawn over the older brother.

"Mary," she whispered as her parents tore Dean's room apart, looking for him.

"Check the bathroom," she heard her mother say. "I'll try his cell." More footsteps. More panic. Alice could hear it in their every movement. A thoughtless hurricane of fear had swept them both up, and with each step, with each word from their mouths, the panic grew deeper. Alice realized she should join in with them, that three people might find her brother faster than two. But she didn't. She only stared at the painting for a moment longer before reaching up and tracing the X with the tip of her finger.

It was still damp to the touch.

"Did you see anything?" Frank asked, running back into the hall. He looked down at the black tips of her fingers, and his hands clamped down on her shoulders, squeezing.

"Did you paint this?" he demanded. His voice was lower now, gruffer. Alice looked from the paint to her father to the paint again. Her eyes were watering.

"Answer me!" He gave her a shake, and her head bobbed forward and back. It didn't hurt, not quite, but it was the sort of thing that would hurt if it kept up. The idea that her father, her daddy, would intentionally do something to cause her pain made the welling corners of her eyes begin to drip. This was the man who had never even spanked her once in her life.

"I said, answer me!"

His hands felt like metal, and she realized, maybe for the first time, how strong he really was. In all the years of her and her mother treating him like the biggest kid in the family, she had never known he was so powerful, so *dangerous*. They would make faces behind his back when he said something silly, when he laughed at his own jokes, when he tripped and nearly fell over his own feet. That was her dad. That was what she knew. The iron grips on her shoulders belonged to someone else, and she was struck by a terrifying thought.

This man had always been there. This power, this awful anger, was always hiding just out of sight; there had been a wild animal living in their house for years, a bear or a tiger, and just because it had never bitten anyone, everyone thought it was a puppy.

Alice couldn't talk. There was too much to take in, too much to process, and her mind skipped between the details, not quite able to make sense of any of it. Just then, her mother swept in and took control.

"What the hell are you doing?" She glared at Frank. He let go of Alice's shoulders and stared at his hands for a split second, seemingly surprised that he had gone so quickly over the deep end. It wasn't like him at all, and Alice could see the mixture of disgust and bewilderment on her mother's face.

"If you want to help, go look around outside."

Frank walked away, a dazed look in his eyes, as Debra rubbed her daughter's shoulders.

"Honey," she said when he was gone, "please, tell me the truth. Did you see anything?" Her voice was soft, kind, healing. It was enough for Alice to find herself once again.

"No. I promise. I was just walking past and…and…"

"It's okay," Debra said, taking Alice's face in her hand. "Just calm down, okay?"

Alice leaned in for a hug, and Debra gave her a solid squeeze. If her mother was panicking yet, she did a very good job of hiding it. She gently pushed her back and stared into Alice's eyes.

"Honey, I have to ask this. Please don't be upset."

"What?"

"Did you paint the X?"

New tears welled up in her eyes. It was all the answer Debra needed. "I'm sorry," she said, hugging Alice once again. "I just had to ask, honey. You stay here. I need to look around—"

"No." Alice grabbed her mother by the arm. "I don't want to be alone."

Debra had that familiar look, that *give me a second of peace* look. It faded in an instant.

"All right," she said. "Let's go find your brother."

They spent the next hour combing through the house as Frank circled the perimeter in his snow boots. The entire scene, the way it all unfolded, was unlike anything Alice had ever witnessed. The closest thing she could compare it to was when Dean was spending the night with his buddy James. They had only been thirteen at the time, and James's mother, Crystal, was taking them to a Minor League Baseball game. It was late afternoon when they got the call.

A pickup truck had rear-ended them as they came off the interstate. Alice could remember the drive up there, the nearly thirty minutes of strangeness in the air, of dread slowly filling up the car. She hadn't exactly been *afraid*, mainly because she wasn't old enough to be afraid. It was a wreck. Okay. Those things happen. She'd seen the ambulances stream by. She even considered how it might be fun to take a ride in one. The possibility that anything bad or fatal could happen was beyond her capacity to imagine.

That moment returned to her now, the feeling of escalation, of something out of control, out of her parents' control. Dysfunctional or not, they always knew what to do, how to handle whatever situation popped up, so to see them panicking, to see that rising dread swallow them, was more than she could handle. It was all in Debra's voice, something that started steady, calm, in control, as if with her tone, she could change what was happening.

"Dean," she said loudly, clearly, with Alice trailing behind her. "Come on out."

They checked every room downstairs, and halfway through, that voice began to change, to crack and break.

"All right, Dean. This isn't funny."

She was still in control, but the edges were beginning to fray. Alice kept at her heels, silent, out of the way. She didn't help – how could she? Her very presence was an added bother that her mother didn't need in that moment. This wasn't her "helping" cook dinner or change a tire. The best thing she could do was stay clear.

"Dean!" Debra said, the façade almost completely gone as they took the stairs two at a time. "This isn't funny."

Her tone had changed from demanding to asking. She wasn't telling anyone anything. She was begging.

"Please," she said, her voice watery as they went through the rooms upstairs, one after the other. All of them were empty, all of them silent. Alice was crying as well; their last hopes seemed to be fading.

"I won't be mad," Debra cried, too soft for anyone to hear, even in the next room. "Just please, come out."

They stopped in front of the crawl space, the little half door that led up to the attic. Debra wiped her nose and opened it, peering inside. The wall of junk loomed just inside. Old, weathered outdoor toys. A red wagon, rusting. A cast-iron bed frame, like a gate. All of it pressed to nearly a foot in front of the door. There was room up there, but not much, and certainly not enough to hide Dean. She closed the door and turned to Alice. It was in that moment that she saw a strange thing happen to her mother's face. The terror and grief seemed to melt away, replaced by a sudden hard mask. It was clear that she had closed some part of herself down, locking the door on it until it was needed. Was Debra doing it for Alice's benefit or her own? Alice wondered.

"Let's just calm down," Debra said, placing a placid hand on Alice's shoulder.

"Mom, where is he…?"

"Hush," she instructed. "He's fine. He's just…gone out."

Debra had to struggle to find the answer. It was, of course, absurd, but there was nothing to be gained from pointing that out, not now. Sometimes, absurdity was all you had to lean on, so Alice just nodded. If there was any moment that she might be helpful, perhaps this was it.

"I bet he went over to Max's house."

A small twinkle of light appeared in Debra's eyes. Was it appreciation for Alice's willingness to be part of her lie? Or was it simple hope?

"You're probably right," Debra said. "I'll bet he just didn't realize how bad the snow was going to be. Max just swung by and picked him up. Come on downstairs; let me make some calls."

Alice followed her mother downstairs and sat at the table, listening to her mother's phone calls. Debra was going through the list of Dean's friends one by one. Every conversation went the same.

"No, we haven't seen him this morning."

"Are you sure you haven't heard anything…anything at all?"

"Yes, the snow is bad."

"I'm sure he'll show up soon. Thanks for checking."

It wasn't like Dean to disappear without a word, but it wasn't completely unheard of. He'd occasionally stay out later than his eleven o'clock curfew, even though he had to know he would catch hell for it. Alice always tried to stay up on those nights, just to see the fallout from his poor decision-making. Frank, always the easier going of the two, would usually just send a text and head to bed. But not Debra. She would make sure that the first face Dean saw when he walked in was hers.

Alice kept thinking about what her mom must have been

thinking, about what it felt like. She knew exactly where her own mind had gone, to a dark place, to a painful place. She wondered if all people did that.

Debra was finishing another phone call when Frank came into the kitchen, covered in snow, his cheeks and nose flushed. He glanced over at Alice, a strange, untrusting look in his eyes. Quickly, he looked away. She couldn't shake his strange behavior, the new, crazed look on his face that seemed to keep popping up.

This place is changing him.

"Yes, thank you.... No, really, it's fine. I'll let you know."

Debra lowered her phone and looked straight at Frank as he kicked snow off his boots. "Well?"

He looked up at her, calm, almost bored. One look, and Alice could see that Debra was fuming.

"What is there to say?" he asked. "No tracks in the snow, which – who knows? – as fast as it's coming down they probably wouldn't last long. I don't know. What is there to say?"

Debra's mouth hung open. "What is there to say?" she asked, her words sharp on both ends. "Our son is missing."

"Now hang on—"

"Don't fucking tell me to hang on. I've dealt with your laid-back shit for the past eighteen years, but if you can't get emotional about our son *missing*—"

"Really?" he said. "Look at this situation with just a pinch of logic. Just look at it."

"After what happened to—" She glanced over at Alice, who kept her face trained straight down on the kitchen table. "After the cat, I don't think this is something to just brush off."

She was staring at him as if he were from a different planet, some cold, unfeeling place where parents treated their children the way that spiders did. *Off you go before I eat you.* This was, without a doubt, the most intense moment that Alice had ever witnessed between her parents, and she was actually holding her breath, waiting to see what might happen next.

He smiled.

"Logic," he said, tapping his forehead. "You always accuse me of not having any common sense, of jumping into things without looking first, of going off on some big scheme. And you know what? Maybe you're right. But I swear to god, I'm the only person in this house who has any damn logic."

Debra's lips were so thin Alice couldn't see them. Alice finally took a breath as Frank continued his speech.

"Look at the facts," he said, counting them off on his fingers as he went. "One, we move into a new house. Two, a cat falls into a pool and dies. Tragic, but completely natural. No fucking foul play involved. Three, we find a weird picture in our house. In a bout of pure *coincidence*, it happens to sorta look like us…if you stand twenty feet away and squint. These are the facts, and all of these facts lead up to one, simple, logical conclusion."

"And what," Debra asked through her teeth, "is that?"

"I don't even want to answer that. I want you to answer that. But first, who do you think drew the X over the cat?"

Debra didn't move her head, but for a single second, her eyes cut over to Alice.

"Go ahead," Frank said, pushing harder.

"I don't know."

"Well, let's look at the suspects. Did you do it?"

"No."

"Did I do it?"

"No."

"Do you think the house is haunted?"

Tears were welling in Alice's eyes. She knew where this was headed.

"No."

"Do you think a stranger just strolled into our house, on not one, but two separate occasions? Or, maybe, just *maybe*, someone else in the house did it."

He glanced over at Alice, and she felt the first tear break loose and slide down her cheek. She wasn't sobbing. She wouldn't do that. She wouldn't give him the satisfaction. Alice turned toward her mother, expecting support, expecting to be saved. What she saw crushed her.

It was subtle; something in the eyes, in the softening of her mouth and in the lines of her neck. She was receding somehow, the anger being blown back like the surf in a windstorm.

She believes him.

"Honey," she said, her voice a soft knife. "Do you know anything about this?"

Alice was shaking her head before any words came out of her mouth, shaking her head in denial and disgust. She wanted to be out of the room, out of the house, out of the world, to be somewhere safe, somewhere that made sense.

Mary would know what to do.

That voice again, that whisper, as soft as snow. Alice stared up at her mother, refusing to wipe the tear on her cheek.

"I. Didn't. Do it."

Frank rolled his eyes, but Debra's face tightened in frustration.

"Alice, please. If this is some big joke that you and Dean cooked up, it's not funny."

"I said, I didn't do it," Alice answered, her voice rising.

"That's enough," Frank said, turning toward her, walking closer, putting his tiny daughter in the direct headlights of his gaze. "Tell the damn truth."

Debra's brows shot up in…what exactly? Surprise? Anger? Alice didn't know. Either way, her mother said nothing. Daddy was talking, and she would let it happen, let it play out, let her husband accuse their daughter of being a liar.

There was a shift inside her, a small twinge in her heart as she remembered everything, all of it in the flash of a second. Her daddy, cuddling, watching movies, teaching her to swim, to dive, to ride a bike, tickling her until she couldn't breathe; those perfect, endless days with her and Daddy all rose to the top, like flower petals on the surface of a dark pond.

Push it down.

She couldn't. It was too much to deal with.

Push it down now.

Alice did as the voice asked. She swallowed hard and looked up into her father's eyes.

If he wants the truth…give it to him.

"I already did tell the truth," she said, her voice dull. "You'd know that if you ever listened…if you ever shut your fucking mouth."

It took Frank a minute to realize what had just happened, but the look on Debra's face told Alice that she'd heard it just fine. If the moment hadn't been so serious, Alice would have laughed at the series of expressions that washed over her father's face. Angry to confused to a bit lost, and finally, back to angry again.

"*What* did you say?" he asked, leaning over her, his voice a few octaves deeper than normal, deep enough to send a shudder through her.

Don't bend.

"You heard what I said."

Frank snatched her up by the crook of her arm and started dragging her along, giving her a speech as he went. For a split second, the strange allure of talking back to her parents was washed away, and a genuine fear took its place. She might not be able to make out much of what her father was saying, but she could feel the anger in his grip. He'd never grabbed her like that before, and in the short walk to her room, she was certain she'd have a bruise. He pushed her inside, onto the bed, and stalked back out, slamming the door.

"Stay in there until we get this all sorted out."

Debra was yelling at him now. Alice could pick the pieces out of it.

"…are out of control…that is your daughter…this house is a fucking disaster…"

The fight followed them upstairs, but Alice didn't try to listen along. She was still processing everything that had happened. This was a giant moment for her, the type of thing that she only read about in books or watched in movies. Had she actually talked to her father like that? The idea itself was so foreign, so distant, that she was still struggling to wrap her mind around it.

You did good.

The voice again. This time, it sounded less like a voice inside her head and more like a whispered secret in her ear, a phantom's voice, something dark and familiar. She thought of Mary, of Dean, of what was happening to all of them, and as the sounds of stomping feet rumbled overhead somewhere, she reached out her shaking hand and grasped the diary.

CHAPTER THIRTEEN

There was a story there. Somewhere in the diary's jumbled entries, the truth was hiding. Alice was now certain, and though the story wasn't laid out in chapters or scenes, it was there all the same.

Mary's story.

It was like a box of puzzle pieces, dumped onto the floor, scrambled and messy, but hiding something. A message. A tale of a girl and, as Alice was learning, a tragedy. She skimmed through the pages frantically, trying to make sense of it all.

Something is wrong with my parents, one page began. *Or maybe, something is wrong with me. I should have known it when I drew on the wall that time. I was just a kid, only seven. I thought they would like it, I really did, and I know that somewhere out there, a different mother and father would have handled that situation differently.*

No yelling. No screaming. No...belt.

Alice gasped, and one hand slipped instinctively to her arm, which was still tender to the touch. She read on.

I can see parts of them in me, but the whole is so different. If I found out that I was born on another planet, that aliens had left me in a basket, I wouldn't be surprised.

I won't be here forever.

Something in the writing was changing, blooming, and she could imagine this child, this little girl who drew on walls, becoming an adult, right there on the page in front of her. She flipped forward, reading more, growing closer to this girl whom she had never met and would never meet.

Do all kids hate their parents?

I heard someone say that the other day. A girl in class talking about how much she hated her mom and dad, about how they didn't buy her this or that, or that the vacation they took was lame, or that she had an eye on a certain car when she turned sixteen, but her dad said she would just get a hand-me-down.

I started laughing at her. When she asked me why I was laughing, I told her it was because she was so funny. Because she was so stupid. That she had nothing to hate her parents about, so she made something up. Invented her anger.

One time, I was with Mommy at the store, and I asked her for… something. I honestly don't remember. Was it ice cream? A toy? I was probably eight then, maybe younger.

She told me no, which I was used to at that point. But it wasn't the answer. It was the way she said it.

Accusing.

Blaming.

Angry at the request itself.

It was like I should know better. That I'd pushed her too far too many times to really expect anything kind or decent from her. That reaction…I don't know. It did something to me. Something new and different.

I started screaming.

Mommy didn't know how to react to that. She threatened to spank me. Said she would tell Daddy when I got home. Then she got desperate. She grabbed my arm and started squeezing.

"Stop this." She spat the words in my face.

I looked down, saw her white knuckles, saw the red skin of my arm, felt the pain growing.

"You WILL stop this," she said. "Or I'll break it."

The world stopped spinning, and tears formed in my eyes. I stopped just as an older lady passing by paused to see. And what did she see? A mother abusing her child?

No.

She only saw a disobedient child getting what she finally deserved.

"You know what they say?" she said to my mother as I rubbed my arm. "Every daughter hates her mother."

I can't stop thinking about that moment, about the idea that the two of us becoming enemies was something that was bound to happen.

"No," I told the woman.

"Excuse me?" she asked, staring down the barrel of her thick glasses.

"I said no. I don't hate my mother."

I felt the iron hand on my tender arm once again, and I glanced up to see Mommy standing next to me, glaring down.

"Don't talk to strangers that way," she said before her grip loosened.

"Don't worry," the lady said as she walked away. "With you for a mother, she'll learn soon enough."

Alice read on. Each new line, each new passage, painting a picture, a dark, terrifying picture.

On one page…

I can't write this down. I can't. If they find this book, it will be even worse, so I can't. I can't.

On another…

I'm going to sneak into their bedroom one day. I'm going to sneak in, and I'm going to take that fucking belt. I swear to god, I'm going to burn it in the woods, burn it and bury the ashes.

Every word became more chilling than the next, and Alice was certain she could have spent the entire day reading that book, doing nothing but wearing the bruised skin of a lost, forgotten girl. Something was here, Alice was sure of it, and with each passing page, she became more convinced that Mary was trying to tell her something.

That Mary was crying out for *her* help.

Footsteps. Sharp, impatient. Down the stairs, straight to her door. Alice had just enough time to slide the book under her pillow before the door opened. Her mother stood there, stone-faced. She walked in and closed the door behind her.

"I'm…sorry," she said, standing just next to the bed, seemingly wanting to sit on it but not quite able to. "Your father. He's…under a lot of stress. But, he had no right to grab you like that."

Debra's eyes were cast down. She tried to raise them, but she seemed to lose her nerve. Instead, she turned and sat on the edge of the bed, her back to Alice. It looked to Alice like an easy way out.

"You shouldn't have talked to him like that, but he had no right to grab you."

After the time alone, Alice had returned to her usual self. The dark little voice had crept back down to wherever it slept, taking all of her nerve with it. Even so, she imagined answering with something clever and sharp, something like, *Well, you had no right to accuse me, did you?*

She didn't say that. She didn't say anything. It felt more appropriate to let her mother sizzle for a bit before offering any sort of olive branch. Debra seemed to feel it as well – she shifted uncomfortably on the bed before standing abruptly.

"I'm sorry too," she said a moment later. "I shouldn't have let it get that far."

She shuffled around, turning toward Alice. She still wouldn't look her in the face.

"I'm not going to ask you again," she said softly. "But I want you to know that I'm calling the police. If Dean is really missing, we… we need to get some help."

She paused, clearly waiting for Alice's reply. It never came.

"If there's anything I need to know, please, tell me now."

Again, Alice was silent. Just once, she cast her eyes over to the pillow and the diary hiding underneath it. She was gripped with the wild thought that this was all a test, that the entire scenario was something her parents had cooked up to see how honest their little girl was. Even so, she said nothing.

"Okay then."

Debra waited for a second, for what, Alice could only guess. Then she leaned over and wrapped an arm around her daughter. Alice winced, but she leaned into her all the same.

"Everything's okay," Debra whispered. "We'll find him, and everything will be okay."

Alice let her leave, and she considered pulling the diary back out. She glanced over at the clock; it was almost nine. Somehow, she was actually hungry. She didn't want to venture out any farther than she had to, but she decided to slink out and grab a box of cereal from the pantry. Debra was in the kitchen, already on the phone as Frank skulked around behind her, pacing like a dog at the edge of his leash.

"No…yes…I mean, not that I know of. No, not at all. There's no reason for him to… Please, just let me finish."

Her mother wasn't crying, not quite, but it was clear that something in her demeanor had cracked. The image was deeply disturbing, terrifying even. Before now, part of this entire scene had felt like a bit of a game to Alice, just a young girl testing the limits of her parents' boundaries. Now, seeing Debra so broken made it real, and a sick feeling surged inside her.

That's guilt you're feeling, a voice whispered. *No less than you deserve.*

Frank met her gaze as she walked in, and for a moment, Alice was certain that he would grab her again. He didn't. Instead, his face softened. A tight, guilty smile stretched across it.

Alice didn't want to be here. She didn't want to see any of this. She quietly opened the pantry and pulled out a box of sugary cereal, the kind of thing her mother would frown upon, then hurried back to her room, glancing up at the painting once again.

Alice couldn't help but wonder what was next or, more importantly, *who* was next. She sat, silent, in her room, eating sickly sweet handfuls as her parents continued talking in the other room. It was, without a doubt, the most surreal morning of her life, and she couldn't stop thinking of Dean. The memory of Baxter dead in the pool made her feel queasy, and she could only imagine what the sight of her brother might do to her if they found him the same way. Mangled, bloody, facedown in the snow. Silent tears rolled down her cheek as she munched away at the cereal. Her mind drifted again.

"Mary," she whispered between bites.

She was there, in the room, with Alice every waking moment. She was all around the house, part of it, staring into windows, hiding in shadows, wandering through the woods. It was silly. It was impossible.

But it's true, and you know it is.

That whisper again. Alice couldn't deny it. There was no proof, none that anyone else could believe, but the truth was sometimes deeper than that, could push beyond what was visible – or even possible.

Yes, Mary was here, and she was angry. But the question remained: why? What did she have against Alice's family?

When she had eaten all she could stand to, Alice started back for the diary. She was just opening it when she heard the footsteps. She quickly slipped it under her pillow and glanced up, expecting to see her mother opening the door, but instead found Frank in her doorway.

"Hey, kiddo," he said, his voice normal, plain, a bit goofy. Alice said nothing. Instead, she waited for him to speak.

"I… It looks like the cops are going to send someone out if they can get through this weather. There's a lot to keep them busy today. We never get snow like this, so there's wrecks, outages…"

He trailed off, a rare case of self-editing. He usually would talk himself hoarse, explaining something that no one asked him to, but he was different as well, shaken in the same ways that Debra was, even if the results might have looked different.

"I'm going out for a bit," he added as Alice glanced down, away from his eyes. "I want to double-check around. Check the driveway, the road, the woods. Make sure there's nothing else to see."

See what?

Alice looked up from her feet and stared at him. He wasn't looking directly at her, his gaze shifting, unsettled.

He looks guilty.

"I'm sorry I got so fired up earlier," he said softly. "I'll be back in a bit."

Alice let him leave without a word. She was still stunned by everything that had happened – and by her parents' reactions, to her defiance to Dean's disappearance. A small, aching feeling began to burn inside her, blooming, becoming a genuine sharp pain in her chest.

She wanted to go home. Her real home. Her lost home.

She'd seen it in Debra's face. This place was breaking them, the same way it had broken Mary.

No, the voice inside insisted. *It wasn't the house. It was* him.

The front door closed, and even from halfway across the house, she could feel the cold seeping in, the cold tendrils snaking through every room. What if Dean was out there? Would he be able to survive?

He's already gone.

No. She wouldn't hear it. She wouldn't even entertain it. Alice shut the door to her bedroom and pulled the diary out from its hiding place. Reading it would be the only way to silence the dark whisper in her ear. She scanned the pages, looking for names, for references, for people. She wanted more of this broken, disjointed story to make sense, for all of this madness to make sense. And so, she read. Over the course of the next hour, she noticed a trend slowly emerging, a story within the story.

Dad was hunting again today, an early entry read. *He's always gone, even when he's home. I should go see him sometimes. It's not a long walk down there. We used to do things together all the time. Fishing. Hiking. Spending time together.*

Alice thought about her own father, about the undeniable drift between the two of them. How long had it been growing? She thought about the last time she had jumped into his lap to watch TV. Of the last time she reached for his hand in public. From what she could tell, this entry was written when Mary was thirteen. How much farther would they drift in the next three years? She skimmed forward, looking for more references to Mary's father.

Dad wants to know what I want for my birthday. He actually suggested that I ask for a puppy. It's like he wants one for himself but he's too afraid to ask for it.

Once she noticed it, that slow drift between father and daughter, it was all she could see.

Alice continued skimming the pages, and she saw an even greater sign of the wedge between Mary and her father.

Walker was in his mood today.

The name threw her at first. It was like a book or a movie adding a character in the last act, something strange and unsettling about it.

The pills ran out. It always gets like this when the pills are gone. He doesn't want to admit it, but he's a different person. I wonder if I would still hate him as much if he never took them at all. I'm pretty sure I would.

It was her father. Walker was Mary's father. He had to be.

He doesn't think I know about them. Mom doesn't either. But then again, they've both got plenty of secrets.

Another clue, subtle, powerful. She still called her mother 'Mom'. Mary still had some connection with her.

He hasn't been the same since he hurt his back. It never would have happened if he hadn't been so stupid, so lazy. She talks about him when we're alone, just the two of us. She tells me what he used to be like, how sweet he used to be, back before the fall. What kind of man falls down the stairs when he's trying to fix them? A drunk one, that's who.

"He was better then," she tells me, talking to me like less of a daughter and more like a friend. I don't blame her though. I know she doesn't have any friends. Walker ran them all off.

"He's not even much of a man anymore."

She told me that once, and I don't think it sunk in at the time. That was back when things were different, simpler.

"He'd rather spend all his time out there in the woods than with his wife. Than in his own bed."

How could I have known what she meant? I was just a kid. I'd have probably never known what she meant if I hadn't seen it for myself.

Daddy's place.

I've seen the pictures of them, dating, back before me and Peter came along. He was thinner then, stronger looking, not this shell. This bitter thing that just exists to yell at us, to…

…no. I won't write about that. I promised myself it was dead, it was gone, it was something I left back in the shed, in his special little place.

"Our secret."

Bastard.

Bastard.

Bastard.

She tells me how sweet he used to be, and for the life of me, I can't tell if it's a lie or the truth. If she's trying to convince me or if she's already convinced herself.

She's weak. I see that now. I'm only fourteen and I see it.

"Fourteen and looking like a full-grown woman!"

The bastard had the nerve to say that in front of me.

I won't be like her. I won't be so weak. And if he ever tries it again, I'll kill him.

So, there it was. Mary, not quite a little girl anymore, was living with a monster for a father, someone who did things to her, things she didn't want to dwell on for even a moment. But, whatever his crimes, he didn't break her. Mary was a fighter, a bold little warrior. She was everything that Alice wasn't. The two of them were separated by life and death, and the only thing that connected them was words, simple words sketched onto a yellowing diary.

Not the only thing.

As her mother paced around the house, double-checking every room, Alice slipped under her covers, still reading.

CHAPTER FOURTEEN

The hours passed, and Alice stayed in her room, wrapped in the almost ghostly silence of the house. From time to time, she'd hear her mother's nervous footsteps pacing in the hallway, stopping in front of the painting before moving on. Alice kept expecting to hear a knock on the door, to hear the muffled discussion between her and the officers. But the knock never came.

Pieces of Mary's story rose up like bits of paper burning in a bonfire. They'd had a dog, named Buster. Peter, Mary's older brother, liked to hunt with Walker. Her mom, always nameless, was an avid gardener. As for Mary, she was popular with the boys at school, but she only had a few girlfriends. They didn't seem to like her because, as she wrote, *I don't put up with all the bullshit.* Once, an older girl who had been bullying her tried to get physical with her. She'd gotten in Mary's face, calling her a whore, pointing her finger into her chest.

I grabbed her finger and started twisting it. I didn't care. I didn't stop until I heard it pop and she started screaming.

She was nearly kicked out of school for that one, but she didn't seem to mind, for reasons she made all too clear.

I've sat there and taken it before. I've been quiet when I should have been loud. I've let things happen that should never have happened. Mom is the type of person who lets things happen. She accepts things as they are.

I've seen what that gets me. I'll fight until I'm dead.

The details of Mary's life thrilled Alice, and despite all the fear and uncertainty of the past few days, she imagined the two of them as friends. They would have gotten along, she knew it, and Mary would have made her stronger. Made her better. Taught her how to fill in those missing gaps in herself so that no one, not her parents or Dean or kids at school, would ever take her for granted again. The more she read, the more she saw the world around both of them as a forge, a place that tested them with fire, made them into something new. She would never have asked to trade places with Mary, but Alice couldn't help but admire how strong she was in the face of such awful things.

The house, its own character in Mary's story, began to reveal itself through Mary's eyes. The pool, once pristine and blue, started to deteriorate first. The plastic liner began to split and break in places, and instead of having it fixed, Walker let it fall into disarray. Soon, it was ruined, filled with algae and a chorus of frogs. Mary wrote about the attic, how much bigger it was than she thought, but how it began to fill with old junk, packed so tightly she couldn't get in there anymore. She talked about the basement, that almost nightmarish, subterranean world with walls so caked with mold and grime that it looked like the inside of a cave.

It's a weird house, she wrote. *We've lived here since I was seven, but I've never really gotten used to it. Mom said it was built in the Thirties, that they had to add on to it. She loves that about it, loves how unique it is. But I'd kill to live in a normal house, a house that doesn't get so cold during the winter. I swear, it seems like it's haunted sometimes.*

Alice certainly understood *that*.

The worst are those stairs, she added. *It's like they didn't connect them to the wall right or something. They just feel so rickety. I hate even going upstairs, to be honest. If Walker hadn't been drinking so much, things would be better. He never would have fallen and hurt his back.*

No fall.

No pain.

No pills.

Imagine that. Just a regular fucked up family instead of...this.

Alice glanced over at the clock. Half the day was gone now, and she'd never even heard from her dad or the cops. She closed the diary and moved to put it back in the hiding place while she got dressed. But something in Mary's words, about the way she painted the picture, of a family as a slow-motion train wreck, made her stop. There were ways to stop things from going forward. Despite everything that had happened, she believed it in her bones. So, with a deep breath, she ventured out in search of her mother, diary in hand.

Debra was sitting in the living room, the uncovered windows revealing the world of white that was slowly, surely, swallowing the entire house. Had it ever snowed this much here? Alice couldn't be sure, but it certainly hadn't in her memory. She sat down next to her mother, who was staring at the blank TV, one leg twitching up and down rapidly. At first, Alice wasn't sure her mother even noticed her.

"I've never seen this much snow," Alice said, slipping the diary under one leg. It was warm through her jeans.

Debra looked up, surprised. "Oh. Yes. It's a lot."

Her eyes were red-rimmed, dark blue wells that spoke of unspeakable fear and grief. All of Alice's bluster, all of her pride at standing up to her parents, vanished when she looked into her mother's stricken eyes.

"Probably five or six inches. Haven't seen it like this since...I don't know. Maybe since I was a kid. I can't remember, honestly..."

The thought died away, another rabbit disappearing into the woods.

"Where's Dad?"

Debra seemed shocked by the question, as if she had already forgotten her husband existed.

"He's...out there. I think. Somewhere. I saw him walk past earlier. It was almost like he was checking everything out. The pool. The fence. The porch...maybe the woods."

She looked down at her phone, which rested on one leg, a quiet little square of black plastic and glass. She checked it for what had surely been the hundredth time.

"He's been out for a long time now," she said to herself.

The seed in Alice's brain rattled like a can of spray paint.

What's Dad up to?

"What about the police?" Alice asked.

"I called them back a little while ago. They said they were slammed. There was no one to send yet. People aren't used to this kind of weather. Lots of people in worse spots than we are. Wrecks. Things like that."

She laughed a bit. It sounded like a puppy whining. "I guess we're on the list."

"When will they be here?" Alice asked.

"I don't know, baby." Her leg started twitching again, dancing up and down like a piston, the fabric of her pants shuffling with a *thwip, thwip, thwip* sound. After a few seconds, the sound of it was wearing thin.

"Mom," she said, finally placing a hand on her mother's knee. Debra stopped bouncing her leg and looked over, her eyes still dazed, glassy.

"What is it?"

"There's something I want to talk about."

Debra's eyes brightened. Alice read the hope springing in them, the hope that maybe, somehow, this was all still a joke that had gone on for too long.

"I found something," she said. "A diary. I think it belonged to the girl who lived here before us. The girl who drew that picture on the wall."

She held the little book up, pausing long enough to give Debra the opportunity to confess, to tell Alice that *she* was the one who put the book there. Debra was silent.

"Have you ever seen it?" Alice asked.

"No."

"You're sure? You're absolutely sure?"

"Yes. Honey, what does this have to do with anything?"

"Mom, I think there's something...wrong with this house."

Debra tried to smile, Alice could tell. She watched as her mom tried to do that motherly thing that she always did. *Honey, there's nothing in the closet*, or, *Alice, you're being silly, it's just the wind.* It never worked, even when she was right, and this time, she couldn't just smile, nod, and ignore what was happening.

"What are you talking about?" she finally asked, her voice skeptical.

"There's so much, it's hard to explain it. But this book, it tells about what happened here. What happened to her."

Debra's face darkened. "What do you know?"

Alice glanced down at the diary. "I know her name was Mary. That she lived here with a brother named Peter. A dad named Walker. Not sure what the mom's name is." She paused, waiting for Debra to respond. Her mother only stared at her with numb eyes.

"Walker was…bad, I think. He did things to her. Stuff that she doesn't want to think about. And…I think she died. Here."

A look of pure, grim sickness washed over Debra's face. "How do you know that?"

"I don't know," Alice said. "But…I heard you and Dad talking about it last night."

Debra ran both hands up her face, through her hair, smearing her eyeliner. She didn't say anything. She only kept shaking her head from left to right.

"Please, tell me what happened," Alice begged. "I think she's still here. I think she's got something to do with what's happening."

"No."

"I need to know."

"You don't need to know anything; you're just a kid…."

"Did you put the diary in my room?" Alice asked, suddenly angry at her mother's refusal to listen. "Did Dad?"

Debra reached for the book, and Alice pulled it back reflexively, as if her mother's hand might steal it and burn it to a crisp.

"I just want to take a look at it," she said defensively. "I've never seen it in my life. There's some…rational *explanation* for all this. There has to be. Books don't just show up; someone puts them there."

"She did."

"Jesus Christ," Debra said, slapping a hand on her knee out of frustration. "With everything else going on, the last thing I can deal with is you going off on some…crazy fantasy."

"Look at it then," Alice said, pressing it into her mother's hands. "Tell me how I know all of this. Tell me what *you* know. If I'm crazy, at least prove that I am. Then maybe we can figure everything out."

Debra scanned the pages as Alice talked, flipping through quickly. She turned to the end of the book, her eyes narrowed as she studied the pages. Then she turned back to an earlier page.

"It's nothing." Debra stared down at the pages. "It's less than nothing. You could have written all of this in half an hour if you wanted to. And if you're just messing with me, it's not funny."

"Do I look like I'm messing with you?" Alice asked, on the verge of tears.

"What is this then?" Debra asked, holding the book in front of Alice's face. "Look at the handwriting at the back pages. Look at how new it is. Go ahead, compare them. You can tell some of this looks old, but the last few pages are someone else. Someone new."

It was true. Alice had noticed it the first time she paged through the book, even if it hadn't really sunk in – an entirely different hand had written the last twenty pages or so. The handwriting was scrawled and uglier somehow. Like the hand writing it wasn't as steady as it once had been.

"What happened to her?" Alice demanded, taking the diary from her mother and setting it on the coffee table.

"What does it matter?"

"Please, just tell me. Was it an accident? Was it something with her father?" Hope surged through Alice's chest as another possibility dawned on her. "Maybe you got the wrong story and she didn't actually die. Maybe she was just hurt so bad it messed up her handwriting."

Debra took a deep breath and closed her eyes.

"We should have never. Come. Here."

She said it with finality, as if the words were demons that she was exorcising from her own body. She opened her eyes and met Alice's gaze.

"This girl. This Mary, if that was her name. She didn't get hurt. She didn't injure her hand or go into the hospital or anything like that. She died. And I didn't get the wrong story. They have to tell you, you know. Real estate agents? It's part of the deal. If someone dies tragically, it affects the house. It was in the news and everything. And lucky us, it really dropped the price. It was a steal, as your dad says."

Debra sighed and shook her head. "She fell down the stairs. They had been messed up for years. Apparently, the father..."

"Walker?"

"I don't know anyone's name." Debra rolled her eyes. "All we know is we had to have the stairs professionally repaired before we moved in. They were loose from the frame, and she just fell."

There it was. The truth she'd suspected was out in the open now. Alice already knew something had had happened here, but the details were awful to consider. She'd already walked up and down those stairs a dozen times, and she couldn't help but wonder if she'd walked over the very spot where Mary died.

"Was that all?"

Debra shook her head in frustration. "Yes, that was all. It was an accident. A genuine tragedy. And that's the end of it. Honey, I don't know what's going on here any more than you do, but this house isn't... Jesus, I can't even say it out loud."

Haunted.

"There's something else," Alice added, feeling self-conscious.

"What is it?"

"Dad."

Debra's face twisted a bit with...something. Guilt, perhaps? Alice didn't know for sure. "What about him?" she asked, glancing out the windows.

"He's...different, isn't he?"

Debra tensed, as if she expected Frank to leap out of hiding at any moment, as if the entire scenario were some kind of trap just waiting to be sprung.

"What do you mean?"

"This place is changing him," Alice said bluntly. "I've seen it. And I think you've seen it too."

Debra opened her mouth to argue, but she seemed to think better of it. There was no denying the scene that morning or the night before last.

"It's stress," she said softly. "I don't expect you to understand that. Honestly, I don't know if I understand it. He's put so much of himself into the idea of this house. Of what it could mean to all of us. He's…not been doing well since he lost his job. And I think he needed a win – and he wanted all of us to have a win." She shook her head. "I think he hoped that this house could fix something in our marriage. Something that might be broken. That's why he's acting like this. He's a good man. A good father. You know that."

"Of course I do," Alice said. "That's why I'm scared. He's not the same, I know it."

"What are you trying to say?"

What are *you trying to say?* one of the voices whispered. Alice was too exhausted to try to figure out which one. It was as maddening as it was painful, this split inside her. She wanted her mom to understand, to be on her side, but she didn't want to say it. It felt wrong, it felt like a betrayal, but it felt *true* as well. Debra's eyes softened. She leaned in to Alice, rubbing her shoulder gently. "Honey, just tell me. It's fine. I'm here, baby. It's okay."

Alice swallowed hard. "What if he had something to do with Dean?"

Debra jerked away. The look she gave her daughter wasn't one of fear or disappointment or anger. This was new, something that Alice had never seen on her mother's face, at least not directed at her. It was a look of pure disgust.

"How can you say that?"

"Mom, please…"

"You need to leave this room," Debra said coldly.

"Please…just listen to me—"

"Now. I don't want to see your face for a while. Go. Before I actually punish you. And take this thing with you."

Debra pointed to the diary on the coffee table. Alice stood and scooped the book up before backing out of the room.

"If I see that book again, I'll burn it."

CHAPTER FIFTEEN

Alice left her mother sitting there, a single thought racing through her head, the seed of an idea now in full bloom.

This place is changing them both.

After dropping the diary off in her room, she hurried into the bathroom just off the hallway. It was a simple, square room, nothing more than a toilet on one end and a wide vanity on the other, but like most of the house, it had an oddness to it, something that just didn't seem to fit into the modern world. She pulled the door closed and locked it behind her before dropping onto the toilet, her chin in her hands. She was tired, even then, barely halfway through the day. The entire ordeal was draining her, and there was no end in sight. She imagined the police, the questions, the searches through the house, through her room, through their boxes. She tried to think up the questions that they might ask her.

"What did you know?"

"Did you want your brother dead?"

"How long have you hated your parents?"

It was as if she were trapped in the center of a murder mystery, the kind of thing they showed on network TV at nine o'clock at night. As much as she tried to talk herself out of it, to tell herself that Dean was fine, that Mom and Dad were fine, she simply couldn't. She was almost completely convinced the police would find them all dead, and this house would become an urban legend that people in town shunned, that teenagers drove past on Halloween.

Alice went to wash her hands before gazing into the mirror. Her eyes looked different, heavier now than before.

You look old.

"*We* look old," she said aloud, wondering if she was going crazy.

The mirror took up the entire wall from the vanity up, and it came out a few feet on each side, making two, wide C-shapes of reflective glass. She'd never really noticed the strange effect it made; she climbed up onto the counter and leaned forward, turning her head one way, then the other, finding herself in her own personal hall of mirrors, where an endless string of Alices in a neat row. The effect made her feel smaller, more insignificant, as if she were a speck of sand on a beach.

That's not true. You're everything.

The voice in her head was convincing, welcoming. She sat there, letting herself get wrapped up in the fantasy, in the dream that this house had broken her into all those reflections, knowing she would only be whole again if she could figure out what was going on.

Alice couldn't have guessed how long she was trapped in the world of the mirror – minutes? hours? – but as she stared into her infinite selves, the doorknob behind her began to twist. The squeak of it was soft, too soft for her to hear, and seconds later, the heavy, old-fashioned brass knob fell to the floor with a solid thud, startling Alice from her reverie. She turned. Was her mother trying to come in?

"I'm in here," she said aloud.

No answer.

"Mom?"

She hopped down and walked to the door. A rough wooden hole was all that was left of where the knob had been. Alice tried pulling the door open, but it was stuck, the locking mechanism still in place even though the handle was already off.

"Mom? Dad?"

A scream. It was her mother's voice, somewhere upstairs, from the sound of it. It was too far away for her to hear anything other than the fear, a terror that cut through the walls, through the door, through her heart. Something was after her mother. She could hear it, as clearly as she could hear the thumping of her own heart.

"Mom!"

Alice didn't know if anyone could hear her, but she kept screaming all the same. She pounded at the door, kicking it, trying to turn the mechanism in the hole with her fingers, trying so hard that it hurt.

"Mom!"

She heard shuffling, feet scuffing across the wooden floor upstairs, short, strange bursts of words from her mother.

"No! Don't you touch me. *No!* I said, *get back*!"

She'd never heard her mother so desperate, so *frenzied*. The sounds changed suddenly, the words becoming little more than distant whispers. Whoever it was, the situation became clear: her mother was fighting with someone.

It's him, the voice whispered. *It's your father.*

She was trapped, caged like an animal, and the fear and madness began to spill out of her. She'd been there once in her life that she could remember, a single moment in time that was so awful that it seemed to have changed her DNA. It was the time that she hid in the trunk of her mom's car after she took the groceries out and Dean had slammed it shut, knowing she was inside. It was that same feeling, that throat-closing suggestion that you were just moments away from death, that the only thing that could save you was to get free, to breathe free air.

"Mom, please, let me out!"

All at once, she didn't care about what was happening upstairs. She was cutting her fingers, bruising her hands and knees, fighting the door as if it were something alive, something she could tire out, something she could defeat. But this was a real, solid door, not a hollow thing from her old home. She could beat it for the rest of her life and it wouldn't make a difference.

"Momma, please!"

Her voice was a shriek. Her heart was a drum. Her body shook. The rumble overhead grew louder, and she stopped her assault on the door, listening. There was a scream followed by a heavy thud. Then, furiously pounding footsteps.

"Alice." Her mother's voice, breathless, her footsteps tumbling down the stairs.

"Mom, I'm in the bathroom. I'm stuck!"

The footsteps stopped, and the door began to rattle as Debra pounded on it from the outside.

"Alice, what happened?"

"I don't know; the knob just fell out. Please, help me out of here!"

Her mother's long, delicate fingers slipped through the hole. There was blood on them.

"Mom, please, hurry!"

More footsteps. Heavy. Thudding down behind her.

"Alice…"

Her mother's voice was desperate. Hopeless. Beaten. Suddenly, the fingers disappeared from the hole. Alice dropped to one knee and stared out, trying to see what was happening.

"No, you stay away from me. Fucking get away, stop, *stop*—"

Something flashed in front of the door. It was only there for a split second. Something pink.

Debra moaned and was silenced with a muffled thud as she fell out of Alice's view. Then there was only stillness.

"Mom?" she whispered, staring out the hole.

A long shadow appeared, and a dark figure shuffled out in the hall. Alice turned away from the hole, pressing her back to the door.

There was a knock on the door.

It was soft, slow, a steady beat of three, four, five knocks. Tears ran down Alice's face as she prayed, begged, that the sound would stop, that whoever was out there would leave her be. The knocks subsided, and for a moment, she heard nothing at all, just the thrum of her own heart. The silence was finally broken by the sounds of something heavy being dragged through the empty house. Down the hall. Up the stairs. Finally, out of the reach of her ears entirely.

There was nothing left for her. Everything she knew, the world she inhabited, was gone, washed away in the span of a few short days. When the house had grown completely silent and she worked up the nerve, she picked up the doorknob and slipped the metal rod back into place. Acting entirely on instinct, she fiddled with it for a few seconds. The latch clicked open, and the door swung free, creaking loud enough to echo in the ghostly silent house.

There was the diary. Left just in front of the door. A present. A gift. A thought occurred to her, an image so grotesque and yet somehow perfect, somehow true. This house was alive, hungry, and she, sweet little foolish Alice, was slowly feeding her family to it. And what did she get in return? Words scratched onto a page.

She stood there, frozen for a moment, not wanting to touch it, not wanting to move. The painting was across from her, angled so she couldn't see it from where she stood. All she needed to do was move forward, a step, maybe two, and there it would be. But Alice didn't need to look. She knew exactly what she would find. Beside the doorway to her right were a few drops of blood. So little of it, like someone had dripped a bit of paint.

She's dead.

Alice hated the voice now, but she didn't have the strength to argue with it. It felt inevitable that her mother was dead now, that Alice would find her and Dean both dumped into the frozen pool, their eyes glazed, still surprised, still amazed that they were no longer among the living. Her mind went in reverse, playing back the scene like a DVR, and she saw Frank carrying the bodies, throwing them in one after the other, and if her imagination went forward, she would no doubt see him dumping her in as well.

Why?

It was her voice this time, the usual, quiet, meek voice, and it was a fair question, one she couldn't answer. This scene was a puzzle plagued with too many missing pieces.

Was the house haunted? Had it somehow taken control of her father, turning him into something closer to Walker, the first iron-fisted parent? Was it Mary, a bloodthirsty spirit hungry for revenge?

Though tempting, none of those answers felt possible. They were still *wrong* in their own ways. Alice put one foot forward, carefully stepping over the diary, afraid that it might jump up and attack her if she got too close. Once she was safely past it, she looked up at the painting and found what her mind had already told her would be there. The family had changed, the black paint still wet where the crude X had been drawn over the mother. The sight of it made Alice burst into a fresh round of quiet tears. This was it, then. This was what the world was, what her life had become. Her family, the most important people in the world to her, had become nothing more than a series of check boxes being ticked off, one after another.

A grocery list.

Yes. That felt about right. There were no answers, none that she could find, only a silent house filled with the echoes of her lost family.

A noise echoed from the other end of the house, cutting through her tears. The front door rattled. Unlocked. Swung open. The winter blew in, the very sound of it bone-chilling.

"Debra?" Frank called, stomping off his feet again.

It's him. You know it's him, and you know what's next.

"I can't believe it, but there's almost eight inches out there. I don't think we've had snow like this in twenty years."

Why was he talking to a house if he knew it was nearly empty?

You know why. He's playing dumb. He's putting on a show for you, to make you feel better. To put you at ease.

"I walked all the way to the road. It's completely shut down. Unless the cops have four-wheel drive, I don't see how they'll get up here."

Alice stared down at the drops of blood, at the diary, and back up at the dripping X on the wall.

You don't have much time.

Alice picked up the diary and darted into her room.

CHAPTER SIXTEEN

Alice could hear him moving through the house. He was in the kitchen, rummaging through the cupboards, the fridge. Usual dad stuff.

"You see anything of Dean?" he asked his nonexistent wife.

Alice didn't reply, and she didn't hesitate. She knew it wouldn't be long before he came looking around the rest of the house; she ran to her closet and began to bundle up. A hooded sweatshirt, boots, gloves, anything that she could find quickly that would keep her warm. She didn't have a plan, not a real one. All she wanted to do was put distance between them.

You're afraid of him, the voice whispered. *You should be.*

"Debra? Alice?"

He was closer now, maybe even in the hall. Alice pulled on her other boot and froze.

"What happened to the door?" he asked.

She held her breath and slipped into the closet, immediately thinking of spiders – brown recluses – and centipedes. She pushed into the curtain of hanging clothes and pulled the door closed to a slit.

"What did you guys do when I was—"

He was there now, just outside the bathroom door, surely close enough to see the drops of blood and the newly painted X on the wall.

"Oh my god…"

The fear in his voice. Was it real? It sounded genuine, but how could she trust it? Was it just another part of the game he was playing?

It sounds like he's scared, the quiet Alice said, speaking up and making herself heard. *I don't think he's that good at acting.*

"Alice!" he screamed, bolting into the room, throwing the door open. "Debra!" He tore out of the room, his heavy boots clomping their way through the house. It was now or never. If she was going to make a run for it, this was her only chance.

But where would she go? What would she do? The closest neighbors were probably half a mile away through snow the likes of which she'd never seen in her life. It was foolish. No, it was fatal, a mistake that would undoubtedly take her life.

Frank's voice boomed from every corner of the house, but Alice merely slunk down to the floor, hiding like...a rabbit in a hole. It was all she knew to do. She waited there, quietly, patiently, until the footsteps drew closer. Frank barreled back into the room, breathless.

"Alice?"

She could hear him, striding across the room, checking under the bed, behind the curtains. There was nothing left to do. He was coming; she slipped the diary under her sweatshirt and prepared herself.

The closet door flung open, and there he stood, red-faced from both the snow and his furious run through the house. He looked confused to find her there, as if he expected her to already be gone.

To already be eaten.

"Alice, Jesus, what happened?"

Don't be fooled.

The competing voices inside her argued, but they both agreed on one thing. This game wasn't over, and if she didn't play it, she might never know the truth. Alice decided to play the game. Until she knew more, it was the only choice she had.

"Daddy," she said, leaping into his arms. He hugged her back, and despite her fear, her mistrust, it felt good. He picked her up and squeezed her tightly, and she wondered how this man could possibly be the cause of what had happened.

Don't fall for it.

But she did, and when he carried her over to the bed and set her down, she felt part of herself breaking.

"What happened, Alice?" he asked, wiping the tears off her cheeks.

"I was in the bathroom, and someone took the doorknob off. I…I couldn't get out, and I heard Mom yelling at someone."

"Who? Did you see anything? Anything at all?"

Why does he want to know what you saw?

Alice considered the question carefully, making sure not to hesitate too long. "No. I didn't see anything. I just heard her screaming, and she came down the stairs, and it sounded like people fighting. And then…it just got quiet."

Frank was shaking his head, as if the details were too impossible to imagine. "There was someone here?"

Alice stared at him, studying him. "Yes. I don't know who."

"And the cops?" he asked. "Did they ever show up?"

She shook her head.

"Jesus," he said, stomping his foot. "What the hell is going on here?"

He turned to leave the room, and Alice felt a twinge of fear; despite her suspicions, he was the only thing standing between her and certain doom.

After all…it will be dark soon.

The dark was coming, and the only thing worse than being alone in this house was being alone in the dark.

"Wait," she said, grabbing his arm. "Don't leave. Don't go upstairs."

"Why? I need to keep looking, and she might be up there. I need to—"

"That's where it took her."

Frank's brow creased and he slipped his arm away from her. "It?"

"I…I don't know. But you can't go up there alone."

Frank leaned out of her bedroom, into the hall, and peered up the stairs.

"Dammit," he said under his breath. She'd never seen him so jittery, so breathless, her calm, easygoing father. It only deepened Alice's conviction that he wasn't the same anymore. That something had changed him somehow.

He's becoming like Walker.

He grabbed her hand and dragged her into the kitchen, where he rifled through the bills and mugs that littered the counter, a search that quickly became frantic.

"Where is it?" he asked.

"What?"

"My phone…my fucking phone, it was *right* here."

He was in full panic mode then, his rising terror making her feel sick to her stomach.

"Did you see it?" he asked. "Mine or Mom's?"

Alice didn't have an answer.

"Where the *fuck* is it?" he yelled as he slammed his hand on the counter, hard enough to knock a glass loose inside one of the cupboards. He turned back to Alice and stared. "You heard footsteps?"

She nodded.

"Any of them coming from the kitchen?"

She nodded again.

"Come on." He led them down the hall. Alice's feeling was growing, the feeling that the house was against them, that it was alive and hungry, that it was stalking them as if they were a family of rabbits, saving the youngest for last.

Frank took a quick detour to the unfurnished den and dug around in some boxes. He finally found a toolbox and tested out a handful of weapons. A screwdriver. A box cutter. Finally, he settled on a claw hammer, which he held in front of himself, testing its weight. He swung it once, twice, then met Alice's stare. The mad gleam in his eyes was a shocking thing to see, as if he were mentally preparing himself to kill someone.

Again…

"Stay close," he said, going up the stairs.

The house creaked as they ascended, each step whining as if it were alive, as if it didn't want to be stepped on.

This was where it happened.

No. Not now, Alice thought desperately.

But this was the place. Right here. Maybe on that step. Or that one. Do you think he pushed her?

Stop it, she thought. *Stop it now.*

Frank walked in front, hammer held at his side, taking each step slowly, carefully, as if he expected something to leap from the landing at any moment.

I bet he made it look like an accident. Just blamed it on the rickety stairs. I wonder if her neck broke on that step there, just where your foot is.

The house was a tomb; the only sounds were the creaking stairs and the endless, rushing howl of the wind and snow. If Mom and Dean were still here, where could they be?

Alice and her dad reached the landing, Alice's heart beating so hard she worried, dimly, that she was having an asthma attack like she did when she was younger, that she might pass out. Her lungs felt strange; the stress of everything was tightening her chest, making it hard for her to take in air. Frank heard her breathing, and he glanced back, a look of concern in his dark eyes. He reached down, took her hand, and squeezed it. It was a small gesture, but enough to bring her back from whatever brink she'd been standing on.

They checked the empty room to the right of the landing, found it empty, untouched. Down the long hall they went, past the crawl-space door. Frank strode by it without a word, but Alice stopped, pulling him back. He turned, and without a word, she pointed at the small door.

The small metal hook was unlatched.

Frank nodded and carefully opened it, hammer raised. The same pile of old junk greeted them, just as it had before. Frank leaned closer, peering in. There was nothing but more darkness hiding within. He silently closed the door.

The bedroom at the end of the hall loomed, darker than normal.

When they approached, the reason was clear. Snow had covered the skylight overhead, and without the lights on, the room was pitch black. Frank flipped the switch and methodically searched the room. Under the bed, in the closets, in the bathroom. It was empty.

"There's nothing here."

His voice was swallowed in the cold silence of the house.

"There's nothing here."

There was bitterness in his voice, a raw, sore pain that spoke of deep loss.

"*There's nothing here.*"

And there it was, a sudden change, as quick as a bolt of lightning on a sunny day. The grief was gone. In its place was something darker. Something accusing. Frank turned and looked at his daughter, his baby, his sweetie, with a curdled stare.

"Daddy…"

"What the fuck is going on?" he asked, taking a step forward.

"Dad…"

"There's no one here!" he yelled. "Explain that to me."

"I don't know. I…I was stuck in the bathroom."

"You said you heard them upstairs, right?"

"Yes…I mean, that's what it sounded like."

"That's what it sounded like?" He laughed, a chuckle that bled into a cruel, bitter groan. "We're talking about *sounds* now?"

Alice realized she'd been backing out of the room. Her eyes were fixed on the hammer, on her father holding it like a gun, like something unpredictable, something that might go off if you weren't careful with it. She could see the white lines of his knuckles as he gripped it.

"I'm sick of this shit," he said, marching forward slowly. "I'm tired of these games, Alice. I'm your father."

She was halfway down the hall now. Tears were running freely down both cheeks.

"Stop that," he said, stomping the floor. "Stop that damn

crying. You always do this whenever things get hard. You cry. It doesn't do you any good, do you understand that?"

She had her hands up, tracing her finger tips on the wall, careful to steady herself, to keep from falling. When her fingers brushed across the banister, she cried out, a weak, soft cry. She sounded like a small animal, a creature too pitiful to do anything other than cry.

This is it, the voice whispered. *This is where he does it.*

"This isn't a game," Frank said. "Your brother and your mother are missing. This is your last chance."

She stepped onto the landing, felt the breeze coming up from the steps. The cold air kissed her cheek, and goose bumps ran up both arms, an electric feeling, as if her skin were anticipating what was coming.

He'll use the hammer. They won't notice. You'll be covered with bruises once you hit the bottom, so they won't notice at all.

"If you know anything, I mean, *anything*, about where they are, you better…tell…me…now…."

She glanced down; her boots neared the edge of the top step.

Six inches or so…that's all that's left.

"Tell me…"

Alice opened her mouth to speak, but there was too much to process, and her mind stumbled. The hammer, the snow, the painting, the wind, the stairs, the little drops of blood, the glimpse of pink, the madness, the rooms that didn't fit, the face in her window.

In all of it, Alice could find no words.

"I said…"

Did he raise the hammer?

Yes.

Or was he just leaning forward, leaning down in that way that grown-ups always do? Always looking down, always telling you no, never listening.

No.

Was this it, the moment that her father, the one who gave her piggyback rides and played hide-and-seek, who double bounced her on the trampoline and once spent an entire weekend putting together a little toy kitchen for her...was this the moment that he killed her?

Yes. Yes, yes, yes; you have to move, you have to get out of here, you have to do something*!*

Alice leaned back, intending to run, intending to dash down the stairs, intending to dodge out of the way. Instead, she felt the world tilt back. It was an awful feeling, one that she'd known before, whenever she leaned back too far in a chair, her parents warning her to keep all four feet on the ground, and that moment coming at last, inevitable, impossible to escape now that it was in motion.

She was falling.

The world slowed. Her mind reeled. All of the voices inside her cried out at once, each and every one of them knowing, understanding, that this was the point in time they'd all cease to exist.

Alice fell.

And in the blink of an eye, Frank's hand darted out to catch her. He snatched her by an arm, and with a single, powerful motion, he pulled her back to the top of the step, where she melted into him, sobbing.

"Alice, Jesus...what are you doing?" he asked.

Once again, she had no words.

"You can't do that," he added. "You could have killed yourself... and...and..."

Frank squeezed her tighter. "I can't lose you too."

He patted her back, and for a moment Alice could believe that the world wasn't upside down. There were parts of it, small slivers, that still existed as she had known them before. After a few moments, Frank spoke again.

"I'm sorry," he said, his voice watery. "I'm just...I'm looking for answers. I'm trying to fix it. But I don't know how."

He straightened up suddenly, as if overtaken by some urge to be the man of the house, someone who didn't cry, even if the situation called for it.

"Let's go back downstairs," he said plainly.

Alice went without any hesitation. She was still dazed, still lost in the woods after everything that had happened, so she went along, holding her daddy's hand like the little girl she was. It wasn't until he had taken her back to her room that she began to sense something was amiss.

"Dad?"

Frank walked her in and sat her down on the bed.

"Dad, I need to ask you something."

He looked annoyed, as if he had better things to be worried about. All the same, he entertained her question. "What is it, honey?"

"What happened in this house?"

Frank didn't look surprised at all. "Your mom doesn't give you enough credit," he said with a tired smile. "She's always surprised when you figure things out. I don't think she understands how clever you are."

"Dad?"

He shook his head. Alice could tell he was wondering how much she knew and how she figured it out. And she could tell he was too exhausted to really care.

"A girl died here. She fell down the stairs." He looked at Alice, his eyes searching her face. "But you already knew that, right? Your mom tell you?"

She nodded, and Frank shook his head again, eyes closed in frustration. He took a deep breath. "We agreed we wouldn't say anything to you kids. I guess that doesn't matter now."

"What happened to the family?" she asked.

"Same thing that would happen to most families when something that awful happens. They split up. The mom moved away with their son. And the dad stayed for a while. Then he stopped paying the mortgage, and the bank took over."

He managed a pathetic smile. "Deal of the century."

"There's more to it," she said. "I know there is."

Frank was clearly done talking about it. "Maybe. But it's gone. Past. All of it. And we got bigger things to worry about."

"But the girl—" Alice said.

"No buts," he replied. "She's dead. That's the end of it."

Alice tried to talk, but he wouldn't let her. He looked haggard and spent, like a man who hadn't slept in a week. "I need you to stay here," he said calmly. "I need to keep looking. I need to find your mom and Dean, but I can't let anything happen to you."

"No, I…I…"

"Look," he said, turning around to the bedroom door. "These are strong doors. Solid. If you lock it when I leave, no one will be able to get in. I won't go far, I promise. I just need to keep looking around. Hopefully, the cops will be here, and we'll get all of this sorted out."

Alice wanted to protest again, but she let herself sink into her bed, let it almost swallow her. The truth was she was tired of trying to figure everything out. She *was* just a kid after all. And the bed, god help her, was so inviting. She nodded as Frank leaned in and kissed her forehead.

"It's going to be fine," he said.

For once she believed him.

She closed the door behind him and locked it tight, checking it twice to make sure it wouldn't open. Then she fell into her bed and let the world drift away.

CHAPTER SEVENTEEN

The world was silence.

Had the house ever been so utterly devoid of sound?

Had any house?

Alice, still in her boots and jeans, crept out of bed and approached the door. It was dark outside by then. Even through the blinds, she could see that the sun was gone, and that somehow, through some impossible turn of events, the cops still weren't there. She opened the door and peered out. Frank was nowhere in sight. The wind had died down, and all she could wonder was how much snow had fallen.

The hall between her room and Dean's was dark enough to make bile rise in the back of her throat. More than ever, her room seemed to be a little haven in the midst of a cloud of ink, a lighthouse on a black sea. Light had become a commodity, something precious and rare, and she hated herself for wasting it. The thought of going out there, of venturing into that abyss of empty gloom, was more than she could bear. She slipped back inside, closing the door behind her and locking it once again.

She was alone.

No.

Yes. She'd never felt more alone in her entire life.

No, not alone. Mary is here.

Alice glanced over at the bedside table, at the book she had set there, the diary, *her* diary. There was nothing left to do. She was all alone in the world, floating at the edge of the universe with nothing more than a book to keep her company.

She read.

The last third of the book told more of the story, more of the tragedy that was Mary's family. She was older now, maybe in her late teens, but the wounds of what had happened were still raw, still burning in her mind.

It was only once, she wrote. *He knows better. He knows I'll tell, knows that everyone will know if he tries to take his little girl back to his fucking shed.*

And the truth is I know better. I used to be afraid that someone would find this book, would use it against me. But nothing scares me anymore. I made the first mistake when I went back there, when I walked in on him in that place.

His place.

The thought that it was ever something pure. That I even wrote his stupid name on it. I was too young to know what he was doing in there. I walked in there like a lamb into the slaughterhouse.

Most of the pages toward the end were like this. The story became a once living thing, something that had been brutalized, stabbed, beaten, left for dead. Now, all that remained was the blood smeared onto the page.

One entry simply said the following:

You won't touch me again.

You won't touch me again.

You won't touch me again.

Dozens of times, across the page, crazed, zigzagging patterns of the same phrase over and over again. Alice realized she was crying as she dove deeper in, as the truth she tried to conceal from herself came crashing down. In this silent house, unspeakable things had happened, and in her hand, she held the screams, the pain, the torment of a girl like herself, agony made solid.

She could have stopped it. I know she knows; I just fucking know it. But she never did, and here I am.

Fuck.

Pieces. That's what I am. Broken glass. A porcelain doll. A china plate, always in the cabinet, keep the dust off!

I'll use it, do you understand? I won't let it grind me down, make me like him, like both of them, I'll let that fire burn me down to nothing, let it swallow me, let it change *me, and when I'm gone, when I'm* nothing, *I'll be more than both of them combined, because I'll be free of it, free of him, free of what he did.*

Alice didn't want to keep reading. She knew it was wrong, knew it wasn't her place to unearth this past, a past that was never hers to begin with, but she couldn't stop. A part of her felt as if all of this, every moment, every single step she had taken, had brought her here, to this place in time to be the single person on this planet to bear witness to the crime that happened in this house.

She turned the page and saw an entry with a single line.

I know what I have to do.

The line stared up at her, threatening her, taunting her. This was the moment that Mary decided. The moment where she made her final stand, if only in her mind. Alice reached down with a trembling finger and turned the page. And there it was. The plan.

He can't get away with it.

I won't let him get away with it.

I was a kid then, but I'm not anymore.

I'm telling.

Everything.

She can hate me if she wants.

But I WON'T let him get away with this.

Alice leaned back on the bed, her breath catching in her throat. There it was. The end of the story. The reason for her accident. The reason for everything.

An unspeakable crime had been committed, and Walker had snatched away the only hope for justice, along with his daughter's life. A faulty staircase was an easy thing to blame it all on. An accident. Unfortunate, but these things happen from time to time.

And with the truth, a terrible weight was lifted. It wasn't over, at least not in any way that Alice could imagine, but the puzzle looked clear, finally. One question was answered, and another remained.

Why?

Why was her family missing, taken from her one by one? Why was the cat killed? If Mary still existed in this house, why was she doing this?

More than ever, she felt the malevolence of the place pushing down on her, that the house wanted her dead, wanted all of them dead. And the book in her hand felt dirtier than ever, a living infection. With a sneer, she dropped it onto the bedspread. The book fell open to a page she hadn't yet read.

Alice lifted the book and studied the page. The handwriting was different, cruder, more scrawled. It was near the back of the book, the same section that her mother had pointed out earlier. There were a handful of blank pages in between, but Alice turned to the first page with the new handwriting and began to read.

I'm fine. The fall hurt, but I'm fine. Daddy was there. Daddy caught me. Daddy always catches me.

I feel fine.

I feel fine.

I feel fine.

Alice flipped to the next page and the next. She found more of the same, a complete and utter change from the earlier pages. She flipped through them, frantically, picking up pieces here and there as she went.

Daddy loves me. Daddy always loves me. When everyone else leaves and the house is quiet and I'm all alone, Daddy is the only one there for me.

I'll always love my Daddy.

★ ★ ★

Daddy never hurt me. People lie all the time. Mommy lies. Brother lies. The world lies, but Daddy would never do anything to hurt me.

I thought something happened, but it didn't. What I thought was real was fake. What I thought was hurt was love.

Daddy loves me forever.

No hurt.

No hurt.

Never, never, never, never, never.

* * *

I never fell. Daddy was there. Daddy caught me. Daddy made me safe. Daddy made me whole. Daddy was there. Daddy chased the monsters away. Daddy is all I have. Daddy is all I need. Daddy wouldn't let me fall, so I never fell.

Promise

Promise

Promise

* * *

I NEVER FELL

NO NO NO NO NO NO NO NO NO NO NO NO

LIES LIES LIES LIES

MY BRAIN TELLS ME LIES

NEVER TRUST MY LIES

THE STAIRS ARE DANGEROUS

DANGEROUS STAIRS MAKE LITTLE GIRLS FALL, MAKE LITTLE GIRLS DIE, BUT IT'S OKAY BECAUSE DADDYS ARE THERE, DADDYS ALWAYS THERE TO MAKE LITTLE GIRLS NOT DIE

NOT DIE

NOT DIE

NEVER FELLLLLLLLLLLLLLL

There was no air in the room. Alice clutched at the collar of her shirt, opening it up, pulling it away from her neck, trying to breathe as her mind wrapped around the madness that was spilling out of the page in front of her. The diary was alivc in her lap, she was sure of it, but as much as she wanted to stop reading, she couldn't; if she closed the diary, she'd never open it again.

She turned the page.

A bit of the madness had died down. The handwriting, still scribbled, still messy, was more controlled now.

I watched them come in.

Why are they here?

They're not the same. They aren't supposed to be here. But...maybe they are. Maybe they've come home. After all this time, they've come home.

My family.

Mine to rebuild.

One by one.

It was like reading her own gravestone, and yet, in some way, it wasn't a surprise at all. She'd known it had to lead *somewhere*, that all of this madness had to lead to some conclusion. And this seemed to be it.

Mary. The dead girl. Rebuilding her family.

Alice turned the page again and gasped aloud.

Alice.

Little Alice.

What will we do with you?

The diary slipped through her fingers and fell to the floor, an electric, burning thing, and the moment the cover closed, her mind was swirling with excuses, with rationalizations. It was all she had to hold on to, to keep her mind from splitting, fracturing, breaking beyond repair.

That's not what it said, the dark voice insisted, just as afraid as all the other voices. *You read it wrong. You had to have read it wrong.*

Then pick it up. Pick it up and see, prove yourself right or wrong.

The moment stretched, endlessly, the voices arguing, her heart throbbing in her ears so loudly that the silence of the house was temporarily defeated, pounding, pounding, pounding.

Alice held her breath.

She bent down, and she picked up the book.

The pounding continued as she flipped through and found the page again.

Alice.

Little Alice.

What will we do with you?

She didn't drop it this time. Instead, she closed her eyes and steadied herself, waiting for the world to settle, for the pounding to stop.

But it didn't stop.

The noise wasn't inside her, not anymore. It had escaped somehow, gotten free, become…something else. It was above her, high above her, upstairs, on the roof, somewhere.

Thump…thump…thump.

Steady. A tree branch against the house. Yes, of course, the wind. She cocked her ear and listened, eyes still closed.

Thump. Thump.

Not steady. The wind is never steady. Why should it be? The wind did as it pleased. There was a long pause, and she stayed, frozen, silent.

THUMP, THUMP, THUMP, THUMP…

It was a violent sound. A living sound. The sound of a struggle. There was no denying it. Someone or something that was very much alive was making that noise. It could just be her pounding heart, but…no, there was no more room for lies, no more room for games. Something was up there, upstairs.

Was it her father? It was impossible to know for sure, but her heart told her it was, told her that the sounds she was hearing were the final, desperate gasps of her family dying in some strange, horrible way.

THUMP, THUMP, THUMP...

With every passing second, the sound grew worse, and her mind showed her awful things that she didn't want to see. Animals stuck in traps, gnawing at their limbs. People strapped to tables, operated on, helpless to do anything but flail. And worst of all, her father, the man who loved her, who took care of her, who moved them into this nightmare in an attempt to make them all happier, to fix them. She saw unutterable atrocities carried out on him, and she knew they were true, every one of them.

You'll die up there.

And that was true too; she knew it as surely as she knew her own name, but it didn't matter. Alice placed the diary down on the bedside table. She was afraid of it, afraid of what it might mean to have it in her hands when she finally found the source of that steady thumping, as if it were a bottle rocket that had already been lit.

She was opening the door, she was going up there, and whatever fate awaited her and her family, she would face it with him while there was still time. It wasn't noble or brave. It was an act of pure terror, of unimaginable fear because she *knew* she was next, and the thought of being alone, of facing the night, the darkness, the utter silence of that house *by herself*, was a fate worse than death. And so, Alice stepped out of her bedroom, walking away from that small beacon of safety and into the darkened hallway.

One step. Another. Still, the noise carried on upstairs, unending and tireless.

THUMP, THUMP, THUMP...

She left the light of the bedroom behind, and walked around the corner. She knew what she would find, what would be waiting for her there. She didn't need to look, but she did anyway.

The picture on the wall was nearly complete now. Three Xs in a row where the cute little family had once been. Only the little girl with dark pigtails remained.

Thump…thump…

The sound was growing weaker now.

He's almost dead.

Alice turned toward the stairs, shuffling up to the bottom step. There she stood, at the place where Mary died, where her blood surely soaked into the floorboards, already a deep, dark red. She couldn't do it. It was impossible. Walking up those stairs would be like a cow walking into a slaughterhouse, a conveyor that her family had already been fed to. It was more than she could even begin to consider.

Then why are you doing it?

Alice looked down at her feet, aghast. She was already on the third step.

Thump…

There wasn't a dry spot on her face, the sweat, tears, snot all mixing. She was crying like a baby, her chest hitching, the fear greater than any she had ever known. The stairs stretched, almost endless, a path beyond the wall, the roof, into the darkness of the woods. She would never be off these steps, even if the horror upstairs didn't kill her. She would die here, just like Mary did, and they would stay here forever, waiting for the next family to feed to the demon house.

And then, a second later, she stood at the top of the stairs, shivering, burning, dying all at once. It was dark up here, the only light issuing up from her bedroom below.

The sound…it stopped.

It had, and an even deeper, relentless silence fell over her, engulfing the world. There was a light hovering on the wall of the hallway. It was wrong somehow, something impossible, something her brain struggled to make sense of.

You know what it is.

She tried not to admit it, but Alice knew exactly what she was seeing. The half door leading to the crawl space and attic was open, and from within, a faint light was shining out.

There was no going in there. It was packed full, she knew it; she had seen it for herself more than once. And yet, when she walked a few steps forward and peered inside, she found a path cut through the wall of junk. She had to lean down to slip under the short door, and then she was inside, in another world. The weak light emanating from the back of the space dimly illuminated a narrow hallway constructed from random pieces of the former family. The cast-iron bed frame was pushed aside like an open gate, and the walls of the makeshift corridor were constructed of lawn toys, playhouses, picture frames, and long-forgotten pieces of furniture. A face stared at her from a moth-eaten painting, a young girl standing on an orange hillside as the sun set behind her.

The floor was creaking, unfinished wood, flat pieces of pressboard that had grayed with time. It was like venturing into another dimension, a place of the forgotten, where all the things that people lose or don't need go to spend eternity in silence.

The path veered left, and she realized the light was above her now, on some higher plane than it had been before. Her foot bumped against the first wooden step, and she finally understood where she was going. Her father had told her, but like everything else in this mad house of mirrors, it didn't make sense until she saw it. There was one entrance to the attic in the master bedroom, but there was no ladder going up. Now this was the only way in, a secret passage that threaded the perimeter of the second floor and ended in a narrow staircase that led to the attic itself.

She took the first step, and the smell hit her hard enough to almost knock her back down. It was a mélange of odors hitting her all at the same time – the strangely familiar scent of untouched dust, the universal flavor of attics and basements. The sharp tang of sweat. And something else. Something darker. An earthy smell, like mulch, like shit, like unwashed bodies that stank so violently you couldn't tell whether they were alive or dead.

Trembling, Alice crested the top step and walked finally into the light. It was an assault on her brain. There were too many things to see, too much to process.

Candles burning in a small circle.

Faint, crude crayon drawings pasted on every wall, pictures of families, smiling, Xs drawn on faces, blood drawn on crotches. A mattress, filthy, draped with an ancient comforter designed with My Little Pony characters. Floors, walls, ceiling painted pink and decorated with misshapen flowers, rainbows, clouds. Something dead, furry, curled up and rested on the floor, at the edge of the candlelight, something she knew even if she couldn't quite spare the brainpower to *admit* that she knew.

And of course, her family.

Dean.

Mom.

Dad.

The three of them sitting in a semicircle on the opposite side of the room, their faces bathed in the yellow light radiating from the candles.

And the blood.

Around foreheads. Dripped onto shirts. Oozing into the ropes that bound their hands, around the gags in their mouths. Blood that had dried into crusty, brown splotches.

Dead.

No.

Frank moved, raised his head, looked up, and saw her. And in his desperation, he began to stomp his foot. It looked to be the only thing he could do.

Thump, thump, thump.

Was he asking for help? Begging her to set him loose? Alice didn't know, but it didn't matter either. She couldn't have helped him if she tried, because she was a ghost herself, already dead, already carried to some impossible place where nightmares were real.

Frank's head lurched forward, and his eyes darted to the side, past her, behind her, and Alice suddenly understood.

He's warning you.

Of what?

Of the thing standing behind you.

CHAPTER EIGHTEEN

It felt familiar somehow. That sensation.

Where was she?

A cave.

A cave?

Yes. It was a field trip, silly. It was only a few years ago. Don't you remember?

Yes, of course. The cave.

They told you to stay close to the group, but something about the place just kept drawing you in. You wanted to stand there, in one of the huge, wide-open caverns by yourself, without the other kids. They were ruining it with all their chatter, the boys trying to wrestle, the girls playing with each other's hair, the kids with phones already taking selfies.

Yes, that was it. Alice could see it in her mind, the quiet grandeur of the place, a sort of dignity to the yawning, black emptiness that was wasted on her classmates. She wanted a moment, just a moment, to see the cave as it was, to experience the truth of it.

So, you lingered farther and farther back until it was just you and one of the distracted parents. And when you saw your moment, you slipped behind a section of jagged wall and let them all pass.

Alice had held her spot until the cave grew quiet. Then she walked out and stood there, alone, feeling the open majesty of the place, equal parts humbling and terrifying.

But why was she thinking of that now?

There had been some intangible quality in the cave, a feeling on her skin, an almost imperceptible kind of sonar that told her, even in pitch blackness, that this place was bigger than she could ever imagine. That feeling returned to her in the attic, a feeling that she was standing at the edge of some vast expanse, that the room was bigger than she would have thought possible.

Frank was stomping the floor in front of her, flinging his head back, trying to speak through the gag in his mouth. Something stirred in the immense, cavernous darkness behind her. Alice turned and stared. Something shuffled. A shape growing, towering, a head taller than even her father. And in that sickly yellow candlelight, it came for her.

There was no time to think, to consider, to plan. She only caught pieces of it, the vast height, the wide shoulders, and, somehow, a delicate, ruined splash of pink. Her family didn't matter. Her plans didn't matter. The only thing that mattered was the deep, all-encompassing thought that ran through her head, all of her voices singing in unison.

Don't let it touch you!

The feral part of Alice took over, and she ran, sprinting down the stairs like a gazelle. Something brushed against her back, a strong, heavy thing.

Its hand! A monster's hand!

As she made it halfway down, the stairs began to rattle as something heavy took to the steps above. Alice screamed and leapt. Her body folded as she hit the bottom. One knee bent up and slammed into her lip, and she tasted blood as she clawed through the dark, twisted corridor on all fours. Her pursuer, that *thing*, was at her heels. It knew the winding tunnel of its lair better than she did; something heavy thudded down on one of her shoes, nearly pulling it off.

It wants you! It's hungry! Don't stop, don't stop!

The air at the end of the corridor was fresher, colder, as if she were emerging from a buried coffin. Alice shot out like…

…a rabbit…

…and she clambered to her feet, turning the corner of the stairs and gazing down them, gazing down at the precipice, the cliff that had taken Mary's life.

No! Not the steps! It wants *you on the steps. The window. The ladder. Hurry girl, hurry!*

She sprinted to her parents' room and tore open the window.

Glancing over her shoulder, she saw her pursuer appear from the crawl-space door, an impossible shape, too big to even fit through such a tiny opening. That struggle was the only thing that saved her; she was out the window before the thing could stand, out into the cold, hands on frozen metal, feet slung awkwardly over, climbing, slipping, plunging, the ground rushing up to meet her while a filthy hand reached down, trying to grab her. She landed flat on her back in the fresh snow, the breath rushing from her lungs. For a moment, she only lay there, staring up, waiting for the creature to plunge down, to take her, to end her.

Alice was dying. She knew she was. Nothing in her life up to this point had ever felt like this, so there was little doubt in her mind. She was still, wrapped in the frozen white, and waited for her breath to return. A second later, it did, and the fear of imminent death was replaced by the fear of the hunt, the fear of predator and prey. She couldn't tell if it was still snowing or not, but it didn't matter. The wind blew the loose flakes into her eyes, blinding her vision for more than a few feet in front of her as she found her feet and began to move.

The snow slowed her down, and as she plodded around to the front yard, she was struck with how absurd her love of snow had been before this moment. It was a rare thing, a special little slice of time that was gone as soon as it appeared. But that was before, in a different life, a life where she wasn't being hunted. Now, this snow, the deepest she'd ever seen, was just another punchline in a cruel joke.

She stopped in the front yard, staring up at the mostly dark house. There were no tracks in sight, no sign that the monster had come this way. Stopping, even for a short moment, was enough to send a cyclone of guilt swirling up inside her.

Dad was almost dead.

She believed it.

I'm sure he is now.

She believed that too. The distance between her and her attacker was just enough for her to experience something other than abject fear, but it wasn't enough to send her back in. She doubted anything would be enough to make her do that.

The moon was bright now that the snow had cleared, and the sheen of white reflected it brilliantly. She could find her way without a flashlight.

And where will you go?

To safety.

The neighbors? You've never seen them. It could be a mile, maybe more.

A mile wasn't so far, she thought, shivering. But it was a lie. The snow was up to the tops of her boots, and even though she was dressed in long pants and hoodie, it wasn't enough. She remembered sledding a few years before, assuring her mom that she was fine in jeans and a light jacket. In less than ten minutes, her pants were soaked up to the knee, and her teeth were chattering. That was with less than three inches on the ground. This...this wasn't like anything she'd ever seen before.

The road then. Yes, the road.

How many cars have you seen?

There was no point in arguing with herself. The road was all but invisible, no tracks to be seen. As far as she could tell, no one had driven this far out for hours. They were home, tucked in, safe and prepared for a storm that would assuredly shut everything down.

"I'll just *walk*," she cried to the silent yard.

Go ahead. Die out here. Die in there. It's all the same.

The cold grabbed her then, cutting through her terror. The fear-driven chemicals in her body had begun to recede, and for the first time, she really felt it, the cold gripping her with icy fingers, and she considered what it promised. Dying out in the snow would at least be quiet.

But it will hurt.

The tears on her face were starting to freeze, and Alice slipped down to one knee, sobbing.

"It's not fair."

Who said it would be? a sharp voice asked. *You're still alive. That's more than some of us have.*

"Mary?"

Does it matter who I am? Either way, I won't help you. The only one who will get you out of this shit is you. So, now comes the big question. Run? Fight? Die? Your choice. But choose quickly.

There was nothing else for her inner voice to say. This was a crossroads, a moment that every other moment after depended on. It was all too abstract, too distant now that she stood alone in the snow up to her shins. She glanced back up at the house, and all at once, it became real again. A shadow stood in the frame of the bay window, watching her struggle, watching her decide. A moment later, the figure was gone.

No! that inner voice screamed, giving her a reason to move once again.

Don't let it touch you.

She ran, not into the white emptiness but back toward the house.

Get inside. Find a way to lose it and get back inside. Call the cops. Call for help. Do something, girl!

She raced toward the opposite side of the house, the side with fewer windows and doors, the safer side. Her lungs were burning when she came to the wooden fence, and she stopped, peering through the boards, watching the area around the rotten swimming pool. Nothing stirred, not even for a second.

Alice flipped the latch and stepped through. If she was quiet, she might be able to sneak in behind it, to make it back upstairs. Her mother had her phone with her, she always did, and if she got up there, she'd have the chance to—

A shadow detached from the wall and reached for her. It was waiting, hidden in the darkness next to the house, and it emerged from the dark, a monster made of hair and pink, a creature with filthy hands as strong as iron. It reached for her, mumbling something incoherent.

Don't let it touch you!

A primal, irrational fear took hold of her, and Alice stepped back, back, back until the ground fell away beneath her and she tumbled into some new blackness. She landed on her back six feet into the deep end of the pool. The dark water was frozen, and her head thumped against the ice, hard; the world began fading to black around her. In the haze, there was something that rose above her confusion, a sound that echoed from one side of the empty pool to the other.

A crack.

The stench was enough to bring her back, to break through the fog that loomed over her head. It seeped up, all around her, a black smell, rising through the cracking ice. She could feel it, the sewage creeping up her back, oozing out through the fissures in the ice. Overhead the shadow peered down at her.

It didn't matter. Death didn't matter. Nothing mattered as long as she was balanced on a thin sheet of ice over a pool reeking of shit. She rolled gingerly onto her stomach, spreading her weight as evenly as she could. Tendrils of broken ice spread out around her palms, her legs, her stomach, and all around her; the stench rose and swallowed her. She crept forward, to the side of the pool, the cracks and pops following her all the way, always with her, a new, awful shadow.

Somehow, the ice held as she crawled to the edge of the pool and began to reach up. The old, torn liner was slick with ice, snow, and frozen algae, and no matter how hard she grabbed it, she couldn't get a grip.

"Please, please, *please*..."

She had shimmied up to her knees, giving up on the liner, reaching higher, but she still couldn't grasp the lip of the pool. The ice was giving way under her, and at the last second, she wrapped a piece of the plastic liner around her hand and began to pull herself up even as her feet broke through the thin ice. She was up, the liner wrapped so tightly around her hand that it was surely bleeding. She pushed her feet against the side and climbed, eyes closed, her entire being focused on the singular goal of getting out of that fucking hole.

Alice was halfway up the wall when she heard it. A moan above her, a sound like an insane child. There was a moment, a split second, when the voice inside warned her, that some deeper, instinctual part of herself tried to take control.

Don't look! Please, don't look!

But it was an impossible thing to ask. Alice had no choice in the matter. She did look. And she saw it, leaning down, so close to her face that she could see the eyes for the first time, dark and wild. A hand reached for her.

She screamed. She slipped. She fell.

There was a crack, loud enough that it felt as if it had come from inside her body, as if a painless, invisible bone had snapped. There was barely even enough time for her to make sense of it before the grimy blackness swallowed her. Even with her eyes clamped and her mouth closed, she felt it, a foulness beyond compare, leaking into her pores. She felt the sloping side of the pool, so slick with filth that her hands and feet could find no hold. She fought back against the revulsion, against dying in the worst, most inhuman way possible. But her fighting did no good; she *was* dying, and she was drowning in a pool of shit. It was the kind of thing that the boys at school would make up.

Would you rather die in a pool full of shit…

Except of course, this was real. This was *happening*. Her breath was catching. She longed to scream but didn't dare. The world fell quiet around her, a cold, damp, awful place.

This is where you die.

There was no peace in the thought. No final moment of clarity before the end. Just fading. A candle burning itself out. And somewhere in the growing blackness that was Alice's existence, she sensed something in the filth next to her.

Water splashing. Strong hands lifting her out.

CHAPTER NINETEEN

There were sensations.

The sense of being carried, through the cold, back in from the shadow world of dark and snow to be eaten by a looming thing with yellow eyes. The house. The warmth. The smell. The taste of shit in her mouth. The feel of it drying in her eyes. Something warm and wet. Harsh light. Her clothes gone. Shampoo in her eyes, up her nose, in her mouth. The taste of it bitter but welcome, an escape from the horrors of the pool. Naked but safe at the same time. Strong hands patting her dry. Making her clean, making the nightmare a memory, something distant, a dream. Something she could forget.

Pajamas, clean, dry, from head to toe. A brush through her hair. The strangeness of it all swirling around her, encompassing her entirely. And, at long last, her bed, nestled into the sheets, warmer and safer than she'd ever felt in her life because she knew the long nightmare was ending. Every moment, from finding Baxter until this one, was finally coming to a conclusion. The dream had been long and awful, but like all dreams, it couldn't last forever.

From the moment she slipped into the pool, Alice had experienced the entire string of events like a person trying to watch a TV screen hidden behind a pane of cracked glass.

Or ice.

There was an urge, however faint, that kept coming to her as she dug deeper into the blanket. It was the same feeling she had every weekend when there was nothing to do, no soccer games scheduled, no errands to run. It was the feeling of the day rising around her, tempting her, asking her to join the world of the living and to leave the world of the dreamers behind.

The only problem was she didn't want to. There wasn't a weekend in her life that she had ever experienced a love of her bed so deep, so all-encompassing. Nothing, it seemed, could get her out of that bed.

A warm, hearty smell began to fill the room, welling up from the vents to the ceiling.

Mom is cooking.

Was that it? French toast? Bacon and eggs?

No. Something richer. Something...meatier.

Her breakfast casserole? The one she always made on Christmas morning? Yes, it was. It had to be. She could practically taste the sausage, the cheese, the spicy bite of it.

No...

But it was. And she knew what that meant. It was Christmas morning. The one she remembered was just a part of the dream, part of the awful nightmare. It all made sense. Everything had started going wrong the moment they moved, so soon after Christmas that not all the toys were even opened yet.

It's not that....

But it was! She knew it was. And she was up, on her feet, stumbling around, trying to find her footing in the dark room. The layout was wrong, though, the bed out of place somehow, and as Alice fumbled for the light switch, the familiar sickness rose up inside her.

You're still here....

The overhead light bloomed, confirming what the cold, truthful part of herself already knew. She didn't want it, didn't want to look at it, but it was *her* room. Mary and Alice both lived here, and she wondered if somehow both of them had died here. Her eyes hurt in the light, and she rubbed them, feeling the grit in the corners of them. There was a taste in her mouth, up her nose, something beyond foul. What was it, this thing that lingered, this awful memory?

It's shit.

There was no arguing with the brutal, simple truth of it. She was clean, true, but there were some things that would always be there, always be with her, until the day she died. Alice's head was spinning when she walked out of the bedroom, her feet wobbly, her knees nearly buckling, the scent of meat still filling the house. The floorboards creaked under her feet, and she froze, listening to the busy footsteps in the kitchen. It was still dark outside, the morning refusing to come.

Alice rounded the corner and peered to her right. Even in the dim light, she could see the picture. The three black Xs had become four. She had been taken, claimed, and devoured by the house as well. Perhaps this was the other side, an endlessly cold place that mocked the life she'd known before. It was insane, but then again, it was all insane.

We're all mad here.

There was nothing else to do but see for herself, see what new world had been made for her. She crept into the sliver of light that beamed out of the kitchen, and stood at the threshold, peering in.

Her family was sitting around the table. Her mother and father at each end, Dean on one side, and an empty spot, just for her, across from him.

Dead. All dead.

She saw it. She believed it. Each of them was tied to a chair, their arms behind their backs, filthy rags wrapped around their mouths, gagging them. All three of them slumped forward, their heads hanging limp.

Your family is dead. You're the only one left.

Alice couldn't move any further. It was as if she were peering into the frame of a grim painting, an artist's rendition of the worst thing she could imagine.

Orphan. Orphan.

From the opposite side of the kitchen, something stirred. The familiar sound of the oven opening, closing. The silverware drawer being drawn before sliding shut. The sound, sharp, sudden, made an incredible thing happen. Her mother flinched.

Alice opened her mouth and moaned, a sound that came from deep within her lungs, a sound of hope being eaten by fear.

The owner of the footsteps must have heard; a figure walked into the center of the kitchen, into the light.

At first, Alice couldn't understand what she was seeing. The figure was tall, topped with a wild mess of long hair that seemed to swallow its entire face. Drapes of greasy hair covered the forehead, but the eyes shined out, blue and mad. A thick beard, scraggly and black, rounded out the bottom of the face.

A man…

Yes, a huge, wide-shouldered man. That was clear, that was easy enough to make out, but the rest of it was so at odds, so *incredible* that she struggled to make sense of it. There was the pink she had seen time and time again, a girl's raincoat that he wasn't wearing so much as bursting out of. The seams were completely torn, and they were held in place by what looked like shoestrings, and the entire thing was cobbled together in places with duct tape. Under it all, he wore yellowing, insulated underwear that covered his chest and arms. It looked to Alice as if a wild animal had somehow come across a high schooler's abandoned closet. The jacket was like a hermit crab's shell, something this creature had grown out of but never discarded.

The two of them stared at each other for a moment. Then he smiled.

"You feeling better?" he asked, his voice a raspy, high-pitched whine. She knew at once that the voice he was using wasn't really his, but some kind of act. "I always feel better after a nice shower."

As he spoke, Debra looked up and stared at Alice. Her eyes instantly welled with tears, and she began to tremble, violently enough to make the table shake and bounce, and the empty glasses begin to rattle. The strange man put a hand on her shoulder, and Debra stilled, but her struggles had been enough to rouse Frank as well; he began shifting in his seat.

"Everything's fine now that you feel better," the man said, patting Debra's shoulder. Her mother's eyes were wide, and they showed a depth of terror that Alice had never seen in anyone before.

It was, she knew, a terror not just for herself but for everyone seated at the table.

Now that Frank was looking up, she saw a similar look in his eyes, but it was almost hidden under a patchwork of bruises and cuts. His right eye was swollen nearly shut, and trails of blood marked his face with lines of various shades of dark brown, maroon, and still-fresh red. The look of him, the man she had been so absurdly afraid of, beaten and bruised, was more than she could bear to look at. Alice looked away, back at their gruesome host.

"Please," he said, motioning to the empty chair. "Come in. Have a seat."

She held for a moment, refusing to go any farther into the madhouse that had once been a kitchen. Then she saw the long, stony fingers close on her mother's shoulder, saw her mother's eyes narrow in pain.

Alice walked in and sat down.

"I've waited so long to meet you in person," he said, turning back to the counter and busying himself with whatever meal he was preparing. "I've been watching you since you moved in."

Alice looked from parent to parent, then across the table at Dean. He was still slumped forward facedown, his forehead nearly touching the table.

He's dead. You know he's dead.

"I gave you the diary," he said, looking over his shoulder. "I wanted *you* to be here. To be with us. To help fix everything."

Alice didn't understand, but in that moment, she didn't even care. All she wanted was for Dean to move, for his chest to heave, for him to look at her. The silence draped over the room again, and Alice realized she wasn't looking at her host; when she glanced up, his face was strained, annoyed.

"Do you understand?" he asked impatiently. As if to make his point, he crept back over to Debra and once again placed a hand on her shoulder.

Alice felt as if she were standing on a tightrope, perched above a drop that would assuredly kill her if she leaned too far one way or the other. On either side was open, dead air, and only her decisions could save her from this point on.

Balance, girl, the voice inside her whispered, suddenly and strangely helpful.

"I understand some of it," she said quietly. "But there's a lot that…I don't know."

Her voice was quivering, and it felt as if she were holding a hand out to feed an alligator. No quick movements. Steady.

Balance.

"I need you to show me," she added.

The crazed man stared at her for a moment. Then he smiled.

"Good!" His voice was perky, a girlish twinge in it that did little to cover up the gravel in his throat. "That's why I'm here. That's why I did *all of this.*"

He finally lifted a hand off Debra's shoulder and motioned at the table. There was pride in his eyes, a true, deep excitement for what he had done, what he was still doing. He was gliding toward her, his bare feet soundless on the floor, so much like a ghost's. Debra and Frank both leaned forward, panic in their eyes, as if through sheer will alone, they could stop what was happening. And there he was, before her, blocking the light as he reached down to her.

"*I did this for you.*"

His blackened fingernails brushed across her cheek, but she never blinked. She was afraid, but simply drinking in the sight of this creature, of what he was, of what he *meant*, somehow overrode her fear.

"Who are you?" she whispered softly.

He laughed, the soft tone gone from his voice, replaced a second later by his reply. "I'm Mary."

Then he was gone, back across the kitchen, to the oven, to the upcoming feast. Alice's head was spinning, but she still used the small opportunity as best as she could. Stretching her leg beneath the table, she nudged Dean's knee with her bare foot. It felt solid, lifeless, but she did it again, kicking him hard enough to shake the chair he sat in. The man who called himself Mary looked back once, then continued with his preparations. Dean slumped forward even further, and then he coughed.

He's alive.

He was struggling with the gag in his mouth, trying to catch his breath against the ropes that held him. He began to shake violently. Debra moaned in response, and Frank screamed through his own gag, his face turning the color of a summer apple.

Alice never saw or heard him walk over, but their captor slapped Frank across the face, sending a small shower of blood droplets across the table.

"I warned you," he said, his voice deeper.

"Please," Alice said. "My brother. Please, can you do something to help him?"

Dean was still shaking, and the stranger turned and watched him.

"Please," she sobbed, "I don't think he can breathe. Please, just take that thing out of his mouth."

Something about her tears, the sound of her voice, seemed to bring some change in him, and Alice saw it in his face, some guilt or fear that hadn't been there before. A split second later, it was gone, the mask now firmly back in place.

"Oh, this won't do," he said as he pushed Dean back in his chair. A loop of rope had gone taut around his neck, and the second he was raised up, the blood rushed back into his face. The stranger removed the gag, and Dean coughed deeply, a wet sound that ended with him vomiting onto the table.

"No, this won't do at all," he said as Dean finally sat up and saw Alice for the first time.

He was barely able to hold his eyes open, but aside from the rope mark on his neck, he looked more or less okay, especially compared to Frank. After glancing around the room, Dean looked straight at their captor. Besides the occasional cough, he never made a sound, not even when the stranger placed a hand on his back and patted it.

"There, there…big brother."

Alice looked from Dean to the man, waiting for some further response.

"You always do eat your food so quick. Not surprised you'd choke. Dinner's almost ready…."

He was gone again, and there they were, the four of them crowded around the family table, like they hadn't done in years. Alice and Dean finally locked eyes, and the confusion that consumed her must have been clear on her face. She started shaking her head, soundlessly trying to ask him, *What is all this?*

She was hoping for some spark in his eyes, some signal that he understood what all this was about. She hated the heavy, leaden feeling of knowing more than they did. She was the baby, a child, too young to deal with this alone; all she wanted in the entire wide world was for her big brother to smile and nod, to grin and wink, to let her know that *he had a plan*. But she saw nothing but fear in his face, a mirror of her own terror. He had years on her, but those years meant nothing, not when a madman was cooking them dinner in their own kitchen.

It's not your kitchen, a voice whispered.

That's not true.

Watch him, the dark voice snapped back. *Look at him move around the place. He's been here before.*

Alice did watch, and she saw it all, saw a man who knew this place, who looked at home here.

Home.

Home.

Yes. Home. But whose home?

Look at the jacket. A girl's jacket. Way too small for a man. I'll bet he got it from someone close.

From his daughter…

Alice's mouth dropped open. It was all there, all clean and neat and simple. The true owner of this house was still here because…

Say it. Say it out loud.

"He never left," she whispered.

Her family heard her words, and they looked at her, their eyes asking why she should be mumbling to herself at a time like this.

Who never left?

Alice looked at each member of her family, one after the other. She knew what they didn't, what they *wouldn't* if she didn't get them out of this situation. For the first time in her life, she was more powerful than all of them, simply because *she knew.*

Say it. Say his name. Say it out loud so your ears have to hear it, so you can stop pretending. Stop acting like the voices in your head make you crazy or different or less *than anyone else. Say it. Believe it. Then save your family....*

"Walker."

The man at the kitchen counter froze, but he never turned around, not yet at least. Alice's heart tightened. Was such a thing possible? She began to process it, to go through everything she knew, to make sense of something so unthinkable, so impossible.

Walker, an abusive father.

Mary, his rebellious daughter.

An accident on the stairs. Mary dead.

A ghost.

No, not a ghost. Gone. Dead.

A broken family. Parents split, mother and son gone, leaving the house. Walker, the sole occupant, disappeared.

What a deal.

No. Not disappeared. Here.

Here!

Always here. At her window the first night, peering in. In the woods, following them. Killing Baxter. Taking Dean. Locking her in the bathroom. Taking her mother and father. Chasing her into a pool filled with shit...

His shit.

And now, here he was. The picture in the hallway filled her mind. That was his family. That was what he lost, what *he* destroyed with his own hands. And now, that was what he was rebuilding. Making new.

Daddy never fixed anything.

That was true. Before now, he never even tried.

But the jacket? The name?

Alice didn't know how it worked, but she had seen it play out in movies, on TV. When someone is so thoroughly unable to deal with reality, that person sometimes breaks from it. Creates a new one. A safer one. And becomes someone else, someone within that new world.

He…thinks he's Mary.

Walker returned with four plates, which he began to carefully place in front of them. Alice had to do something, had to find a way to get them all out of this. Whatever the deranged truth of this situation was, there was no denying one thing. Walker looked at her differently than he did the rest of the family. There was something there, something small that, just maybe, she could use.

"Mary?" she said as he set down the plate.

Walker paused for a minute, and Alice imagined his mind working on overdrive, trying to reconcile two truths at once. Then he smiled. "Yes, Alice?"

"What do you want?"

His eyes met hers, and, subtle though it was, she saw it: a conflict. A battle between something passive and something furious, a desire to kill mixed with a desire to give up. It was a terrifying thing to look at straight on, and she didn't dare look for more than a moment.

"This," he said through his teeth, as if the words were painful. "A family. Together."

He was walking away, back to the counter to fetch something else, when she asked another question. "But…what else?"

When Walker faced her, his mouth had turned down, his lips receding into his face behind the wall of beard. She only saw teeth.

"I…know…what I want."

The words were pulled out, like splinters, each a bit more painful than the next.

"I'm sorry," she said, calming him.

He breathed, in, out, in. Slow. The storm cloud slowly dissipated.

"Little girls," he said, "like us...always with the questions." He went back to the oven and opened it. The smell of roasted meat filled the kitchen as he drew the pan out and set it on top of the stove. Alice tried to remember her mother's roast, a sweet memory that felt so distant in that moment. It was always her favorite, but it took so long to cook she wasn't expecting Walker's anytime soon, not until they all got settled.

"I used to ask my father questions," he continued. "He was busy. He was always busy, but he always had time for me."

He took the lid off, and steam rolled up into his face. For some reason, he sneered.

"*He* was a good man. The best man. I was lucky to have him."

Trying to convince himself, the voice whispered. Alice watched him the same way she might watch a rattlesnake that appeared at the foot of her bed. Something was rising up in Walker, something dark and even more dangerous than anything she'd seen so far. She could see it in the tensed muscles of his neck as he dug into the pan with a two-pronged fork.

"I was *lucky*, Alice. Do you understand that? How *lucky* I was?"

A large chunk of meat, brown and glistening, slipped out of the steaming pot and onto a platter.

"Unlike this one," he spat, pointing the fork across the kitchen at Frank, who winced. Alice expected him to use the fork on her father, to dash across the linoleum and dig one of his eyes out with it. Instead, the voice calmed back down, slipping back into the higher register.

"You don't know what you've missed, Alice. To have a father. To have a *real* father."

Alice was trembling, filled with a mixture of fear, disgust, and rage. She'd let this place get hold of her, let this awful man control her in subtle ways. Hours earlier, she was convinced that her father was a murderer. He wasn't perfect, but at his heart, he was the sweetest man she'd ever known, a man who teared up during sappy commercials, a man who sat up with her all night when she got food poisoning. Somehow, she'd turned on him, siding with the awful thing standing in their kitchen. The mere thought of it made her tremble, the anger pouring out of her skin, so hot it was painful. She looked up and saw something in Walker's eyes, something that took her anger to new, untold levels.

He was smiling. The look in his eyes was nothing less than beaming pride.

"I have a real father," she spat.

Alice didn't so much speak the words. They escaped. The moment they were out, she could see the impact. Everyone in the room looked at her with wide, unbelieving eyes.

"What did you say?" Walker asked.

"She's barely awake," Dean replied, trying to cover for her.

Walker held a hand to his forehead, as if he were in some kind of unthinkable pain. "I'm trying…I'm…trying…"

Alice held her breath, waiting for another blow to come.

"I knew…that this would h-happen… This family is…is… broken. I have to f-fix it."

He turned back to the kitchen, but he was only gone for a moment. When he returned, he held the platter of meat in one hand, and a knife in the other. He dropped the platter onto the center of the table, the clang eliciting a scream from Alice.

"I'm trying," he said, his voice stronger now, all hints of childishness gone, "to fix what's broken. Do any of you appreciate what I fucking *do*? What I've given up for this family?"

His voice rose to a scream, and he began to wave the knife around. Once, it swung so close to Dean's face that Dean screamed and ducked aside.

"This family has to be fixed, or none of this is going to work. Do you understand that? People die when things don't work!"

The fire in his eyes died away, and he closed them. Mary, or the crude copy of her, appeared once again. When he opened his eyes and spoke once more, the softer tone had returned.

"We can fix this. I know we can."

He reached down and began to cut. In her previous terror, Alice hadn't noticed the steaming hunk of meat. Now, it was all she could see.

"You see," Walker said, slicing into it, "a family has to be perfect. None of the pieces can be out of place. It's like that picture I painted...."

The meat was a strange, misshapen thing, something she couldn't recognize. Even so, it horrified her in ways she couldn't explain.

Not right. Not good.

"I painted it back when everything was just right."

A hunk of brown meat slipped off a small bone. Frank began to gag. Dean shook his head. They already knew.

You know too.

"This family was so close to being perfect...but there was one problem."

The meat had been carved on one side, a series of slices down to the ribs. Walker spun the platter around to get to the other side.

"We never had a cat."

The face was locked in an endless scream, the lips pulled back, revealing the needle teeth.

Baxter.

"This family has to be made right."

There was nothing else in the world. There was no monster hiding in their house. There was no family in danger. There was no swimming pool filled with human shit. There was only him. A madman who had killed her cat.

That is my father, a voice whispered, a voice she assumed belonged to a ghost. *That's why I'm dead. Because I wouldn't stand for another horror to happen.*

Frank was convulsing in disgust, trying to knock over his chair, trying to get away. He had reached his breaking point. Debra might have as well, but in a different way. Her eyes were closed so tightly that she might have been asleep if not for the steady hitching of her chest. And poor Dean stared deep into the corpse of the cat that always bit him, unable to look away like a kid stumbling across his first roadkill. Only Alice was still there, able to see this scene for what it was.

He killed me, Mary whispered. *You can't let him kill you, girl.*

"Please," she said quietly, "I need you to stop this, Mary. I need you to stop this."

Walker looked up from the work, and the anger swelled up in him, changing him from one person to another. He raised the knife so suddenly that Dean ducked away yet again.

"This is the way it is, little girl," he said, pointing.

Little girl.

He turned toward Frank and raised the knife, slicing the gag away and opening a gash on his cheek in the process.

"Jesus, please," Frank moaned, leaning over on the table for support.

"I'll fix this," Walker roared. "I'll fix this fucking family if it's the last thing I do."

He picked up a greasy piece of meat and mashed it into Frank's mouth.

"Eat it. Eat it, you son of a bitch. You killed your family, do you understand that? You fucking killed them!"

Little girl.

"You think you can fix them? I'm the only one who can fix them."

That's what they called you in school, Mary whispered.

"Eat it. Everyone's going to eat it together. We're going to fix this family!"

You know what they called me in school? Mary asked. *They called me bitch.*

"Stop it!" Alice yelled, slapping her hand on the table.

Frank, sputtering and bleeding, spat out the hunk of meat,

silently sobbing. He seemed too tired, too broken to even notice the danger his daughter was in. Debra opened her eyes and strained against her ropes as the tall, gaunt man walked around the table, knife outstretched.

"You," he said, reaching the length of the table to point at Alice with the knife, which hovered in front of her face. "You were supposed to be the one. The only one. The one who understood me."

They called me that because I wouldn't let them do whatever they wanted. Maybe that's what you need, girl.

"What am I supposed to do?" Walker asked. "How can I fix it if you're the one who's broken?"

A good girl won't get you out of this.

"I thought we would be friends."

Alice stared up at him. Her blood had turned to ice. She didn't know if she would ever make it out of this alive, but it didn't matter anymore. If she didn't say it, if she didn't get the words inside her out into the world, she was already dead.

"I would have been friends with her," Alice whispered. "But she's dead."

"Please," Dean said. "She's just a kid. She doesn't know what she's saying."

Alice ignored her brother. "*You killed her.*"

The words landed with a finality that shook everyone into silence. Walker looked over at Dean, then Frank, then Debra.

"I can't fix this," he whispered. "How could I fix this? I couldn't fix the cat…it was wrong. It was just *wrong*…."

He was circling the table towards her, knife twitching in his hands. Debra tried to scream through her gag, while Dean kept pleading.

"Please, no, she's just a *kid*…."

If Walker heard the words or saw the desperation, he made no sign. Instead, he walked calmly over to Alice.

"I can't fix you," he said, placing a hand on her shoulder. "Because this family already has a daughter."

With his free hand, he swept the dead cat away to the floor, and with a swift, sudden move, he grabbed Alice by the neck and swung her up onto the table. She landed flat on her back, with the knife hovering over her face.

"*This family will be right again*," he spat, his voice that of a thoroughly mad man once again.

You can't beat him! a voice called from within. It was the soft voice, the scared voice, the voice of the good girl. Then another voice took over. The voice of the bitch.

Mary's voice.

Yes you can, girl, just not like this. Your mind can beat him, so use it!

"Daddy!" Alice yelled out as Walker forced her head back, pushing it flat against the table, exposing her neck. She could feel Frank rattling the table next to her, fighting to get free, but she ignored it.

Deeper, the voice said. *Your words can cut, so use them!*

"Not again, Daddy," she said. It was an act, some strange bit of dress-up, mixed with real tears and true fear. Walker held the knife aloft, but the words seemed to weaken him.

"Please," she sobbed as he stared down at her, mad. "Not again. Not there…"

You know what to say. You know that words are weapons.

It was true. She did know. Mary had told her.

So stop fucking around and use them*!*

The table had grown quiet, none of them daring to breathe as they waited for Walker to make his choice. In that beat of silence, Alice spoke.

"Not the woods. Not the shed. Please, Daddy, don't make me go back there."

Even then, even after everything, Alice still didn't know what had actually happened back there in the woods. It was a gamble, her last card to lay down, and if she was wrong, then nothing would save her. She gazed up at the insane face of Mary's father, and she saw him begin to crack. The knife was shaking in his hands, and his eyes slipped closed, the lids trying to keep the tears at bay. He sniffed once, again, and Alice could see the snot running down his nose.

"N-n-no…not there…"

You have him.

Alice could see it. Walker slowly lowered the knife, and the entire room seemed to breathe a sigh of relief. They weren't out of it, not by a long shot, but Alice knew Mary was right. She *did* have him.

"Daddy never hurt me," he said, his voice pitiful, wounded.

Alice was scrambling. She had him, but the question was, could she *keep* him? She leaned up onto her elbows.

"He was a good daddy," Alice assured him, and Walker nodded. She glanced down at his hand. The knife was still there, still gleaming and dangerous, as if he were holding a poisonous snake.

"Yes," Walker whined.

Alice didn't know what to do next. She didn't have a plan, but she did have something. The beginning of a plan perhaps.

That's not good enough, the good girl pleaded.

Shut the fuck up, honey, Mary replied. *A bit of a plan, a bit of luck.*

Alice wasn't confident, but she knew that if she left Walker alone, he would come back to the same spot eventually. She had to be the one in charge.

"It's that place," she whispered, sitting up on the table and speaking to Walker as if the two were sharing a secret. Walker's brow furrowed, but he leaned closer to hear.

"That place in the woods," she continued. "It's a bad place. It made Daddy bad."

"No," Walker said, raising the knife, holding it just in front of her nose, driving her back down to the table. "Daddy was good. He was always good—"

"I know," she said, cutting him off. "It wasn't him. It was never him. It was that *place*. That was the only thing that ever made him… different."

Walker's eyes darted back and forth as he backed a step away. Alice sat all the way up.

You're in charge.

The feel of her feet back on the floor gave her a surge of adrenaline.

You're doing it.

"We have to fix this," she said, reaching out, daring to place a hand on his shoulder. Walker flinched, but he didn't chase her away.

"We *can* fix it," she assured him. "We just need to get rid of that place. To…to burn it!"

It was pure inspiration, something she hadn't planned. Even so, she could see the beauty in it. There were a million things that could happen between the house and the shed, and while most of them might be awful, at least a few scenarios ended with her saving herself and her family. She looked into Walker's eyes and added, "When that place is gone, everything will be right. Everything will be fixed again. And the best part is you'll be the one to do it."

Alice froze, locked between the two possibilities, between salvation and damnation. Then, Walker gazed at her, his eyes watery, his face broken. And nodded.

CHAPTER TWENTY

Walker watched her dress, layering sweats and a light jacket over the pajamas before slipping on a knit hat. Her heavy coat, her *real* coat, was still lying in a pile of sewage next to the back bathroom along with her heavy boots. A pair of tennis shoes were all she had, but they would have to work.

There was a subtle truce between them, a house built on shaky ground that neither of them quite trusted. He held on to the knife, and as she had passed from room to room, she kept looking for a way to slip a weapon into her pocket. A knife, a pair of scissors, even something as innocuous as an ink pen. She never got the chance, and once she was dressed, her plan felt beyond foolish.

He'll walk you out there and kill you.

It wasn't Mary's voice. She had gone silent, saving herself for the end perhaps. Alice brushed the voice aside, but there was no denying the weight of the words. Was she walking to her death? It certainly felt that way, especially in her flimsy clothing, a poor defense against the snow.

Alice walked out of her room, looking like a kid on Christmas morning who wants to take her new sled for a ride without actually getting dressed. Walker stepped aside and pointed the knife at her.

"I'll follow you," he said.

"Do you have matches?"

He nodded. "Just go."

She followed the foul smell of shit through the house, back to the pool. It looked like a slug trail. She walked past her family, the three of them still locked in place. Dean's chair looked slightly askew, as if he'd been trying to work himself free after they left the room.

"Take me instead," he said as they passed, but neither she nor Walker looked for more than a second. "Take me, you sick fuck. Leave my sister alone!"

Alice cut her eyes at him for a few seconds, just long enough to hiss, "Shut up, Dean."

To her amazement, he did. They walked out the same way she had been dragged in, past the slug trail of human shit and out into the cold. The pool stretched before her, bigger somehow, an open pair of jaws that wasn't satisfied since she got away. Even from a distance, Alice wondered if she might somehow slip into it, if she might find herself once again in the black frozen world of ice and human waste. She pressed against the wall of the house as Walker opened the wooden gate.

"Go," he said, motioning her through.

Once she was past the gaping blackness of the pool, she felt the cold for the first time. Her feet were the worst. With the flimsy shoes on, it felt as if she were wearing nothing more than a pair of thick socks. Once she rounded the corner of the fence, the wind hit her face full on, a bitter assault that made her long for the awful scene she just left. She glanced back at Walker who was stumbling through the snow behind her. The weather was a lot, even for him, but he was still in control.

"Go!" he yelled over the wind. "Keep going!"

The two of them plodded forward, less adversaries in that long walk than teammates, allies in some long, brutal struggle against nature itself. The snow had stopped falling, but the wind was as violent as ever, and the loose powder blew up, into their faces and nostrils. Once, Alice slipped to her knee, and the cold of the snow bit into her, right through the thin protection of the pajamas and sweats. Walker was there a moment later, lifting her as the melting snow soaked through down the front of her leg and into her shoes. She stood, taking one glance back at the house. It shone like a lighthouse, a beacon in the darkness behind them.

"Go!"

Onward, they went into the dark. Alice could almost imagine they were walking on the surface of an alien planet, something so barren and empty that it couldn't possibly hold any life. The trail stretched before them, a corridor into blackness, and she walked mindlessly, one foot in front of the other. The pain of the cold grew, multiplied, became something else entirely. The cold turned to heat, the ice to fire, the pain to nothingness. When she realized that she couldn't feel her feet at all, a surge of white-hot panic rose up in her.

They're dead. Those feet are dead. The rest of you will be soon enough.

Alice looked back and gasped when she saw how far they had come. The lights of the house were mere pinpricks on the horizon. Walker was staring back as well, the pain of this trip clear on his face as it surely was on Alice's.

When you die, he'll use that knife. He'll cut you open and stick his hands inside to warm up.

Alice felt like crying, like screaming, like curling up and letting the windswept snow bury her. Her pace slowed, and she readied herself to tumble face-first into the powder, to give up once and for all. That was when she saw the tracks. They were small, narrow things, a neat, tidy row of paw prints, two small ones followed by two larger, flatter ones.

Rabbits.

Of course. These woods might look dead, but they were alive. There were coyotes, foxes, things that ate rabbits, and somehow they survived. A voice spoke to her, something from the past, a book read aloud whose name she couldn't place in that moment.

If they catch you, they will kill you...but first, they must catch you.

It wasn't Mary or any of the arguing voices this time. It was her father, reading her books at bedtime. There *were* real fathers in the world, not this abomination that followed along behind her.

That's right, girl, Mary whispered. *That's right, little rabbit. Don't let him beat you. If you can't do it for yourself, then do it for me.*

Alice straightened up and walked on. Soon, the shed loomed before them. Had it looked so grim during the day? In the dark and the blowing snow, it looked crooked somehow, bent and evil, as if all the malice and terror that still lived in the house had originated here. This was the mouth of a river made of grief, despair, abuse, pain, fear, and of course, human shit. And at the sight of it, hopeful energy surged through her.

That's right, Mary said. *Win or lose, it's time to put an end to all of this.*

Alice stopped a few feet away and leaned on her knees. From the corner of her eye, she saw Walker reaching into his shirt. The key for the heavy lock was hiding near his chest, tied with a piece of thick twine. His hands were shaking when he reached for the lock, but she couldn't tell if it was from the cold.

He's afraid, the gentle voice whispered.

He should be, Mary spat.

The door flung open, and a bitter smell of old, unwashed bodies drifted out from within.

"In," he said gruffly, motioning with the knife. He seemed to have given up on trying to sound like Mary.

He doesn't know who he is.

Alice stepped into the dark, and Walker pulled the door shut behind them. For a moment, she stood there in the semi-darkness, wrinkling her nose and trying not to touch anything. Then a struck match into a kerosene lantern revealed the saddest, most disturbing apartment she had ever seen. There was a table on one end, filthy, scattered, with metal plates and cups, faded silverware, and even a few deer antlers lying loose, trophies that were never hung. The walls were lined with more of the hand-drawn pictures. At first, she assumed they were all Mary's old drawings, but they were too neat. Too well drawn. She realized that these were all drawn by Walker, a child's crude illustrations filtered through the mind of a grown man. On the opposite wall, another tattered mattress rested in the corner. Beside it, stacked in the corner, were a compound bow, some arrows, and a rifle. Behind her, just beside the door, was a can of kerosene.

This was the life he had lived for the past two years. Hunting and trapping what he could. Maybe scavenging the nearby houses for supplies. Drifting between his two bachelor pads, one here, one in the abandoned attic. It might have gone on like that forever if they hadn't moved in, if they hadn't shaken up his world. Alice hugged herself tightly, not wanting any part of her or her clothes to touch the walls. The madness might seep into her.

Alice took it all in, trying to imagine what his life had been. That was when she noticed the cardboard box in the corner, tucked under the table. The top was folded outward, and she could see the contents plain as day. Magazines, old ones with naked women on the covers, the page curled and filthy. There were small cases as well, DVDs from the looks of them, the details all a blur, but enough for her to know exactly what she was looking at. It was the boy at the fair all over again, the porn that Walker hid out here, away from his family.

A special place.

Walker stood in the center of the room, his back to Alice, staring at the pictures on the wall, his crude crayon drawings contrasting luridly against the women, with their splayed legs in the magazines. Was there some story here, one that only he could see in the wall of drawings?

Little girl. Sunset. Father's hands. Rabbits running. Rainbows. Storm clouds. Grassy hills. Gray woods. Mother. Brother. Dog.

Family.

He stared at it. She could hear him breathing.

"It happened here," he whispered, so softly that Alice could barely hear it. Was he talking to her at all?

"He had to pay. He couldn't fix it."

Alice swallowed hard. The wind whistled outside. The sound of it made her cold all over again, as if she were cold for the first time.

"Did he pay?" she whispered back.

Walker began to sob. "Yes..."

Alice could hear him crying, and numbly, she wondered if the sound of his grief would make her cry as well.

No, Mary said. *Cry later. Cry for yourself. Cry for me if you want to. But not for him. Never for him.*

She reached down and picked up the can of kerosene. "Here."

Walker was still sobbing when he took the can and began to spread the kerosene around the room from corner to corner. Alice watched. She still didn't know how it would end, but a calm had fallen over her. There was some peace in him now, and while she didn't expect him to just walk into the woods and let her go, she wasn't afraid of him in the same way. The monster had been burned away. Only a pathetic, pitiful man remained.

Walker dropped the can and reached for a pack of matches that sat on the table. He picked them up, fished one out, and held it to the side of the box. Suddenly, he froze.

"What is it?" Alice asked.

He was shaking his head. The sobbing had stopped.

"It's still not right," he said to himself, the high pitch returned to his voice. "I can still fix this."

"What?"

He stepped toward her, pushing her back against the table. She bumped the lantern, which nearly tipped over behind her.

"You're just an extra daughter we don't need. I'll burn this place, and I'll burn you too," he said, looming over her. "Then you'll be out of the way. It will be perfect."

"Wait, please…"

"We'll be a family again."

He raised the knife, and Alice's hand brushed against something hard, curled, bumpy. Every voice inside her spoke a single word at the same time.

Antler.

Time ceased to exist. There was only that moment, the two sides of the coin, the knife above her, the curled, bony antler below, and her in the center.

She was the fulcrum.

She was the edge of the coin.

Mary's voice.

Do it.

Alice swung. Then she pulled her hand back, leaving the antler behind. It jutted out from his neck, sticking out like a strange growth from under his chin. He opened his mouth to scream, but he couldn't. His mouth was filling with blood. Deep in that bubbling hole, a bit of yellowish white. The tip of the antler, piercing his tongue.

He gurgled, dropped the knife, and began pawing at the hunk of antler protruding from his neck. In his madness, he spun around, knocking Alice back into the table with a swipe of his long arms. Her weight threw the table back, and it tilted against the wall. Alice saw the lantern, just next to her, both hovering and slipping through space as Walker spun and screamed. Alice was able to catch herself, to regain her footing as the lantern hit the ground a few feet away. She didn't need to see what happened. She could hear it. Stumbling, she made her way for the door as the lantern burst. A whooshing sound rose up behind her as she flung open the door and spilled out into the snow.

As she reached for the door her mind took in the scene before her, a hundred images overlaid in the span of a single second. It would take her years to parse through what she saw, to try to make sense of it, but even then, it was a fool's work. Her mind had done her a kindness and broke the image into pieces, small enough to process.

A circle of flame, spreading, a wreath of fire swallowing everything. A man in a pink, shiny jacket, the plastic fabric not so much burning as melting, seeping down his body in shiny ribbons. A plume of blood running down from his neck, covering him like a red bib. A hand, strong, wild, clutching a hunk of deer antler and ripping it free.

And most of all, the eyes. Mad. Cold. Pitiful. Staring straight at her. Alice backed away, her body shaking from the cold, the fear, the pain of the flames that were rising in front of her, threatening to swallow them both. Walker reached forward with blood-soaked hands, and those wild, mad eyes began to roll back.

Was it blood loss? Pain? Smoke?

Alice never knew. But as she backed away, she saw him slump down, the smoke and fire consuming him. She turned to run, but froze just a few feet away. A part of her, the kind, sweet part, didn't want to know that a man was dying a few paces from her. It was torture to run away, to listen to the crackling fire chase her through the dark woods. But another part, the sliver of her mind that she called Mary, a part of her mind that had always been there, always with her, told her there was no saving him, no other way. And in the long, frozen trek back to the awful house, Alice believed it.

Her family, still tied to their chairs, turned their heads as she walked into the kitchen, their faces telling the story, waiting to see if she was returning alone. Dean was halfway across the kitchen by then, trying to slide his chair across the room to get a knife to cut them free. Frank, whose face was now a pale greenish color under the blood, had to peel his face off the table to look at her. Debra's eyes told Alice all she needed to know about how much her mother loved her.

"Where is he?" Dean asked.

"Gone."

Alice's voice was syrupy. Her eyes felt like she had bits of gravel rubbed into them. As she cut them free, the other members of her family went back and forth between watching the door behind her and gazing at Alice. They looked at her as if she weren't the same person who had walked in, as if maybe Walker were wearing her skin.

"What happened?" Dean asked as she sawed at his ropes.

"He...burned."

No one asked again.

When Dean was free, he took the knife.

"I'll do it," he said, looking at her with an unsure glance. Alice sat down again, back where she was before as Dean freed their parents, first Frank, then Debra. Everyone had something to do, something to keep them busy. Dean helped Frank to the couch and fetched a handful of paper towels to stop the gash on his face. Then, once his dad was settled, he ran to his room and came back out with a baseball bat as he scanned the back door. Debra hugged her daughter furiously, then began checking her for wounds. Finally, convinced that her daughter was at least physically safe, she grabbed a garbage bag from the pantry and put what was left of Baxter into it.

"I can't believe you did that," Debra said when she returned. "You saved us."

Alice nodded. There was no pride in it. No sense of accomplishment. Just a simple confirmation. Debra was on the phone moments later, screaming at the dispatcher. Alice sat there on the couch as the family swirled around. It was busy all of a sudden. It was like a real family again. From the sound of it, the cops were on the way. They would be there soon in one of the four-wheel drives that had been running all day. They were finally bumped up on the priority list.

The house was alive again. No more ghosts. Just a family, busy as families always were. Alice stared at the blank television, same as she had yesterday afternoon. It was an odd feeling, knowing the events that had bridged those hours.

Tap, tap, tap…

Alice heard it, but she didn't glance away from the black screen. She couldn't. She had nothing left to give, no energy left to expend.

Tap, tap…

It was just the wind anyway. A sound as familiar as her own breath at this point. If she didn't look, it would always be the wind. It couldn't be anything else. All she had to do was not look, never look, never, never, never…

Tap…

Alice looked.

Walker stood at the wide, sliding glass door. His clothes had burned away, almost everything except his boots. His beard was gone, and ribbons of pink, melted jacket covered his body in patches. His penis was a curled, black stump between his legs.

"Daddy," he whispered into the glass.

"I'm cold, Daddy. I want to come back inside. Please, Daddy..."

Alice screamed.

EPILOGUE

It's hard to explain how long it's taken me to get to the point where I can actually write about this. I've held this diary a thousand times, pen in hand, feeling like the simple act of touching it, of holding it, might somehow conjure the past back up. I almost always end up tossing it to the floor or dropping it with a scream, only to pick it back up hours later with a scarf or a pair of gloves, something to keep it from touching me.

To keep *him* from coming back.

I thought he was coming in that night. I was so sure he would smash through the window and grab me, take me away, take me back into that world of snow and fire, of pain and fear.

But he didn't. Walker just stood there, tapping his finger, talking in that girlish voice. The pink jacket was burned to him, sticking to his mangled, red-and-black body like a second skin. I could see his dick too, a black, shriveled thing, like a sausage forgotten on a grill, burned to nearly nothing.

I screamed, and I swear to god, I thought I might never stop, that I might still be there screaming, screaming until my throat bled and I started coughing up blood.

Maybe I am still screaming.

A part of me feels that way. It's that little whisper that I started hearing in that house. Back then, back when I was too young to know the difference, I would have sworn that it was Mary, and in some ways, maybe it was. It felt like...a ghost whispering in my ear. Telling me secrets. Telling me to feel things I shouldn't feel, to know things I shouldn't know.

I realize that it wasn't a ghost, not literally anyway. It was just some deeper, buried part of myself. A truer part of myself. And it wanted out. It needed out. But now that it is out, that it is with me every second of every day, it has a mind all of its own.

It's that voice that tells me how dangerous this book is, how the past won't be gone forever until I take care of it. There are plenty of times I think this voice is lying to me, trying to convince me that the worst fear inside of me is the truth, that every dream I've ever had will wither and die, just like me.

This isn't one of those times.

This diary isn't magic. It's just a bundle of old paper and ink, but it does have a bit of power to it. I knew this immediately, once everything was said and done. I should have given it to the police, but they had all they needed. This book was, in some ways, something I had earned, and though I was afraid of it, I didn't want to let it go.

The first thing I did do was to tear out those last pages, the false pages, the *wrong* pages. This book was Mary's, and if a part of her spirit or soul was bound up in it, it felt horribly wrong, a desecration even, to let Walker's words live on in there.

Oh, Walker.

That sick son of a bitch.

I've learned a lot about mental health in the years since, most of it firsthand knowledge of post-traumatic stress disorder, depression, suicidal thoughts. Fun things like that. So far, I've won those little skirmishes, but every one of them takes a piece of me with it. I feel a bit like a puzzle that's missing pieces, and I can imagine all too well a world where I *don't* win those fights. I hope it never happens, but I'm also not so bold to say it won't.

All that is to say, that in some strange way, I sympathize with Walker. He was, quite clearly, a broken man. And, in turn, he broke me as well. I know what that feels like, and so, foolish though it may be, I sympathize.

But let me make one thing clear. He was a bastard before anything happened. He was simply, a man who broke himself.

I did nothing to deserve what happened to me, and that's why he will forever be a sick son of a bitch.

Yes, I expected him to kick the glass door to pieces to carry me away, to continue his insane assault on my family. But he didn't. When I screamed, everyone came running, and by the time my dad opened up the door with a still-greasy butcher knife in his hand, Walker was gone.

And so, we waited.

I wanted to be mad at the cops too, but the truth was this entire scene was more than the town was used to. It's what you would call a prototypical small town. Maybe there were fewer cops than they needed, but then again, no one could have seen that kind of weather happening.

The news ended up calling that entire week the "Snow of the Century," something that hadn't happened this far south in decades. There were only a few four-wheel drives in the police force, and most of them were working wrecks, literally driving injured people to and from the hospital while ambulances skidded all over the road. Apparently, there was even a wreck involving an ambulance that was carrying an elderly lady who had slipped and split her head open when she was getting the mail. The ambulance got rear-ended on a small bridge, and the entire vehicle just slipped off into the water. The EMTs tried to get her out, but she ended up drowning in a frozen creek.

So, no, I don't blame them. It was about half an hour after Walker ran off into the woods that a single, unmarked pickup pulled up in the front yard, lights flashing. The cop's name was Officer Simmons. A nice guy. He was actually off duty at the time, and after trying and failing over and over, dispatch asked him to check the situation out. Luckily, he lived a few miles away.

I wish I'd never known that little nugget of information. I could have died, not happy, but maybe a bit less unhappy knowing that a police officer was within walking distance the entire time. Dean saw the lights before he knocked, and let him right in. Officer Simmons was a young guy, probably not even thirty at that point. He wasn't ready for this…whole scene. But he handled it well.

Dad told him what happened while I sat in Mom's lap in the living room. I kept glancing up as they talked, and I kept seeing Officer Simmons looking away from Dad, just a second at a time, catching glimpses of the turkey dish still sitting on the floor or the splatters of blood on the table. When Dad finally got to that part of the story, I knew, just *knew*, that Simmons was going to puke.

He never did.

The young man wasn't in uniform, but he did have his gun and a flashlight, and after calling in the situation as best he could, he told us all to sit tight. It was a strange sight, seeing Simmons in a snowsuit, probably bought for some ski trip, and a thick wool hat on, pistol in hand, as he ventured out in the woods. He wasn't gone long.

Simmons found him a few hundred yards away, clutching a tree, nearly naked.

Dead.

The snow was already beginning to cover him, and in a few more hours, it would have likely buried him. It took another hour for the rest of the police to arrive. I can remember standing in the front room, gazing out the wide bay window, and watching the world of solid white turn blue and red with lights. They filled the room, chasing the shadows away, chasing the ghosts away. Here, again, were people, proof that the world didn't end when you walked out of our driveway, that the last few days hadn't taken place on an alien planet.

I stood there for a long time, watching the police make a perimeter, check the house, do all the things they needed to do. At some point, I realized that someone was standing next to me, so close and so sudden that I couldn't believe that I hadn't noticed it before.

It was Dean. He was crying, but he wasn't making any noise. I got the feeling that he wanted to tell me something, but he never did. I've wondered about that for years now, trying to figure out if he wanted to thank me, to apologize, to just tell me he loved me. I never knew.

A few moments later, I felt a hand on one shoulder, a soft hand, my mother's hand.

"Never seen this much snow," was all she said in a quiet voice.

I heard Dad approaching, his footsteps too heavy to sneak up on anyone. He stood behind all of us, one hand on my left shoulder, the other on Dean's. He pulled us together in a wordless embrace.

I remember riding to the hospital in Mom's lap, Dad and Dean piled into the back of Simmons's extended cab pickup. We were all bruised, cut, battered. But somehow, the family that had walked into that house was walking out again, forever altered.

And that was what happened.

It was thirteen years ago, a lifetime for the little girl who survived it. I've tried so hard to put it behind me, but something has been missing, something I couldn't quite grasp until years after the fact. I feel it every time I pass a tall guy on the street, especially if he has a beard or long hair. I feel it on more nights than I'd like to admit, when the wind blows cold and I hear something brush across the window. I feel it in the shower, always taken with my eyes open, so I can see any faces peering against the curtain.

Walker is still with me.

I've known it since the moment he tapped on that glass and fled into the cold night. Here are the things I know:

I *know* he died in the woods that night.

I *know* he was buried in the ground with no fanfare, no family to watch them shovel the dirt.

And I *know* that he can't hurt me anymore.

But everything I know is pointless in the face of what I feel, and what I feel are eyes watching me sleep, hands brushing through my hair, and a mixture of blood and snow running through my fingers. He's with me every second of every day, and only now, after all these years, have I finally figured out how to put him to rest. It was a simple thing, something I learned from a powerful, strong, stubborn girl I never actually met.

Mary.

Mary's still with me too. I don't feel her every waking moment like I do Walker, but when I do notice her; it's stronger, more meaningful. It's in the way that I don't take shit from the guys I meet, whether in bars, online, at work, you name it. It's in the way that I carry myself, my posture, my voice, the way people look at me. Most of all, it's in the way that I understand the vital power of words, of the weight they carry, of the damage they do.

I'm working as a journalist now, just local stuff with a few internet articles mixed in. I'm not setting the world on fire, not yet at least, but I'm using my words for something good. I'm making a living off them, changing people's perspectives with them, and most of all, I'm telling the truth.

I wonder a lot about what I would have been like if I hadn't gotten that diary, if Walker hadn't left it for me to find. Would I have been my mother – strong, tough, rarely backing down? Or my father – flighty, fanciful, always willing to risk something on a dream? I don't know the answer. But I do have a sense that I fall somewhere in between. A dreamer, sure, but a dreamer with a voice, with the conviction to make it real. And what is a dream that you don't chase? It's just a cloud, breaking up, disappearing, impossible to say whether it had ever been there at all.

Mary gave me something, something I was lacking, something vital.

No.

That's not right.

She helped *me find something*. It was there, but I just didn't know where to look. I walked into that strange, awful house a silent child. I walked out with a voice.

We never went back, by the way. I think maybe Dad did, once we shuffled things around, living in hotels for several weeks while the banks took one more risk on us. The house we landed in was in a neighborhood, an older one with houses on each side, far enough away to have a nice yard but close enough for neighbors to be there if you need them. Once I started driving, I decided I'd go see the place, just a quick drive by. I thought it might help. But the fact was I couldn't get within a mile of it. I had this overwhelming feeling that I'd get a flat just as I drove by, and there I would be, stuck next to the house as night began to fall. I never tried it again after that.

I even avoided the woods for years, but I've actually started to go hiking recently. I like it during the summer and spring, even the fall. But not in the winter. Not when the leaves are gone and the trees look like gray bones in a graveyard. The winter woods are too full of secrets, and my life doesn't have room for secrets anymore.

Dean ended up doing better than me, which is understandable, I suppose. He was always easier, always bending in the wind, just like Dad, in a strange way. There was a difference though. He was easygoing, but he was focused too. He went to college, got a solid job at a corporate office, and within five years out of college, he got married. He's satisfied. You can see it all over him. I think that was the difference between him and Dad. He got the smooth edges, but not the butterfly chasing.

His wife's a sweet girl, and they're expecting a baby later this year. I think about him a lot. We don't see each other as much as I thought we would, but that's okay. He moved, I moved, and life just goes that way. Only once did we really talk about what happened. He had just graduated high school, and he was getting ready to go to college out of state. It felt almost like a funeral, that last day he was at home. That might sound dramatic, but he was part of my life from day one. All of a sudden, that was changing.

I caught him in his room, finishing the last bit of packing. I sat down on the bed, acting like I owned the place. Nothing had changed.

"Things are going to be different without you around," I said, trying to be cool about it, acting like I was too stoic to be crushed inside.

"You'll be fine," he said. "You always are." He paused, seeming to think for a moment. Then he added, "You always will be."

I didn't go in there intending to grill him about everything that happened. I'd come close for years, going as far as walking up to his closed bedroom door and holding my hand up to knock. I never took that step though, but something about that moment, his last day before leaving, the finality of it, grabbed me, shook me.

"Do you ever see him?"

He froze in place. I can still remember what he looked like standing there. He was holding a Pop Figure. I'm not sure which one, but I think it was King Kong.

"See who?"

The tone told me the truth, told me everything I needed to know.

"I see him everywhere."

There was a moment there, that edge-of-a-coin feeling again where the conversation could have gone either way. He could have called me crazy, told me to get over it, to leave the past in the past. Instead, he nodded.

"I might not see him as much as you do. But yeah. I see him."

"How do I make it stop?" I asked, throat thick, the tears just there, always waiting.

Dean never looked at me. But he did sit down next to me.

"I don't know. Every day it gets better for me. There are whole days, almost weeks even, where I don't think about it."

I felt a pang of jealousy. The idea of going an entire week without thinking about him was unthinkable.

"I hear you," he said. "Sometimes. At night. I don't think Mom and Dad do. Their room is too far away. And...I think about it. About you. About what you did. I think, maybe, that you did...more. That for the rest of us, it was something we went through. Something we survived. But..." He paused, seeming to struggle with the words. "...for you, it was something bigger. That it took something from you. That maybe you left a piece of yourself in that shed. That you had to. And if you hadn't, we all would have died that night."

There were no dry spots left on my cheeks when he finished talking. We sat there a while as I waited to get my voice back.

"So where does that leave me?" I asked.

He sighed, telling me what I needed to know before he even spoke another word. "I don't know."

It was hard for him to leave me like that. I know it was. But it was also, in some ways, a kindness. He didn't sugarcoat it. He didn't tell me what I wanted to hear. He gave me what he had, and that would have to be enough.

Mom and Dad both tried to connect with me in their own ways, Mom trying to keep me busy, trying to make me happy. That first year, I got to do pretty much whatever I wanted. I tried not to take too much advantage of the situation, but it was hard when the offers were always in my face. I tried to play guitar, piano, and violin that first year, all three at considerable cost, I'm sure. None of them stuck.

Dad, always the talker, would try to dig into the situation whenever he found a moment that seemed right. I'd give him bits and pieces, just enough to make him think that I was doing fine, that this awful chapter of our lives was finally closed. It was a lie, but it was a kind one, and I think he was finally able to find some peace with the fact that he had gotten us into that situation in the first place.

It wasn't his fault, of course, but I think Mom always saw it that way. As soon as I graduated high school, they finally separated. They lived apart for a full, awkward year. Holidays became two-step affairs, with one Christmas or birthday at the suburban house that had finally become home, and another, smaller, sadder one at Dad's apartment. I'm still young, but there are few things more pathetic than the apartment of a single fifty-year-old man, but we made the best of it.

Somehow, through some black magic I still don't understand, they got back together the following spring. Maybe the holidays were too sad even for them. They've limped along ever since, but I think there's something hopeful in them. I don't know for sure, but it seems like they've found a bit of that spark that got them together in the beginning. I'm surprised to say, but I think they'll make it.

Which leaves me. Just me. I'm alive. I have a job. Maybe I'll get a boyfriend if I feel like it. But it's hard. I already have one awful man in my life.

I think a lot about that conversation with Dean. About that idea. That I left something behind to save us all. He's right. I know he is. But the question is, what happens when you lose a part of yourself? What takes its place?

I've always known that Mary was with me. That she got me through all those awful moments. That, in some way, she was the one who did what I couldn't. I don't mean literally, or at least, I don't think I do. Peering through the window of that diary showed me what was possible. Showed me what a girl could do.

Mary saved me.

And finally, after all these years, it's time for me to do the same for her. I've already gotten rid of Walker's pages, purged him from the records of this place. And now, I've finished her story. You see, that was the only way for me to continue mine.

I found her. The records are all public, not hard to find if you look. She's right there, in town. Gardenside Cemetery. I haven't been yet, but I already know what I'll say.

I'll tell her what happened, even the worst parts, the parts I've never told anyone.

I'll tell her I'm sorry, for everything she went through.

And most of all, I'll thank her. I'll let her know that her life, no matter how painful, no matter how short, was not in vain.

You saved me, Mary.

I thought about the best way to do it. I don't own a grill or a fireplace. I walked around the store, looking for something that would work, and I settled on a big metal pot. It's too big for me to use for soup or chili. I never have that many friends over.

When I'm done here, I'll go out back, set the diary inside, and set it on fire. It will be hard to lose it in a way. It's become almost a security blanket for me. And another part of me thinks that she's in there somehow, like a part of her is still locked away, and that if I keep it, I'll keep her.

But it was never mine. And Mary is long gone.

When it's done, I'll take the ashes and I'll finally visit her. In person.

And finally, after all these years, I'll give Mary back what belongs to her. I don't know what comes next. But I think it's time I found out.

—Alice